RICHARD BLADE . . .

regained consciousness when cold water was dashed in his face. Stung and shocked by the icy blast, he sat up quickly.

"There," said the girl. "That is better. I was sure you were not dead. Now you must help me. At once. I, Princess Taleen, command it!"

Blade sat up and stared at her. It was typical of Blade—a facet of his character which had saved his life many times over—that he accepted immediately and without question the realities of a situation. Not for a moment did he believe himself mad. Something had gone wrong with Lord Leighton's experiment. As simple as that.

"Do hurry," the girl's voice rose imperiously. "They are getting very close. If they find us they will kill us. I will not go back to be a captive of Queen Beata. I will not. I will die first!"

Blade got to his feet, conscious for the first time that he was entirely naked. For a moment, the girl ran her eyes over his body and he saw approval, then she handed him a short, bloodstained sword. "Listen—they are coming this way and getting closer."

She spoke truth. There was only a little time left.

THE RICHARD BLADE SERIES

THE BRONZE AXE

The Richard Blade Series

Jeffrey Lord

PINNACLE BOOKS • NEW YORK CITY

This is a work of fiction. All the characters and events portrayed in this book are fictional, and any resemblance to real people or incidents is purely coincidental.

THE BRONZE AXE

A Pinnacle Books edition, published by special arrangement with Lyle Kenyon Engel.

ISBN: 0-523-00201-7

First printing, June 1973
Second printing, January 1974
Third printing, August 1974

Printed in the United States of America

PINNACLE BOOKS, INC.
275 Madison Avenue
New York, N.Y. 10016

Chapter 1

Richard Blade, quite by coincidence, had been reading that very morning in *The London Times* of the scientific marvels to come. The writer in *The Times* had labeled his piece: "What's Ahead In Technology." He had been considerate enough to include a tentative time schedule for the miracles he was writing about.

Blade, folding his paper neatly at the place, and heartily enjoying his bacon and eggs, read through it with no look of skepticism on his handsome face. He was a skeptic, but not about science. It was what men *did* with science that was a cause for concern, and cynicism. Blade had been a top man in British espionage circles for nearly twenty years—he had been recruited while still at Oxford—and he held no delusions about the human animal.

Thinking of animals, he noted that the year 2000 was given as a probable date when intelligent animals might be used for low-grade labor. He poured himself more tea and pondered. Just what did it mean? A gorilla foreman directing a crew of dogs, mules and horses? While a graduate chimp kept the time and pay sheets? Mutants of some sort, bred especially for the job? Blade's mobile mouth quirked in a smile as he helped himself to more bacon. Cats might be very good at espionage work.

He ate contentedly and read more of the article. He was between jobs; spring had come to London and his chief, J, was leaving him alone as he had promised. Zoe Cornwall, the sloe-eyed beauty he eventually meant to marry, was waiting for him at the cottage in Dorset. When he finished breakfast and attended to some minor matters, he would drive the little MG down to the Channel coast and spend the weekend with Zoe.

For a moment the image of Zoe, her tawny and expectant body awaiting him on a crisp and fresh-smelling bed, interposed between Blade and the paper. He banished the image with resolution and read that as early as 1990 the scientists expected to establish direct electromechanical interaction between the human brain and a computer.

Direct electromechanical interaction. It had quite a ring to it! Blade, who had always had a vague distrust of computers, wondered just what it meant. Would they make the man into a computer, or the computer into a man?

The phone rang. Blade, a fork halfway to his mouth, stared at the offending instrument. He had two phones and the wrong one, the red phone, with connections directly into Copra House and J's desk, was ringing. It had to be J, then. Simple logic. That meant a job. Blade swallowed, cursed and considered not answering. J had promised him this little vacation. And Zoe was waiting.

Blade answered the phone. He was always on call. And duty was, quite simply, duty, and that was an end to it.

"Hallo."

It was J, of course, an elderly tweedy type with a voice so mellifluous that it flowed around the omnipresent pipe without hindrance.

J said: "Good morning, my dear fellow. Lovely morning, eh? Or have you looked at it yet? No matter. Will you scramble, please?"

Blade pressed the button on the base of the phone. "Done, sir."

"I know," said J, "that I promised you a vacation, that there would be no jobs for a time. You will be happy to know, dear boy, that I am going to keep that promise."

"I am indeed," said Blade. "You are making me very happy, sir. Not that I was worried. I know that you never go back on your word."

"Quite," said J. "Quite, my boy. However——"

Blade stared frowningly at the phone. "Yes, sir?"

"A little something has arisen," J said. "Nothing to do with your line of work, really, but they seem to want you. I really don't have much of the picture myself, except that it's all terribly top secret and urgent. I understand that it won't take very long—say a few hours at the most. If you'll drop by the House, Richard, I'll tell you more about it. Which, as I say, isn't a great deal. I can expect you?"

Richard Blade had worked with J for a great many years. He knew an order when he heard it, no matter how tactfully it was couched.

He told J he would see him in an hour.

Copra House, a grimy Victorian structure in the City, was off Threadneedle Street where Bart Lane ran into Lothbury. A well burnished brass plaque announced that it was the headquarters of The New East India Copra and Processing Co., Ltd. There actually was such a company. In one of the offices, reached through a maze of dingy corridors, J ran the affairs of M16A, which was a very special branch of the Special Branch.

J met Blade at the door of the barren cubicle he used as an office. The old man was wearing his bowler and carrying a rolled umbrella; a light Burberry was thrown across his arm. He greeted Blade with an effusion of shiny false teeth. "Come, dear fellow. We'll catch a taxi. It appears that they want us at the Tower."

When they were headed for the Tower J gave Blade an

appraising look as he set about filling his pipe. "You look in the pink, my boy. That's good. Fine. I gather that in this, er, experiment—whatever it is—they're looking for the best possible physical and mental specimen in all of England. That, Richard, would seem to be you. I gather they've been through some thousands of files trying to find their man. You were chosen. It's quite a compliment, I suppose."

Blade was impatient, and canny. It didn't size up as any sort of espionage or counter-intelligence job. Then what the hell was it?

He said cautiously, "Experiment, sir? I'm to be some sort of guinea pig?"

J was holding a match to his pipe. Between puffs he said: "Something like that, I shouldn't wonder. All I really know is that Lord Leighton called me personally, early this morning, and asked if they could borrow you."

"They?"

J shrugged. "The boffins, of course. Of whom his Lordship is the chief boffin, as you probably know. God only knows what they're up to now, but of course I couldn't refuse to cooperate."

Blade stared at his chief, his face impassive. "Of course not, sir."

J nodded. "Wouldn't have done any good to balk, Richard. His Lordship let it drop, not too subtly, that the PM himself is taking an interest in this thing. So there we are, eh? Just be a good chap and go through with it, whatever it is. I was told it wouldn't take very long."

Just as most native New Yorkers have never been to the top of the Empire State building, Blade, a native Londoner, had never been in the Tower. And he did not, now, really get into the Tower as tourists know it. He and J were met by a uniformed policeman and hustled around to where the old Watergate had once been. There they were turned over to two burly men, obvious Special Branch types, who guided them down a long tunnel, into

8

a maze of sub-basements, and to an elevator shaft that bore signs of recent installation.

One of the men pressed a button. A car began to whine upward. The man who had pressed the button looked at J. "He's to go down alone, sir."

"Of course." J held out a hand. "Goodbye for a time, Richard. Call me when you can and let me know how it went. I'll confess that I've got a bad case of what killed the kitty. If they'll let you talk about it, of course."

The car arrived. Blade stepped in. There were no buttons or controls of any sort in the car. A bronze door sighed hydraulically and the car shot rapidly downward, so fast that Blade's stomach felt queasy.

The car fell for a long time. Blade wondered how long they had been secretly mining beneath the Tower. Had it anything to do with atomic blast shelters? Certainly their security was good; he had a finger in a lot of pies, knew pretty much what went on, and this was his first inkling that such a place existed. J hadn't known, either. Blade was impressed.

The car stopped. Blade's stomach returned to its normal place. The door slid open and Blade stepped out into a brilliantly lighted foyer. It was bare except for a desk and two chairs. Behind the desk sat a little gnome of a man who Blade recognized at once as Lord Leighton, top scientist in all Britain. High boffin of all the boffins, as English scientists were called by laymen. In the United States they were called "brains". In England they were boffins. Call them what you liked, they were the men on whom Britain was now depending for her very life as a great power and nation.

Lord Leighton was something of a mystery man. His background was shadowy and very few pictures of him appeared in public. Blade had seen a photo of Leighton years before, in the course of his work, and he saw at once that years had ravaged the man.

Leighton stood up. His thin hair was white, and Blade

had forgotten that the man was a hunchback. Polio, too, Blade guessed as Leighton came around the desk in a halting, crablike walk. Leighton extended his hand.

"Richard Blade?"

They shook hands. Leighton's was small and dry. "Fine of you to assist us," he said. "I trust it isn't an imposition?"

Blade said that it wasn't. Not at all. He was only too happy to help in, er, whatever it was.

Leighton gave Blade an up and down glance, much the same appraisal that J had made in the taxi. The hunchback's smile was warm and tobacco stained.

"If it *is* an imposition, a nuisance, you really have only yourself to blame, Mr. Blade. We were looking for as near a perfect physical and mental specimen as we could get, and the computers kicked out your card every time. Just how do you feel about computers, by the way?"

It was an odd question, pointed up by the fact that the little man had just led Blade into a low-ceilinged room where dozens of computers were humming and clicking and clacking. Leighton, his hand on Blade's arm, guided him through the maze of consoles.

Blade was puzzled. All he could honestly say was: "I don't feel any particular way about them, sir. I just don't know very much about them. We use them in our work, of course, but I personally have very little contact with—"

"Good, good," said Leighton, who did not appear to be paying much attention to Blade's words. "Just as long as you don't really feel any hostility for computers. They can sense it, you know, and it makes them most uncooperative at times. Ah! Here we are, Mr. Blade. Just in through that door, Mr. Blade, and strip down. Naked. To the buff. You'll find a sort of loincloth. Please put it on and rejoin me here as soon as possible. Time is slipping away, you know, and I'm sure you want to get this over with and be on your way."

Blade, who knew when he was out of his depth, nodded

and went into the small dressing room. There was a small linen loincloth hanging on a hook in the wall. Blade stripped and twisted the cloth about his waist. It barely covered his genitals. He went back out to where the computers were humming like giant mechanical bees. Lord Leighton, his hump grotesque under a white smock, was bending over one of the machines and peering at the flashing lights. His lips were moving and Blade realized that the man was talking to himself. He began to wonder if the old boy was all there.

But the man's small yellowish eyes had the clear, cold stare of sanity as they regarded Blade's nakedness. He nodded. "Fine. Marvelous. If your brain is in as fine a shape as your body you're just what we've been looking for. But then it is, of course. Our computers don't lie. Which is more than you can say for most people, eh?"

He took Blade's arm again and led him through another door, into a room that was dominated by a single enormous computer. Most of its inner workings were concealed by gray, crackle-finished shielding, but from the ceiling hung thousands of tiny multi-colored wires, segmented and grouped by clamps, and running through small portholes into the guts of the machine.

Blade followed the hunchback through a twisting labyrinth of narrow aisles until they reached what he guessed must be the center of the machine. Here there was a small square of floor covered with some rubberized fabric. In the center of the square was a glass cage, or box, slightly larger than a telephone booth. Inside the cage was something that, to Blade's by now suspicious eye, very much resembled an electric chair.

Lord Leighton saw the expression on Blade's face and chuckled. "Don't let it frighten you, Mr. Blade. It really isn't what it seems. It's just that the, er, design is perfect for our purposes. Now—let's get you greased up well. There have been some very slight burns in the past. Mi-

11

nor, of course, but annoying. But the grease will take care of that."

He took a small pot from a shelf and began busily applying a viscous dark substance to Blade's naked flesh. Blade sniffed. There was a hint of coal tar in the stuff that Leighton was applying to his temples, the nape of his neck, various spots on his torso and thighs and even to each of his big toes.

"That should do it," said Leighton at last. He put the pot of grease away. "Now, Mr. Blade, if you please—into the glass cage and sit in the chair while I attach the electrodes."

Blade did as he was told. The inside of the glass cage was filled with little wires running in from the sides and down from the top. Each wire was tipped with a shiny round electrode about the size of a shilling.

Lord Leighton began plastering the electrodes to Blade's skin with tape. He was very deft about it. When he began to tape the shiny discs to Blade's temples and neck, the big man made a decision. He had been on the verge for minutes. Now he spoke.

"Before we go any further with this, sir, I think I'm entitled to know what it's all about. It is my body you're using, after all. Just what *are* we trying to do, sir?"

The little man adjusted a final disc and stepped back. He patted Blade's brawny shoulder. "Of course, Mr. Blade. You must make excuses for me—I get so wrapped up in these matters that I even forget my manners. You have every right to know what we intend to do. You will note that I say intend, and not try, because I'm sure it will work this time. Very sure. We have had great success with monkeys, and some qualified success with humans, but in the latter case we were not using first class brains. That, I am convinced, has been the chief difficulty. So you can readily see why we had to search out the best brain in all England—or at least what our computers tell us is the best and they are not often wrong, and—"

Richard Blade was becoming annoyed and he did not try to hide it. His tone was sharp. "Sir! I am not a scientist. So far this has all been gibberish to me. I don't mind letting myself be used as a guinea pig, if it will help, but I damned well want to know what is going on, and in language I can understand." Blade made a motion to get out of the chair. It would not have been easy, even had he really intended to carry it through. By now he was so festooned with wires and electrodes that movement was difficult.

"My dear Mr. Blade!" Leighton gave him a gentle push back into the chair. "I am sorry. I will explain everything—everything. But you must not excite or agitate yourself. Please no! That might be fatal to the experiment. Above all your brain must be calm and receptive."

Blade concealed a grin. Leighton was the one who was getting excited. He peered anxiously at Blade with his yellow eyes and did a little shuffling dance around the perimeter of the glass cage, carefully avoiding the wires.

"Well?" Blade asked grimly.

"I'll try," said Leighton. "Please listen carefully."

He swept his hand around in a circle, indicating the giant computer that loomed over them like some silent and monstrous gray beast. "This is the ultimate in computers, Mr. Blade. I have spent nearly all my life perfecting it. I have spent the last year programming it. It is fully programmed now, Mr. Blade, with a mass of highly specialized material. Material that is esoteric and sophisticated, in the form of symbols and words, and in combinations of both, and at this moment, Mr. Blade, with your brain as it now is, you could not even faintly begin to comprehend it. This machine, Mr. Blade, is programmed to solve problems and utilize knowledge that even *I* do not understand! Do *you* begin to understand at all?"

Blade did. It was beginning to come through. It seemed eons ago since he had been reading *The Times* at breakfast. *Direct interaction between the computer and human brain.*

Blade had spoken the words aloud. Lord Leighton did not appear surprised, but rather pleased. The little man clapped his crippled hands together. "Exactly, Mr. Blade! Exactly. I see that you have been reading the newspapers. I must take the blame, I am afraid, for misleading them a bit about dates. I stated 1990, I think, as the earliest possible date for such direct interaction? Yes, I did. I am a liar, Mr. Blade, but I am sure you will understand. *They* are working along the same lines, and the more we can get them to underestimate our progress the better it is."

Blade knew all about that. It was in his line of work. "So if this experiment works," he said, "I'll be carrying around a lot of high powered knowledge that I haven't had to sweat to get? That I haven't had to *learn?* It will just be there?"

"Precisely." The little eyes glittered at Blade. "It will just be there without any effort on your part. You will know, and be able to use, what it has taken me, and hundreds of my colleagues, all our lives to accumulate. The machine will impart it all to you in a few minutes. The machine is only a machine, after all, and can give you only what has been programmed into it, but nevertheless it will mean instant genius for you, Mr. Blade. Instant genius! And now, with your permission, we will get on with it."

"But," said Blade, seeing the catch, the trap, "I won't be the same man afterward. I won't be *me*. And I don't think I want to be a genius. I'm quite satisfied with things the way they are."

Lord Leighton raised a hand. "Think, Mr. Blade. Think hard and long before you say no—think of your country and the relatively low estate to which we have fallen. I am a genius, Mr. Blade, but I am only one and can do only so much. But if this works, we can turn out geniuses by the dozens, by the hundreds, then England can

14

find her place in the sun again. Without armies and navies. Without economic superiority. We can lead the whole world in scientific genius. Can you refuse, Mr. Blade? Can you?"

Blade was suddenly aware that he couldn't. Leighton had reached behind him and pressed a button. Blade was aware of a low humming sound, of gentle electrical charges surging through his body and making little waves in his blood.

Blade could not move now. He willed his legs to move and they did not respond. Nor did his hands and arms. There was no pain, yet the current held him in the chair like a giant repressing hand, a hand that had solidity but no weight. He was rigid, immobile, bound to the chair by invisible chains of electricity.

His vision began to blur. His head began to swell like a balloon. Lord Leighton's twisted body changed into a ball of color, a flame, a whorl of spinning haze that faded away and away and then was gone. The glass around Blade changed to water and began to run over him, yet he did not feel wet. The wires were tiny snakes now, biting at him with shiny jaws, yet their bites drew no blood, brought no pain.

The roaring began in Blade's ears. He was free now, no longer in the chair, soaring through the sky and rolling and dipping in an absolute freedom he had never known before. He was a spirit without body. He lived, and yet he was *no* thing; he was huge and he was tiny; he was an ant and he was a planet.

Storm now. A mingled wrath of darkness and light. Blade went curving into it at a trillion miles an hour, into an awesome boil of clouds. Lightning stabbed at him. Again. Closer. Blade knew cold and fear and he screamed as the lightning came again.

The massive lightning bolt was a crooked golden dagger slashing at Blade, skewering his head. His brain exploded. The pain was beyond bearing. There had never been pain

15

like this before, never would be again. All the pain since the world began was being poured into his skull.

The pain vanished. Blade, a seared leaf, a crumple of dust, a trace of moisture, trembled upward into void.

Chapter 2

Richard Blade regained consciousness in a strange crepuscular world; he did not, for the moment, open his eyes, but lay quiescent and let a myriad of stimuli impinge on his brain.

He was lying in thick grass. There was a hum of insects and, from a distance, the baying of hounds. Nearby a brook burbled. Even with his eyes closed he was aware of the florid wheel, the burning oriflamme, of a setting sun. Then an intertwine of moving shadow, an intrusion and then—

Cold water was dashed into his face. Blade, stung and shocked by the icy blast, sat up with a muffled curse. What in hell?

"There," said the girl. "That is better. I was sure you were not dead. Now you must help me. At once. I, Princess Taleen, command it!"

Blade sat up, squeegeed water from his eyes with his fingers, and stared at her. It was typical of Blade—a facet of his character which had saved his life many times over—that he accepted, immediately and without question, the realities of a situation. Not for a moment did he believe himself mad. Something had gone wrong with

Lord Leighton's experiment. As simple as that. He would sort it out later.

"Do hurry," said the girl impatiently. Her voice rose imperiously. "And stop staring like an oaf and a peasant. They are getting very close. If they find us they will kill us. I will *make* them kill us. I will not go back to be a captive of Queen Beata. I will not. I will die first!"

Blade got to his feet, conscious for the first time that he was entirely naked. The linen loincloth had disappeared. For a moment the girl ran her eyes over his body and he saw approval, then she shrugged and handed him a short sword. It was bloodstained at the point.

"Here. You take it. I had to kill one of my guards to escape. It is the first time I have killed a man and I did not enjoy it. But you look like a warrior and will know how to use it. Listen—they are coming this way and getting closer."

She spoke truth. Blade, swinging the heavy sword in his right hand, could hear the hounds baying closer now and men called to each other from somewhere toward the setting sun that was now only half a golden orb sinking behind green hills. They were in a small open glade through which the brook scampered, and ringing them was a dark and high reaching wood of oak and yew lightened here and there by stripling birch.

Blade had much experience in hunting, and being hunted, and he knew there was yet a little time. The voices were still a quarter mile off. He looked at the girl, again conscious of his nakedness—which did not appear to bother her in the least—and said: "You say you are the Princess Taleen?"

Her eyes were a soft luminous brown. In another mood, he thought, they would be as limpid as a doe's, but there was a hard glitter in them now. Her small chin firmed at him, and her straight little nose was haughty as she said, "You doubt it?"

Blade, without knowing exactly why he did it, made a

little bow and raised the sword in salute. "It is not that I doubt. It is simply that I do not understand. I am a stranger—in all things."

She studied him, her eyes narrowing. "Yes, I believe that. You are like no man I have ever seen in Alb. But still you must obey me—I am indeed the Princess Taleen, daughter of King Voth of the North. I am in great danger. If you help me I will see that you are well rewarded. My father will pay many scills to have his daughter back. Now will you stop staring like a fool and *do* something!"

She was tall and beautifully made. Dark auburn hair flowed to her waist, held back by a golden band. She wore a dress of dark linen, figured with semi-precious stones, that clung to her nubile body and did little to conceal the small firm breasts. Around her tiny middle was a belt of bronze links from which hung the drinking horn she had used to splash Blade. The dress ended well above dimpled knees. On her small feet were soft leather sandals with long thongs carried up and cross-gaitered around shapely calves.

Blade saluted with the sword again. He smiled, his white teeth flashing in a dark stubble of beard. "I will obey, Princess Taleen. I am your true servant. But just exactly what is it that you want me to do? There is no danger at this moment." He cocked an ear. "They are still ten minutes away."

The girl put her hands on her hips and stared at him in exasperation. Her eyes flickered up the tall trunk of him, over the slim hips, tidy waist, massive chest and wide shoulders and the thick column of his neck. Her gaze softened, as did her tone.

"One thing I know—you are no serf! Possibly you are a nobleman, an aristocrat, from some far-off land. Your name?" Imperious again.

"Blade. Richard Blade. And indeed from a far-off land."

"Blade? Richard Blade?" She pronounced it Rich-hard

19

Bleed. She grimaced. "A strange name, by Frigga! My tongue will not accommodate to it. But we will speak of all this later—now I command you to escort me to the town of my cousin, King Lycanto. The town is called Sarum Vil and it should be somewhere near. My cousin will protect us and give us shelter for the night."

Blade smiled. "Somewhere near, you say? But you do not know exactly?"

She frowned at him. "I—well, not exactly. But I am sure we can find it. There is a path that—"

He chuckled. "If we can find the path. In other words, princess, you are lost. We are both lost."

Before she could answer a great dog broke from the cover of the woods and came bounding at them. It was running far in advance of the pack, eyes glinting red and long muzzle slavering, and it was a killer bent on doing the work for which it had been trained. With bristling hackles and thunder in its throat the huge beast came straight in for the kill.

As Blade stepped in front of the girl he plucked the drinking horn from her girdle. "Behind me," he snapped. "Remain perfectly still."

The animal—to Blade it looked like some weird cross between a mastiff and a wolfhound—left the ground some ten feet from Blade. The long fangs glinted cruelly in the twilight. Blade went into a half crouch, the sword drawn back to thrust, the drinking horn in his left hand and in front of him.

The dog—at close quarters it looked as big as a small pony—crashed into Blade with furious impact, the long teeth snapping for his throat. Blade, taking one backward step, rammed the drinking horn down the red maw and twisted it. Then, in a series of fluid movements, he withdrew a bleeding hand and thrust hard into the creature's belly. He put all his mighty shoulder behind the thrust and felt the hilt of the sword grate against ribs. The dog fell away with a dying squall and went into its death convulsions. Blade thrust quickly into its throat in a mercy stroke.

He put the sword deep into earth to cleanse it and turned to the girl. She was watching, her eyes wide, one hand to her mouth, and for a moment her face bespoke fierce approval.

Yet she said, "A fine animal. A pity to slay it."

He held up a hand for silence. With the going of the sun the darkness had fallen suddenly, an abrupt curtain, and the voices and the baying of the hounds were closer. Blade, studying the thick woods to the west, saw the sudden red sputter of a torch. Then another, and still another. The scarlet flambeaus, danger beacons in the dust, denoted the two horns of a crescent that was closing in on them. Very close now. Too close. They could not go west, and already the horns of the crescent were closing off north and south. That left east, the direction in which the brook ran.

Blade took the girl's hand in his big paw. "Come on, princess. We are going to run a little."

The water was icy. The brook was not deep, never more than a foot or two, but the bottom was rough and stony with countless boulders around which the stream cascaded. Caught brush, snagged timbers and fallen trees impeded their way. It grew cold and a dank white mist began to rise and hang over the water. Blade, naked as he was, began to feel the cold. He was inured to hardship, discounted it, yet he was shivering.

So was the girl. Her hand, clinging to his big one, grew colder by the minute. Blade was setting a merciless pace and soon she was gasping. Several times, but for his support, she would have fallen. Finally, tripping over a hidden snag, she came sprawling into his arms and remained there for a moment. She clung to him, panting, and he was very aware of the lithe body beneath the thin linen. There was a fragrance about her, other than that of clean woman flesh, which he found vaguely familiar. After a moment he identified it. *Chypre*. It smacked of sunnier climes, of the Levant, and he wondered how she had come by it. The last time Blade had smelled *chypre* had been in Alexandria. A man had been wearing it then, a queer who was selling information to Blade, a young deviate who had been murdered two weeks later. What had his name been?

Blade could not remember. His mind was fuzzy and blank. With a great effort, feeling the sudden sweat on his forehead despite the cold, he switched his thoughts and tried—tried—Lord? Lord Leighton! Got it. And his boss? J. Yes, J. He could swear it. J? London? M16A? Yes—yes—then the mist seeped into his brain and he was no longer sure.

He understood it then. His memory of past life was going. Slowly, but inexorably, leaving him.

The girl cried out in pain. Blade, totally forgetting her, had tensed so that he very nearly crushed her ribs.

He released her. "I am sorry, princess. I was thinking and for a moment forgot where I was. I did not mean to hurt you."

She sounded cross, yet she did not move away from him. "You are a great brute, Richard Blade. You crush a woman like a straw."

In the east, over a waving sea of endless trees, he saw the first pale hint of a gibbous moon. He looked back along the tortuous way they had come. The mist, risen higher now, hung like a visible miasma over the stream and drifted in ghostly whorls among the trees. There were no torches, no voices, no baying dogs. Their pursuers, it appeared, had given up for the night.

Blade led the girl to the bank, where they found a grassy enclave which, if not warm, was at least better than the brook. They nestled down together and she came into his arms again.

But first she said: "I am cold, Blade. I seek only the

22

warmth of that huge bear's body of yours. You understand this?"

She could not see his smile. "I understand," he said gravely. "What else? After all you are a princess and I am only a poor stranger—a man with no clothes. What could such a one possibly aspire to? Have no fear, princess. I know my station and I will not reach above it."

None the less temptation was present and he was well aware of it. She was soaked to the skin and her nipples had risen with the cold. Her breasts, half out of the skimpy dress, lay against his naked chest. And he knew, with the sure knowledge that a true man has, that although she would demur, and possibly even struggle a bit, she would in the end welcome his lovemaking. If he so chose.

He did not so choose. That would resolve itself in time. If they were meant to be lovers they would be. Meantime there were more immediate problems—they were lost, hunted, and his belly was screaming for food. If she was as hungry as he, then she was hungry indeed.

She had not spoken for a few moments. She lay against him, shivering like a drenched puppy, with her fine spun hair tickling his nose. Now she pulled away and tried to see his face in the gloom. There was an edge in her voice.

"I think you mock me, Blade. I *am* a princess, but I do not think I like your tone when you say it."

"Again I am sorry, princess. I cannot help my tone. It is the way I always speak."

"If I truly thought you mocked me, Blade, I would have you well whipped when we come to Sarum Vil. I swear I would."

His teeth glinted wolf-like in the moonlight as he held up the sword. "I think not, princess. Not while I am armed and can fight back. Try to have me whipped and there will be blood—perhaps mine, certainly that of your friends."

23

His tone lightened. "Anyway it will not be necessary to whip me—I do not mock you."

Taleen regarded him with something of caution, and a new respect. She smiled back. "Very well. We are friends again. You may hold me, Blade. I am freezing."

But before she came into his arms again they both heard it—the sound of chanting voices coming from the deep black woods to the east. Taleen stared at Blade and made an odd gesture with her right hand across her breasts.

"Frigga protect us! It is the Drus. They are meeting tonight in the sacred glade. And now I know where I am, Blade. Come. We will circle around them and find the path to Sarum Vil." She extended a hand to Blade.

He stared into the depths of the wood, trying to locate the chanting. As he strained his eyes he gradually made out the flickering red stain of a fire, seen intermittently, now and then obscured by the great boles of the oaks and yews that lurked like mute giants in the tenebrific shadows. Blade felt an odd, uneasy and yet exciting, stirring in his blood and could not explain his atavistic response to the fire and the chanting. He only knew that he wanted to see, and understand, what was going on.

But when he made this plain to Taleen she recoiled from him in horror. She snatched away her hand and stared at him as though he had gone lunatic.

"No—no! It is forbidden to spy on the Drus. Most especially forbidden to intrude on the Mysteries. If we are caught we will be killed. They will sacrifice us to the God of the Trees. That is what they are doing now—preparing a sacrifice. If they catch us they will cut off our heads and our hands and our feet, and they will gut us like rabbits and cook us over a slow fire. Then they will eat us! No, Blade. We must circle far around them, and very carefully, too, because they always post sentries."

He watched her, his handsome face impassive. There was no doubt that she believed what she said, and that her

24

fear was genuine. In the moonlight, ever growing stronger, her eyes were full of terror.

It only served to whet his curiosity. He reached and pulled her against his big chest once again. He stroked her hair and felt her trembling and knew the cold was not to blame this time.

"You have seen this with your own eyes?" His voice was gentle and he kept it low. She might be telling truth about the sentries. "You have seen these Drus make human sacrifices and eat them?"

Taleen shook her head and muttered against his chest. "No. I have not seen it. I would not dare. I am not a fool and do not wish to die. But I have heard the stories—as has everyone in Alb—and the stories are true. The Drus are very powerful and they are a law unto themselves. *Everyone* knows and understands that, Blade. And you, a stranger who may be forgiven for your ignorance, must understand it also."

She pulled away from him and looked into his face. "Unless you are really a fool, after all, and have a great wish to die. And until now I have not thought you a fool."

"I am not," said Blade, "and I do not wish for death more than any other man, but I would like to see these Drus with my own eyes. I will see them. Now. Tonight. At once."

It occurred to him that if the Drus were so powerful they must also be potential enemies. Blade had survived for so long by adhering to the creed "know thy enemy!" He did not know how long his enforced stay in Alb would last, or how long his memory of another life would sustain and give him an advantage. It would be wise to hedge against the future—whatever it might bring—and to make his position as secure as possible.

When he spoke again his tone was firm. "I am going to look into this matter, Princess Taleen. There is not much danger, for I am at home in the woods and brush, but you

25

do not have to come with me. Remain here if you like. I will come back for you."

She sighed in resignation. He had expected another flare of anger.

"You *are* a fool, after all. You would never find me again. No—I will go with you. If you are determined to be a fool then I must be one too. Only remember my warning when they are cutting off your head."

Blade grinned at her and patted her lightly on the behind. So anxious and unsure was she that the *lese majesty* went unnoticed.

"Follow closely," said Blade, "and do not be afraid. And try not to step on any dry sticks. Try to step exactly where I do. It will not take long. I want a glimpse of these Drus, nothing more. After that we will find your path and get on to the village of your cousin. It is a fact that I wish we had brought that dead dog along with us—right now I think I could eat him raw."

Taleen made a scornful sound in her throat. "We will be the ones to be eaten, Blade. You will see."

All his life he had been a hunter, first of animals and then of men, and now he moved easily through the forest. It was not as dense as it appeared from the brookside, and the moonlight grew steadily. They made their way around the great trees festooned with vines and creepers. The ground beneath them, thickly padded with leaf mold, muffled their footsteps. Overhanging tendrils brushed their faces like tiny dank snakes.

Blade soon discovered that the forest, so formidable from afar, was really a series of interconnecting clearings. He made his way skillfully through the maze, pausing now and again to let the sullen and fearful girl catch up. Taleen, trying to follow exactly in his footsteps, did not always succeed. She caught her dress on the edge of a bramble thicket and Blade, impatiently, went back to free her. There was a long glistening red scratch on the inside of one tender thigh. He tore a small piece from her linen frock and wiped the blood away and felt her tremble. His own brawny naked body was scratched in a score of places.

For a moment they halted by the brambles, silent and unmoving. The chanting was very near now, a high pitched litany that was not melodic and yet bore a kernel of some dark and fearful tune. There was hand clapping, and a hint of contrapuntal values, and Blade began to make out individual voices. The fire—it must be huge—blazed through the black tree stalks like an ominous beacon.

The challenge, because it was spoken softly and without intonation, an arid voice devoid of color, was more frightening than if it had been screeched.

"Who comes? Who dares to defile the Mysteries, to invade the Sacred Grove? Speak!"

The voice came from behind a tree. It was ascetic, neuter, betraying no sex. Taleen gasped in terror and clung to Blade. He pushed her away, whispered "stay" and stalked toward the tree. He saw a glimmer of white in the gloom. He held the sword in readiness.

The voice, steady and dry and without fear, said: "Stop! Do not approach me. I am a Dru, of the Drus of Alb, and whoever disobeys me will suffer the abiding curse of all the Gods for all time. He will know eternal darkness and peace will elude him forever. Stop! I command it."

It was a formidable curse. Blade kept going. The voice, suddenly pitching up into panic, squealed, and the white thing moved around the bole of the huge tree to confront Blade.

"Die, then! You who will not listen to wisdom. Die!"

There was a flutter of white robes in the moonlight. A glint of golden dagger. The weapon struck at Blade, a powerful and well aimed blow. Hollow, fanatic eyes gleamed at him from the shadows of a deep cowl. "Die then. Die—die—die!" It was the larger chant made small and scored for one voice.

Blade parried the blow and finished matters with a vicious backhand stroke that bit into the Dru's throat just below the chin. Arterial blood, bright in the moonlight, spurted to drench the white robe. The Dru went to his knees, staring in astonishment at his bloody hands, words and blood burbling from the hole in his throat in a scarlet froth. Blade, afraid that the Dru would yet manage a cry of warning, struck again with the sword, this time from the side and below the ear. It was a near decapitating stroke. The Dru sank into the blood and twitched and died.

Blade stooped and pulled away the cowl, curious to see what manner of men these Drus were.

The head was long and closely shaven, the stubble showing gray. I have killed an old man, thought Blade. Regrettable, but not cause for too much concern. The man had attacked him. The golden dagger was shining now at Blade's feet and he saw that only the hilt and flange were of gold—the point and cutting edge were of bronze and would have killed him easily enough.

Old man? Something about the dead face gave Blade pause. He did not pick up the dagger, but instead reached to rip open the front of the white robe, where a scarlet circle was emblazoned over the heart. Inside the circle, still visible through the blood, was an emblem of an oak tree worked in golden thread.

The cloth came away in his hand. Blade stared down at the withered breasts. An old woman!

Behind him Taleen said: "Frigga protect us now. You have killed her. You have murdered a Dru! We will both be cursed forever—after we are killed and eaten."

Blade did not allow either his face or voice to betray the slight nausea he felt. He did not like killing women— even old women who were trying to kill him.

His tone sharp, he said: "Stop talking nonsense, princess. Nothing is going to happen to you. I wish it had not happened, but it has and we must make the best of it.

Why did you not warn me that some of the Drus were women—I would have been more careful." He stroked his black stubbled chin and stared at the bdy. "Not that it would have made a lot of difference that I can see. She did try to kill me. What would you have me do—wear that trinket in my heart?" He kicked the golden dagger to one side.

Taleen did not look at him, nor at the corpse. But she picked up the dagger and wiped it clean on a clump of grass. "I need a weapon now. So that when we are taken I can kill myself before the torture begins."

She tugged at his hand. "Come, Blade. If we run for our lives now, at once, there may still be a chance. Only hurry! There will be other sentries about."

Blade shook her hand away. He gazed moodily at the corpse, brooding. His jaw was set. J would have recognized the look, and have accepted it with resignation.

Blade gazed toward the fire and the chanting. "I have come this far, Princess Taleen. I will go on. I must know about these Drus and their Mysteries. And you have not yet answered my question—how many of them are women?"

"All of them," said Taleen quietly. "I did not mention it because I did not think it was important. You are not only a stranger, Blade, you are *strange*. How did I know that you would be fool enough to spy on the Drus? No one else in all of Alb is that much of a fool—but then I keep forgetting that you are not of Alb."

Blade ignored that. "You say all the Drus are women? No men at all? It is an order of priestesses then?"

Not, then, so formidable after all. He should be able to handle a gaggle of women, probably all of them elderly, who ran about in white robes and chanted weird songs. And yet—he glanced at the golden dagger now tucked into Taleen's girdle. The old crone had come at him in a very businesslike manner.

The girl, cajoling now, said, "You are very interested in

29

the Drus, Blade. I will tell you all about them—if only you will come away with me. Now. While there is yet time. For me, at least. *You* will never be safe now. You have killed a Dru. They never forget and they will look for you always. You are going to have to trust me a great deal, Blade."

Taleen did not try to conceal the malice in her tones. She gave him a sly smile. "I said before that I would have you whipped, Blade. I did not really mean it. But now I have your very life in my power—and I do mean that. One word from me and you are a dead man."

Blade did not look at her. He plunged the sword into the earth to clean it. Only then did he glance from the sword to Taleen and back at the sword again.

She narrowed her eyes and tilted her chin high. "Do not try to frighten me, Blade. It will not work. I know you well enough already to know that you will not kill me."

His grin mocked her. "Yes, I admit it. You know me that well. But you forget something—*you* are also involved. *You* are here now. Who will believe it was not all your idea, your doing, this spying and the killing of a Dru? I am a very credible liar when I want to be."

Taleen glared at him, then fell into a pout. She muttered something he did not understand and again signed across her breasts with her right hand. "Frigga save me from the Drus—and you. I begin to wish I had never met you."

It was a sentiment that Blade was beginning to share. Yet he needed her, badly needed her, as a guide and mentor in this strange land of Alb—curse Lord Leighton and his confounded computer—but he was beginning to see the Princess Taleen for what she was. Beautiful, desirable, and absolutely not to be trusted. A wild child, capricious as the wind, a lovely little barbarian Princess whose only guide was her own wilfulness. Blade had spoken boldly just now, had blunted her spleen for the moment, but he

30

knew that he must watch her constantly from this moment on. She was unpredictable.

So he scowled at her and spoke more harshly than he felt. She was not to blame for what she was.

"I go to have a look at these Drus," he said. "Come with me or stay. It is all one to me."

He began to move cautiously toward the red eye of the fire. He did not look back. Presently he heard her stumble over a root and mutter something to Frigga that was more a curse than a prayer. When he sank to his belly in a thicket, with the fire and the chanting and dancing Drus in plain view, she was beside him. Strangely enough, once the thing was done, she whispered, her soft mouth close against his ear, and again he caught the wanton scent of *chypre* so oddly out of place.

"You see the one who stands aside, who does not dance or sing, she who carries the great golden sword?"

Blade nodded. There were perhaps fifty of the robed and cowled Drus, their faces hidden in shadow, dancing slowly about the huge fire. They were all clapping hands and singing as they went through the convolutions of the dance, an antic movement that yet was somehow measured, stately; the natural merriment of the swirling tropes being smothered by the weight and gravity of matters yet to come.

The Dru pointed out by Taleen stood well off to one side. She was thin and straight as a birch, her face hidden by a cowl, her hands crossed over the hilt of a golden sword so long that, with its point in the earth, the hilt came to the scarlet cord that girdled her waist.

Taleen whispered again. "That is Nubis, the High Priestess. My cousin Lycanto is terrified of her. So am I. So would you be if you were not a fool. Look yonder, Blade, in the shadows beyond the dancers and then tell me if I am a liar."

Blade looked and did not like what he saw. A naked

31

young girl, bound and gagged, lay on a crude hurdle to which leathern pulling straps were attached.

The big man, straining to see, made out a glimmer of white as the girl rolled her eyes at the dancers criss-crossing around the fire. Blade knew stark terror when he saw it, and he was seeing it now. She was not a pretty girl, and she was fat and dumpy, her too large breasts already broken and sagging. Her legs were fat, her ankles thick and peasant was written all over the dull white nakedness of her. Blade, watching her strain against her bonds, moving a little on the hurdle, all the while rolling her eyes in fear, felt a tinge of pity. It was not a familiar emotion and was probably misplaced. He did not really believe in Taleen's wild stories.

The chanting stopped suddenly. The dancers broke ranks and began to scurry about in apparent confusion, but after a moment Blade saw that a pattern was emerging. Until now he had been feeling the night chill; now sweat began to bead and roll on his forehead.

The Drus were well disciplined. They worked fast and in perfect harmony. Forked sticks were driven into the earth on either side of the fire and a long pointed spit of bronze was laid over the fiercely glowing coals. One of the Drus, carrying heavy bags of charcoal, began to bank and build the fire into an even bed of white hot flame.

Taleen hissed softly in his ear. "See. Over there. The big oak stump. I have heard of it. They call it the King Oak."

The High Priestess, carrying the long golden sword, was walking to the stump now. The oak stump, a massive flat table some eight feet across, was capped by a wheel of thin stone that was darkly splotched.

Four of the Drus seized the leather straps of the hurdle and pulled it toward the stump. Blade could see the girl's mouth contorting under the gag as she tried to scream. His hand closed hard around the hilt of his sword. Sweat ran into his eyes. It was crazy, impossible, insane—but he would have the element of surprise. He just might—

Princess Taleen sank her sharp nails into his bare arm. She was reading his thoughts.

"No, Blade! Do not even think it. Do not think that because they are women it will be easy. They are monsters, all of them, and they fight like men. Even if you could save the girl, even if we escaped, that would not be an end to it. They will go to Lycanto and demand our lives. Our bodies. He will give us to them. He is terrified of them. At the very least he will turn us away from Sarum Vil and we will be without food, or shelter, or protection. Listen to me, Blade! For once do not be a fool!"

He forced his great muscles to uncoil. For a moment there he had been on the verge—but this time Taleen was right. If he meant to survive in Alb, and he did, then he must suppress the rage, the shock, and the sickness that was moving in his belly. Richard Blade was rock hard, but it has been said that even stones can weep.

So he watched, and with a great effort kept from retching. And noted that the slim barbarian by his side was not nearly as sickened as he. Her sole concern was for herself.

All the preliminaries had been concluded before their arrival and now matters went swiftly. The bound girl was tossed roughly onto the stone-capped oak stump. She lay writhing and contorting in a frenzy, sliding and rolling to the edge of the stump in a mindless effort to escape. The Drus, ringing the stump now, pushed her roughly back to the center.

They were chanting again, a soft, nearly whispered chant that held the sound of death. The Drus locked hands and began to move slowly around the stump in counter-clockwise movement.

"Mother of Frigga," said Taleen beside him. "I think I know that girl. I am sure of it. It is one of Lycanto's serving maids. More than a serving maid, if the gossip be true.

33

Frigga preserve me—there is more here than I can understand."

The moving circle of Drus parted for a moment and the High Priestess came through. She carried the golden sword in both hands as she slowly approached the stump. She moved with great dignity and poise, her face concealed by the cowl, and she carried the great sword as easily as she would a toy. Blade could not deny his fascination; this was a nightmare from which there was no waking.

The High Priestess leaped agilely atop the stump. The movement was graceful, flowing, and not that of an old woman. The cowl, unsecured by the sudden movement, fluttered back and away from the woman's face. Blade caught his breath.

"By Frigga's breasts," said Taleen at his side. "That is not Nubis. She is a stranger. I do not know her."

The High Priestess did not bother to replace her cowl. She threw back her head and raised the golden sword in both hands, holding it high, imploring benediction from the black dome of sky. She began to intone a prayer softly, her lips barely moving.

Blade felt as if the golden sword had been driven into his own heart. He had never seen anything like this woman. With the masking cowl removed it was like seeing beauty emerge from a dungeon, and he guessed that the white robe also lied about the body beneath it. Her hair was a cloud of silver, the face a perfect heart with a thick cream skin. Her mouth was wide, moist and tender, and superbly drawn in scarlet, the nose beautifully straight and haughty, the eyes wide set and narrowed now as she lowered the sword and gazed down at the writhing victim.

Taleen was right, Blade thought. He was a fool. Otherwise he would not be thinking what he was thinking—that any woman so lovely could not be a murderess in cold blood. Fool indeed. He *knew* better. He had not been born yesterday. He still retained enough of his memory to

34

recall what his former world had been like, and certainly nothing had changed in Alb. Quite the contrary.

And yet he did not believe it, really believe it, until he saw it done.

The High Priestess raised the sword high above the cringing girl. She held it with both hands on the golden hilt, point down, and she smiled around at the Drus. There was total silence now, but for the muffled sounds of the terrified girl. The High Priestess smiled again. Her teeth sparkled like nacre against blood. Sweat stung Blade's eyes.

She brought the sword down with tremendous force and drove it into the girl's heart. Blade would not have attributed the strength to that slim body. The point drove on through the flesh and beating heart and grated against the stone capping of the stump. The naked victim, impaled on the golden blade, writhed and heaved in death agonies. Blood covered the heavy breasts and crept across the stone. The body stopped jerking and was still.

For a moment the High Priestess remained standing astride her victim. Her head was bowed now, her arms hung at her sides, and her manner was listless and depleted. She swayed and for a moment Blade thought she would fall, then she straightened and looked about her. Her eyes swept the silent circle of Drus and, for a long moment, lingered on the thicket where Blade and Taleen were concealed. He could not discern their color, and it was impossible that she knew of their presence, yet Blade felt the intensity of those eyes and something rippled cold along his spine.

Then it was over. She replaced her cowl, could once more have been a spry old woman, and leaped down from the stump. Without a word or gesture she stalked away from the crowd of Drus and disappeared into the trees on the far side of the glade.

The rest was mere butcher's work. Blade felt his sickness grow as he watched and listened to Taleen's whispered taunts.

"So I lie? So I am a credulous fool? I listen to foolish tales and repeat them, do I? It is a lie, then, that the Drus eat human flesh?"

She nudged him with her elbow. "Why, then, are they gutting that poor slave girl like a capon?"

They were stuffing the body now with small leaves of some kind. Blade felt that he had seen enough. He might even have conceded that he had seen too much. He did not care to linger and watch them spit the body and place it over the coals. It was past time to go.

Taleen whispered the same thought bred by a different concern. She was again fearful for her own tawny hide.

"In the name of Frigga, Blade, let us go! We have been lucky but it will not last forever. By some miracle we are still alive, no one has seen us, and no tales will be carried. If we go now it is just possible that—"

She was interrupted by a loud cry from the glade. Then another cry. Then a series of muted screams followed by a great hubbub.

A Dru was standing at the edge of the clearing. She was carrying the body of the Dru Blade had killed. She stood there, chanting and moaning, and her own white robe was as scarlet as that on the dead priestess she carried. The Drus rushed to gather about her, all gabbling and moaning and screaming as it suited them. Blade glanced across the glade to the spot where the High Priestess had disappeared. She did not reappear and he guessed that she had left the vicinity on some errand of her own. Perhaps, he thought viciously, she does not like the taste of human flesh.

Taleen was doing her share of soft moaning beside him. "Frigga save us now! They have found the slain one. We will be cursed forever, even if they do not kill us. I told you, Blade. I warned you. I—"

Blade put his big hand over his mouth. "Shut up, princess. Not another sound until I tell you. Now crawl backwards, very slowly and very carefully, and then follow me. I think it is time to run again. But softly—very, very softly."

Chapter 3

Taleen found her path just as the moon was setting. It was narrow and made rough underfoot by stones and flints and, judging by the depth below embanking hedges, had been trodden for centuries. Blade's feet suffered, while the Princess went easily enough in her buskins.

As they went Taleen poured out all her knowledge of the Drus, as though the horror she had just seen had triggered her tongue. Blade, by nature a skeptic, was too much shaken by the recent scene not to be attentive. He listened and learned. Later would be time enough to sort fact from fiction. One thing he already knew. The Drus could not be ignored. They were a fact of life in Alb. They did evil and they did good. The Mysteries—all knowledge and education, all medicine, all the higher arts and crafts and, most especially, all magic, were in Dru keeping. And woe to he who tried to usurp their prerogatives.

The princess, Blade learned, had been returning home after four years in a Dru school on the Narrow Sea when she had been attacked and captured by the minions of Queen Beata. The Queen was sister to King Voth of the North, and there was a great hatred between the two.

"She thought to hold me captive as long as it pleased her," Taleen said now, "and to bring a great ransom and many concessions from my father. He has great love for me, my father, and I am an only child. That bitch of a Beata would have succeeded, too, had I not had the foresight and the courage to bide my time and watch for my opportunity. I played very meek and frightened, Blade, and then I wept and told Beata that confinement was killing me. On my knees—and I will make her pay for *that*, by Frigga—on my knees I begged that I be allowed long walks in the woods and fields. I said I would die for lack of sun and air. Was that not clever of me, Blade? I pointed out that she, the queen, could have no profit of a dead princess. That was sly, eh, Blade?"

"Most clever," said Blade gravely. "Very sly, princess. So you watched your chance and seized a sword and slew one of your guards. Yes. Clever indeed. There is just one thing that puzzles me a bit."

The path had widened now, the going was easier, and she was swinging along briskly by his side. She cast him a sidelong look. "What puzzles you, Blade?"

Blade kept his face expressionless. "It was a brave thing, a great thing, for a girl like you to kill a warrior. I admit that. But how was it that you were alone with this guard? Was there only *one* guard? From the little you have told me of this Queen Beata she is no fool, so there must have been other guards. Where were they?"

He saw her scowl and kept his glance averted. He wanted to laugh and dared not. For the past few hours they had been getting on well and he did not want to spoil it.

Taleen was still frowning. "You ask too many questions, Blade. And the wrong questions. What business of yours is it that I—"

"None," he said hastily. "None at all, princess. Forget that I spoke."

For a minute or so they trudged on in silence. Then Taleen sighed heavily and said: "You are right, of course.

39

I think you must have been a wizard in your own land. There *were* other guards. But I selected one that I judged weak, the weakest of all, and cozened him with certain promises. He was a handsome rogue, and he knew it, and so believed me when I said that I desired him. He arranged for us to be alone, for I swore that I would not do anything but in private. When were alone I suffered his embrace, but only to get close to his sword, and then I killed him and ran. And found you sleeping by the brook. As naked as you are now!"

She scowled again, her lips a red pout, and her luminescent brown eyes traced up and down his brawny nakedness. "And I tell you this, Blade. Your bare hide now begins to offend me. There is just too much of you!"

Her eyes fell and lingered on his genital area. She made a face and averted her eyes in what he knew was a feigned disgust. "Get you some cover, Blade. I command it. I am sick of looking at you."

He raised the sword in mock salute. "Gladly, princess. Just where do I get it. You will perhaps weave me a breechclout here and now, on the spot?"

The problem solved itself a moment later in a manner neither could have foreseen. They rounded a narrow bend in the path and came upon an open field. It was a cultivated field, bordered by a crude fence of piled stones, and just beyond the fence a man rushed at them with upraised sword.

Blade leaped before the girl, his own sword raised. "Keep back!"

She was first to laugh. Followed by Blade, who put his sword down and joined her, doubling over in merriment. So ridiculous!

Yet, in the first shock of surprise, the scarecrow had looked human enough. The sword, of wood, threatening enough.

Taleen was helpless now, holding her flat belly, her breasts shaking, as she pointed from Blade to the scarecrow and then back again, powerless in the throes of peal after peal of manic laughter.

"You—you," she grasped, "tried to protect me from a scarecrow—"

Blade leaped the fence and tugged a pair of tattered linen breeches from the scarecrow. They fitted well enough, though a bit tight around his powerful thighs. He went back to Taleen, pondering the odd security that a man can derive from a simple pair of pants.

The sky was beginning to gray now, with a first hint of false dawn in the east. When the girl had laughed herself out they resumed their way. Blade was thankful for the incident, and did not mind seeming a buffoon. Her good humor was restored and she chattered like a magpie. Blade kept mostly silent, and noted the changing nature of the countryside. They left the woods, crossed a vast expanse of wold, and entered a region where cultivated fields were intersticed with fenland and marsh. As the true dawn came on and the stars paled, Blade made out the blurred shapes of thatched cottages, all of them on stilts, standing well back from the path. A drift of wood smoke, accompanied by the odor of cooking meat, made his belly churn. Cattle and horses, evanescent against linear pearl light from the east, moved and sounded as they made their way past. A goat trotted to a fence to give them a baleful inspection, then bleated in derision.

After the sights of that night Blade had felt he would never eat again. Now his stomach rumbled indelicately and he was ravenous. He said as much to Taleen, who had stopped chattering for a moment, and she bade him be patient. The town of Sarum Vil, and her cousin Lycanto, was not far now. They would be well fed.

After another small silence, during which Blade caught a whiff of salt air and knew they were near the sea, Taleen said: "Blade!"

"Princess?"

"I think it best that we do not speak of the things we

have seen this night. The Albs are a suspicious lot as it is, and I am going to have enough trouble explaining you. I do not think we should mention the Drus, or what we did or saw. If you agree I think we must make an oath on it."

It was agreeable enough to Blade, in fact suited his purpose, yet it was in his nature to probe a matter that interested him. Without looking at her he said, "You knew that girl who was killed tonight?"

After a moment: "I did not say that. Or did not mean it so. A princess does not *know* a serving wench. But I recognized her—she was of my cousin Lycanto's household. So what of this?"

He prodded her gently, unsmiling. "You mentioned gossip, and matters you did not understand. What of this indeed? I must know. You do not walk in peril now, but I do. How will these things affect me? And how came that poor girl into the hands of the Drus?"

He heard her sharp indrawn breath. "I spoke true when I said you were a wizard in your own land! Your wit is sharper than a sword—you go straight to the heart of matters. But you are right. It is another reason why we must not tell of what we have seen tonight."

"I am flattered," he said. "And yet a little confused. So tell me, straight out, wherein do I go to the heart of matters?"

"It must have been Alwyth," said the Princess. "She is wife to Lycanto. She is a shrew and a bitch, and I do not like her, yet she is a good wife and mother. And my cousin, Lycanto, is a fool like most men. He is like a rooster that thinks all hens are his personal property. The gossip of which I spoke is true—Lycanto has been bedding with that serving girl for months. Now Alwyth has found it out and has given the girl to the Drus for sacrifice. That much is simple. What is not so simple is what Lycanto will do if he finds this out. My cousin is a great warrior, very brave, and also very stupid. He is easygoing and hates trouble. He will suffer much to avoid it, espe-

42

cially with Alwyth. Yet if he finds out that his whore has been slain and eaten by the Drus, and with the aid and consent of Alwyth, then Frigga only knows what will happen. Lycanto will not attack the Drus because he is afraid of their magic, but his rage is terrible when it comes and who can tell who will feel his hand. Perhaps even you. Or me."

Blade gave her a cool stare. "You mean me, of course. You are kin of this Lycanto and he will not harm you. But me, a stranger—"

She nodded, and for a moment seemed to gloat. "Yes. I am glad you understand, Blade. The Albs are a cruel people. But if we keep our mouths shut tight, and Lycanto is in a good mood, I can have my will of him. I will ask for an escort of armed men, and insist that you accompany me north to my father. I am very grateful to you for saving me from Queen Beata, and my father, King Voth, will also wish to thank you in person. So that you understand, Blade."

He nodded. "I do understand."

Taleen smiled at him. "And besides, Blade, I have no wish to lose you yet. You frighten me a little. You puzzle me. Most of all you intrigue me. I have a feeling, Blade, that Frigga has cast a future for us. Love? Or perhaps death. Who can know?"

Frigga, as Taleen had explained, was the Goddess of all women in Alb, in Voth, and indeed in the whole land as far as the Princess knew. She was a trifle vague about her pantheon. She added, with some indignation, that Frigga was not recognized by the Drus and that worship of her, or even mention, was forbidden—a ruling which the common folk ignored, as did the well born.

The male deity in the land was Thunor, equally in bad grace with the Drus, and so invoked as often as possible. Blade filed the name of Thunor away for future reference, conceding that when in the land of Alb it might be as well to do as the Albians did, always within reason, of course.

Blade knew his own weaknesses all too well—temper and stubbornness. Plus a curiosity that would have slain a thousand cats.

They were climbing now, up a gradual slope, until at last they stood atop a long ridge. Below them the fens stretched in flat monotony to a sea that was mirror calm, reflecting the first rays of the sun. Inland the mists still shrouded the fens, and Blade noted that the intricate network of paths approaching Sarum Vil were all carefully marked by poles bearing tattered bits of cloth. The town, he saw at once, was well situated for defense.

"Something is amiss," said Taleen. She was frowning. She pointed down to the town. "Such hubbub is not usual so early in the morning. My cousin is a lazy man and usually sleeps as late as Alwyth will permit. You see, Blade? All those armed men!"

He was carefully studying the little town and the surrounding terrain. It was a fortified place, carefully laid out in rectangle and surrounded by a high wall of earth surmounted by a stockade of sharpened logs. Before the earthen ramparts, on all sides, was a deep ditch some twenty feet across. There was a high tower at each corner of the stockade, but unbastioned, and he judged that the Albs had not yet learned that trick of defense. He could see but one gate in the stockade, facing them, and it was open now. Through it, converging from the web of fen paths, poured a steady stream of armed men. Arms and armor glinted in the sun. A few of the warriors were on horseback, followed by a retinue on foot, but most of them were walking, in groups or alone, armed with sword, spear and shield, and wearing round metal caps that sparked in the sun.

Because of their elevation they could see well into the town, beyond the walls to a large central square where there was a great flurry of excited movement. More armed men were moiling about a huge bonfire, eating and drinking, while the drivers of war chariots dashed madly to and fro in the throng. Now and again a man was knocked down by the horses and there was a great outcry of cursing that could be heard by Blade and Taleen. He smiled to himself. Discipline was evidently not an Albian virtue.

Taleen pointed suddenly. "There! There is my cousin, Lycanto. Just to the right of the fire. You see? Now he is drinking from his horn. He does not look happy, my cousin." She laughed shortly. "That I can understand. Lycanto is a miser, as well as a lecher, and all these warriors will be eating him out of house and home. But there must be trouble, a war, else he would not have called them together. Trust Lycanto not to share his provisions lest he is driven to it!"

At that moment Blade heard a jangle of weapons on the path behind them. He spun about, his sword alert. He and the Princess had been so intent on watching Sarum Vil that neither heard the warriors approaching.

Taleen seized his sword hand and forced the point down. "No danger here, Blade. It is only Cunobar the Gray, Lycanto's chief man. A Captain. I know him, though I doubt he will know me. It has been many years since last we met. Stand back, Blade, and keep you quiet. I will handle this."

The man she had named Cunobar the Gray was leading a band of eight warriors. At sight of Taleen and Blade they halted and whispered among themselves for a moment, then Cunobar came forward. He was a tall man, narrow shouldered, and Blade guessed he was not as old as he looked. The silver gray of his hair and thick beard was premature. He wore a pointed bronze helmet bearing the design of a hawk in flight. The same design was worked into the boss of his heavy shield. He had drawn his sword, but lowered the point as he approached them. There was pride in his walk, and poise and confidence, and a lack of swagger.

Cunobar the Gray paid no attention to Blade. He fell to one knee before the Princess Taleen, jabbed the point of his sword into the earth, and doffed his helmet. His voice was deep and melodious, vibrant as a skald's harp. His eyes, above the heavy brush of gray beard, were a curious reddish brown and missed nothing of Blade without deigning to see him.

"It has been many years, my princess. Too many. I remember you as beautiful, but my memory is a traitor. How beautiful I did not know until this moment."

Taleen was greatly pleased. She shot a look of smug triumph at Blade, who discreetly stared at the ground and watched Cunobar from the corner of an eye.

Taleen touched Cunobar lightly on his gray head and laughed. "The same old Cunobar, I see. Even as a child you flattered me and turned my head and quite spoiled me." She pretended to frown. "For which I had to pay when I returned to my father. But rise now, Cunobar, and tell me what goes on in Sarum Vil. Why are the warriors gathering?"

The man stood up and sheathed his sword. He did not glance at Blade. His men had retired a little distance and were chattering among themselves.

"It is Getorix again," Cunobar said. "From over the Narrow Sea. He is raiding. Already half a dozen villages have been burnt and looted, and the people slain. Last night the beacons spoke that Getorix is near, and so King Lycanto prepares to go against him. What else? If Getorix is left unhindered he will blaze a path of murder through half of Alb. So all freemen and warriors have been summoned."

He glanced past Blade, still not seeing him, to the bonfire and confusion in Sarum Vil. "I do not know the why of your presence here, princess, and I do not ask. I doubt it is a concern of mine. But my men are hungry, as I am, and if we wish to break our fast we had best hurry. That pack of wolves will pick the King's larder as bare as bones on a beach."

They both laughed. Taleen said, "You are right. But if

I know my cousin he will save something back for himself. We will make him share it with us, Cunobar."

Only then did Cunobar appear to notice Blade. He said nothing, but he gave Blade a steely look, then glanced at Taleen and waited. She smiled and made a careless gesture toward Blade.

"It is all right, Cunobar. I vouch for him. He is my man—a freeman and entitled to bear arms, but not of our station. Of no importance, yet will I have him treated as well as he has served me."

The warrior, now that he had consented to notice Blade at all, was scrutinizing him from head to toe. "It is said that a favorite trick of Getorix is to send spies ahead. They travel as freemen, or serfs, and even as warriors. They mingle with the people and find out many things, study all our weaknesses, and report them back to Getorix."

Cunobar's men stopped chattering. They had heard. They all stared at Blade and one drew his sword. Another hefted his spear a little higher.

Blade turned his back on the lot of them and began to whistle a contemptuous little tune. Boldness was his only ploy. He stood no chance against all of them.

Taleen's voice took on an edge. "I have said that I vouch for him, Cunobar. Is that not enough?"

Cunobar's reply was only half apologetic, with an undertone of stubbornness. "More than enough, princess, in normal times. But you are a maiden, my lady, and cannot know the things a warrior knows. Getorix's spies are very clever. And if this fellow is a man of arms, as you claim, where *are* his arms? His helmet, his leathern armor and shield, his spear? He bears nothing but a cutty sword and wears a ragged pair of breeches that he might have stolen from a scarecrow."

Blade was glad that he was not facing them. He could not restrain his smile, a smile that Cunobar would have misunderstood.

Taleen appeared to have trouble with her voice, but she did not laugh. In a tone as cold and haughty as Blade had ever heard she said: "I do not like this, Cunobar. Have done. His name is Blade, he is my man, and I say once more that I vouch for him. I will not say it again. Now escort us into the town, my old friend, and do not make me lose my temper. I will explain matters to my cousin, to King Lycanto, and no other."

Blade turned to see Cunobar bow and stalk away. Over his shoulder he said, "I am sorry, princess. It is just that all strangers are suspect in Alb—especially now."

Blade and the girl stood aside as the armed men filed past. Cunobar, a bit on his dignity now, ignored them, but his men gave Blade a thorough scrutiny. The last man, a burly rogue who wore no helmet, winked at Blade as he passed. Blade winked back, and smiled.

Blade and Taleen fell in behind the warriors as they made their way down the hill toward the gate of Sarum Vil.

Blade said: "It was nice of you to make me a freeman. Very thoughtful. As long as I am to be *your* man I may as well get all the rank I can."

She laughed at him. "What would you? I did the best I could. It was no time to explain matters, even had I desired to, and Cunobar is not the man to explain them to. I will tell Lycanto the truth." Her half smile was insouciant. "At least I think I will."

Once again Blade reminded himself that this was a feckless and potentially dangerous girl-child. Like it or not, he was dependent on her for much. Too much. Perhaps even his life. He changed the subject.

"Who is Getorix?"

She frowned and her face was sombre. "A demon. A sea raider. Some call him Redbeard. Every few years he raids across the Narrow Sea, and pity is a word he does not know. His men are brutes who pillage and murder and rape, and he is the greatest brute of all. It is said that

48

he is a giant, born of devils, and that he bears a charmed life and cannot be slain."

Blade kept his face straight. She was delving in fantasy again. Even so this Getorix sounded like a tough customer. And he could not forget what he had seen in the Dru glade. As for a charmed life—Blade shrugged. He was in Alb, not London, and in a time and dimension he did not comprehend in the least. He must feel his way along, inching like a blind man, and it would not pay to scoff, or doubt, anything. *Anything!*

The princess had turned gloomy. "I do not think that Lycanto can defeat Getorix. He is brave enough, but he is also stupid. And his men are too few. Yet he must try—it is his responsibility. Each king must defend his own shore of the Narrow Sea, so if Getorix strikes here it is Lycanto who must fight him."

"There must be other kings," said Blade. "Other princes and leaders. Why do they not band together and fight this Getorix? So they would outnumber him and have the advantage, and could attack from many sides at once. Surely they are not *all* stupid?"

There was more intelligence in her answer than he would have credited her with. Again he warned himself not to underestimate her.

"They are not all fools," she admitted. "But they are all envious and greedy and they all hate. Strangers, even those from the next kingdom, which may be but a few *kils* away, are not trusted. Queen Beata—may she rot in her own dungeons—has many men-at-arms and is very rich, but she will not come to Lycanto's aid. Nor will my own father, for that matter. In such matters he is as stupid as the others. He cares only for Voth."

Blade was thoughtful. "And yet the subject might be brought up in war council. Who can tell? It might be worth a try."

She gave him a sharp look and her tone was acid. "And who will bring up this subject? Not I. Women are not allowed in war council. You, Blade? I have laughed enough for one day, when you tried to defend me from the scarecrow. Or perhaps you do not really understand yet. You are on sufferance! Your life is already forfeit—the moment it is known that you killed a Dru. And you heard Cunobar the Gray just now. They will kill you at the wink of an eye, simply because you are a stranger. Your life depends on me, Blade, and on me alone, and you had better not forget it. I will do what I can, because I have plans for you, but you must be like a mouse in a field that is never seen or heard. When we come to the town we will be separated, naturally, because an oaf like you will not be permitted in the great house of the king. I will see to it that you are fed and properly clothed, and armed as befits a freeman. But for Frigga's sake keep your temper down and your mouth shut! If you fall into a brawl, or arouse too much suspicion, I cannot save you."

Blade did not like the prospect and he did not like her tone. Yet he spoke softly enough.

"You have said that I must have been a wizard in my own land, princess. There may be some truth in that— more than I have admitted. It really depends on what you call a wizard and—"

Taleen stopped short and stared at him with wide eyes. She put her hands on her hips and scowled. "You talk like one who is moon sick, Blade. A wizard is a wizard! What else? A wizard knows spells, and magic, and can read the thoughts of others. A wizard cannot be killed—except by another wizard. If you are truly a wizard, Blade, you had better admit it to me now. It will make all the difference. I will tell my cousin and he will welcome you. You will be *his* wizard and help him defeat Getorix. Afterwards we will all live well and happy, just as in the tales the skalds tell children around the fire at night. So, Blade? Are you a wizard?"

There was a mingle of mockery and doubt in her eyes.

Blade sighed and kept rein on his temper. It was a time to tread softly.

"Listen to me," he said softly. "Listen well, Taleen. In my own land I am not a wizard—I spoke true in that. But in this land, in Alb, it may be that I am a wizard after all. I know many tricks, especially tricks of war, that will help your cousin defeat this sea raider. I give you my solemn word for that. But I must have his ear, I must speak with him as an equal, to be treated as a peer. I have no mind to languish in the servants' quarters—or even in the freemens'. You must persuade Lycanto to see me, to speak with me in private. Or, lacking that, to let me speak in the war council."

She took a step backward and put a hand to her mouth. They had been loitering and had fallen behind Cunobar and his party. Around them, to either side of the path, where the marsh was firm enough, were clusters of leathern and linen tents. Several small cook fires were smoking, and the common soldiery lounged about them, cooking meat and burnishing weapons, but mostly bantering among themselves. Set off from the path, but in plain view, were open latrines at which men stood or squatted. Near one tent was a short queue of soldiers patiently awaiting the favors of the laughing woman within.

Taleen, oblivious to this bawdy and natural earthiness, stared at Blade as if really seeing him for the first time.

"You have truly lost your wits, Blade. You are addled! You wish to speak in the war council. You! A raggle-taggle stranger wearing a scarecrow's breeches. Frigga strike me dead if I don't think you mean it."

Blade felt his temper slipping. A man could have too much of the princess. Yet he managed to control his tongue. He was an immense and powerful man, yet he understood that guile sometimes prevailed where power failed.

"You could arrange that I speak in the council, princess."

51

The brown eyes widened still more. "I could? How, then?"

"Through this Alwyth, wife to Lycanto. You have said that he dances to her tune. Speak with her, tell her that I am a wizard, and ask her to intercede for me with King Lycanto. It is all quite simple."

Her red mouth twisted in disdain. "Alwyth? I despise her. I will ask her no favors."

Blade essayed his most winning smile. The one that J had often alluded to as "the bomb."

"For me, Taleen? Who saved you from the dog? From Queen Beata? Who coddled you when you were cold and miserable? Is your memory so short, then?"

He knew the grave risk of overplaying, but she was a child—albeit a cunning one—and he took the chance.

She pouted as she considered him through narrowed eyes. Then she nodded, still sulky. "All right, Blade. I will do what I can. But let us go now. Cunobar is waiting for us at the gate and if I do not mistake that is Lycanto's chief of arms with him. You are already being whispered about, Blade. Come. And heed me again—keep your temper in chain!"

Chapter 4

For all that day Richard Blade languished miserably in the hut. It was a small affair, blackened inside by smoke and with a floor of packed earth. A circular hole in the roof provided the only ventilation. His sword had been taken from him and a guard stationed at the door. This was a saucy rascal with sparse hair, a harelip, and a ferocious squint. He was wary of Blade, yet not unfriendly, and had told Blade that his name was Sylvo. He had been a slave, but was now a freeman. Blade had taken a liking to the man.

There were no furnishings, so Blade lay on the bare floor and itched. He was filthy and his black stubble was fast turning to a beard. He kept having visions of a warm tub overflowing with suds. The hut abounded with lice and he partially amused himself by tracking down the tiny gray beasts and cracking them with his nails.

Now, as a first star was visible in the roof hole, his wrath approached its limits. Either Taleen had forgotten him or she had been unable to prevail. Either way he was ignored, forgotten. All day he had been shut in while the din and confusion increased in the town. Blade could not see, but he could hear, and he read the sounds accurately.

53

King Lycanto was not going to fight today. More and more soldiers kept arriving. The chariots raced and men were trampled. There was a deal of dicing and drinking, and much drunken laughter and ribaldry, and sometimes the squealing laughter of camp followers. Blade, glowering to himself, thought that Lycanto ran anything but a tight camp. If this Getorix, Redbeard, kept any rein on his men at all they would have little trouble defeating such a rabble. Blade, who could accept discipline, and knew how to impose it, chafed as though the prime responsibility for such defeat would be his own. This both puzzled and amused him.

At first, after Cunobar's men had thrown him roughly into the hut, he had welcomed the chance to think quietly and without interruption. He knew that his memory was beginning to fail—though with an effort he could yet summon back what was important—and now in his confinement he tried to reason out what had happened to him. It was not easy, and he knew that there was much margin for error. Blade had always been a man of action, intelligent but not intellectual, and he surely was no scientist. So now he tried to look at matters in their simplest form.

The computer experiment had gone wildly wrong. Either the machine, or Lord Leighton, had made a whopping mistake. As a result Blade's brain had been addled, mixed up. It was not a happy thought, yet it must be faced.

Doctors used electric shock to cure. In his case a sort of reverse effect had been achieved. The shock had not driven him mad, in the usual sense, but it must have rearranged the entire molecular structure of his brain tissue.

His reading on the subject had been that of the usual layman—scant. He did not really understand the complex structure of the human brain, and certainly he did not think in terms of neurons and nucleic acids and the synthesis of proteins. DNA was a blank page to him. Yet he knew enough to realize that the experts knew little more.

54

The brain was still an unexplored continent in which anything, if not likely, was certainly possible.

Blade concluded that his cerebral cortex had been so scrambled that he was enabled to perceive an entirely different world than he had known before. It was a real world, as he was real, yet it existed in a different dimension. A dimension that his old brain, before Lord Leighton, had been unable to comprehend.

Now, cracking a very real louse with dirty nails, Blade became quite pleased with himself. Nearly smug. He did not know whether it had anything to do with time or space, though he doubted it. *Dimension!* There must lie the answer. For the moment he was content with it.

For one fact he was grateful. The computer shock had not affected his lower brain, that mass of spidery cells and nerve fibers just above the *foramen magnum.* He had inherited that lower brain from remote ancestors, as far back as the great lizards, and it was packed with instinctive guile and animal cunning. His convoluted and highly complex cerebral cortex might stand him in good stead, but it was his animal brain, with its lightning reflexes and will to survival, that would save him. If he was to be saved.

Nor had the shock altered his personality, Blade conceded with a little grin. He was *still* Richard Blade. Stubborn, combative, at times inconsistent, given to sudden rages and quick regretting. Restless and impatient of fools. A sensual man of vast sexual appetite. Loyal friend and deadly foe. Large of body and huge of spirit, capable of love and lust, of mercy and cruelty. Not a man molded to adorn a church, and yet no friend of the Devil.

Having disposed of all the lice he had gone back to his musing when the door swung open and the man Sylvo came in. He was carrying a wooden trencher containing meat and black bread, and a horn of the foamy light beer that Blade had tasted earlier, complaining of thirst, and had found good.

Sylvo knew his business. He carried a short, razor edged spear and he gestured with it now. "Over in the corner, master, as before. I would not have you too close to me. By Thunor—I think those arms of yours could throttle a bull!"

Blade obeyed, smiling at the man. Sylvo, though guarding him, treated Blade with a mixture of deference, awe and resolution.

Blade crossed his massive arms and stared at the man. "How much longer am I to be penned in this sty?"

Sylvo placed the trencher in the middle of the floor and retreated to the door. He seemed in a mood for talk, and Blade thought he smiled in return. With Sylvo it was hard to tell. Not only was his balding head misshapen—the midwife had not been gentle in wrenching him from the womb—but his terrible squint and harelip lent him a countenance that must have set infants to squalling whenever he passed.

Blade, bored and frustrated, wrathful—and more nervous than he liked to admit to himself—took a sudden notion to bait the man. He squatted by the trencher and, after a bite of bread and meat and a long quaff of the beer, pointed the mutton bone at Sylvo.

"Do you know, my man, that you are singularly unprepossessing?"

Sylvo's face creased. His eyes, what Blade could see of them behind the squint, were small, beady and black.

"Thank you kindly, master. It is not often that poor Sylvo hears kind words. Cuffs and kicks it is, usually. I thank you—even though I know not the meaning of such high born words."

Blade choked back laughter with another mouthful of meat, and felt a moment's shame for his baiting of the man. The poor fellow was only doing his job.

He swallowed and said, "You do not answer my question. How much longer am I to be penned here?"

Sylvo scratched himself vigorously. He wore a loose

linen tunic, falling free over baggy breeches cross-gaitered from the knee down. On his sparsely haired pate was the usual metal cap, set at a rakish angle. His feet were bare and filthy. A most unsoldierly oaf, Blade thought, yet noted that the beady little eyes never left him and the spear was always at the ready.

Sylvo found a louse in his armpit and killed it before he answered. "As to that, master, I can give no answer unless I lie. And though I am undoubtedly a bastard, and the son of a whore, and Thunor knows that I have more sins than virtues, I have never been a liar. Neither am I King Lycanto, and it is he alone that can answer your question. Content yourself, master. It is none so bad in here. Think of me. Of Sylvo. I am the one suffering."

Blade repressed a grin. "You suffer? How so?"

Sylvo threw out a hand and shrugged in disgust, yet the other hand kept the spear steady on Blade. "I have not been relieved, that is how. I have been forgotten. As usual. The beer is flowing as free as the tides, there are women to be had everywhere for the taking, and I have been stuck with the task of guarding you. Is that not suffering?"

Blade agreed that it was. And offered a solution. "That is easily put to rights. Why guard me so closely? I am alone, one man in an unfriendly camp. I cannot escape. What could I do? Where could I go? And who is to know if you leave your post for a little time? Go and get your share of the beer, Sylvo. Take time for a woman. I will be here when you come back."

The man's scrawny body began to shake. He rocked back and forth and from his malformed lips came a cackling sound that Blade recognized, with some difficulty, as laughter.

"Ar, master. You will be here right enough! And so will I—watching you. My head is not pretty, I admit, but I have no wish to have it struck off and stuck on a pole."

Blade had not really expected the gambit to work. He was convinced there was more to Sylvo than met the eye,

57

though that was horrendous enough. He changed the subject.

Scraping up meat crumbs with a bit of black bread, he said: "What of Getorix? The one they call Redbeard. I had thought that King Lycanto would march against him today."

Sylvo made an odd sound with his mouth. "So likewise had we all thought—at least the common folk. But not so. Men are slow in arriving, those who have arrived are drunk, and there is more gambling and chariot racing than drilling. More wenching than spear sharpening. The captains quarrel among themselves and sulk when they are overruled. The king and his wife, Alwyth, have also quarreled—she threw a pannikin at his head in plain view of all the men—and in general the town is like a hen coop with a fox loose in it. Yet all may be well. We have word that Redbeard plans to land at Penvey, which is only a day's march to the south, and it is yet possible that we will be there to meet him."

Sylvo yawned mightily, showing a few blackened teeth. "I hope so, master, for guarding my betters is not my idea of a soldier's work. There is no fun in it, and no profit." He glanced about the barren hut with disgust. "No loot, master. Not a scill's worth."

Blade came alert at the mention of Alwyth. He still had hopes for his plan of establishing an identity and a status—though it would involve some canny lying—and if Sylvo knew of Alwyth's doings he might also know something of Taleen. Who, he thought grumpily, was letting him down. He set about pumping the man as best he could.

Blade shook his head. "So the king and his queen quarrel in public? That is bad, Sylvo. Of what do they dispute?"

The man squinted at him and chuckled. "None of your affair, master, and yet I will tell you. It is common enough knowledge. The king is a great cock and likes his

58

hens—of late he has been topping a serving wench by name of Gweneth. All knew but the queen—but now she has found out and the wench has disappeared. The king is sullen about it, and very full of beer—else he would not have brought it into the open—and he claims that Alwyth has done away with the girl. Or had it done, since the queen is not likely to soil her own hands with the murder of a servant."

Blade failed, for an instant, to guard his expression. And learned that the man Sylvo was indeed shrewd.

"You have an odd look to you, master. Could you know aught of this?"

Blade managed innocence. "I know of it? How? I am a stranger, as you well know. I have no friends in Sarum Vil, unless it be the Princess Taleen, for whom I did some small service. And she," he added gloomily, "has forgotten me."

For a moment the rude hut vanished and Blade was back in the glade of sacred oaks. That silver hair, the slim body, the lovely and demonic face as the golden sword slashed down. Who was she? Where had she gone? He did not know it at the time, but it was the beginning of a long haunting.

And it explained, or so he would have sworn, how the servant girl had come into the hands of the Drus.

At the mention of Taleen the guard's hideous face brightened. "Ar," he admitted, "there is a woman for you! Only a girl, I know, and no doubt virgin as the high born keep their daughters, but a woman none the less. The man who first cleaves that cunna will be a fortunate knave indeed. Ar, that he will."

Blade frowned at him, pretending anger. "I think you speak above yourself."

Sylvo laughed, not a bit abashed. "Ar, master, perhaps I do. But who is to know? You? Come now, master. You are a beggar with one pair of ragged breeches. I do not fear you. Though I admit that you are probably high born and could strangle me like a newborn babe, yet it serves you nothing. For a time I am master here and you are prisoner. Is that not the truth of it?"

Blade grinned and admitted that it was. And made a vow to teach Sylvo manners, if ever the opportunity arose.

"What of the Princess Taleen. Have you seen her?"

Sylvo was seeking for another louse in his armpit. "Only when the two of you first entered town. Since then she has kept to herself in the king's great house. You seem to have a great interest in the princess, master."

Blade watched the play of speculation across the ruined face. Bawdiness was second nature to the man. Then Sylvo shook his head so hard that his helmet nearly tumbled off.

"No! It is not possible. The princess is of the high blood and you—"

There was a light tapping at the door. Sylvo, who had been squatting on his heels, leaped up and half faced the door, yet keeping the spear vigilant on Blade. The man grinned. "Ar, that will be my relief. About time, by Thunor! I shall have my share of the beer and women after all."

"Best answer it then," said Blade dryly, "and stop your cackling." As he spoke he glanced up at the roof hole. The stars had vanished and a coil of mist hung just over the aperture. The night had turned thick and gloomy.

Sylvo was whispering at the door. Frowning and squinting and mumbling. It was not his relief, then. Blade heard a woman's whisper and the rustle of feminine garments. He took a deep breath of relief. She had not forgotten him after all.

He was puzzled by what followed. Sylvo extended a hand through the narrowly cracked door, took something, then closed the door and turned to face Blade again. "By Thunor's liver," he said, "this matter grows in mystery." He tossed a coin in the air and caught it, then bit it with his snaggle teeth. "And I have come by a whole mancus.

60

Pure bronze. I, Sylvo, who have never seen aught but iron scills in my life. A mancus! With three of them I could buy a farm and cattle. A mancus! Me. Poor Sylvo."

Blade could not restrain his impatience. "That was the Princess Taleen, then? She gave you a note? A message for me?"

Sylvo bit the coin again, then slipped it into a purse on his belt, from which also hung a naked dirk. He squinted at Blade.

"Wrong, master. Ar, very wrong. Therein lies the danger—which I have agreed to risk for a mancus. And great danger it is, by Thunor! Danger for both of us. So listen well, master, and make me a promise that you will never speak of this."

Blade lost his temper. He roared like a bull. "Stop your mumbling, you ugly lout, and speak clearly! Who was it, if not the Princess Taleen? And what is all this prattle of danger?"

Sylvo squinted and caressed a few scraggy hairs on his chin. "It is the Lady Alwyth, master. The queen. She would speak with you. She is waiting now until I have your promise of silence. I must have it. Ar, I am no fool. When two great stones play together it is always the kernel in the midst that is crushed."

"Have done with your cursed riddles," Blade shouted. "It is all the same, then. This lady brings me a message from the princess, that must be it. Admit her at once."

Sylvo was not to be hurried. His face was contorted in thought. "Not so fast, master. It is my head and I must think of it—else who will? You are strange here, I am not. I know stories of the Lady Alwyth that you do not. It is a dour, murk night and she comes alone and without escort and seeks to buy silence. Such nights have a way of breeding dark deeds. And still—a whole mancus to me!"

Blade controlled himself. He shrugged his big shoulders in feigned indifference. "Suit yourself. It is none of my affair and, as you say, it is your head. But I will give my oath not to speak of this and"—slyly—"you will have to give back the mancus if you do not admit the lady."

Blade turned his back, crossed his arms and gazed up through the roof at the roiling mist.

He heard Sylvo mutter. "Return the money? Not by the hairs on Thunor's head. I have your promise, master?"

"You have it."

Sylvo muttered again. "Then I will give you half the time it takes a water clock to empty. No more. I will be just outside, master, with my spear and dirk, so attempt no escape. If you do I will kill you and then try to lie my way out of it—it would not be the first time. You swear this on Thunor's heart?"

Blade faced him and held up his right hand. "I swear it on Thunor's heart. Now admit the lady. And keep sharp watch. I do not wish to be interrupted. Nor, I think, will the lady."

"In that, master, we are all agreed." Sylvo opened the door and slipped out.

The single flambeau guttered and smoked in the sudden draft. It was secured to a beam by an iron sconce—nothing more than a ring—and it gave a dim red light and stank abominably of fish oil.

The Lady Alwyth. Lycanto's queen herself! Blade did not know what to make of it. Yet he took heart. Taleen must have spoken with the queen, had pleaded his cause with some success, or the lady would not be here. Yet why Alwyth and not the princess herself? Why all the secrecy, the furtive payment for silence? Blade shrugged. He would know soon enough. And anything was better than this stinking hut.

The door opened, then closed swiftly. At once Blade caught the scent of *chypre*. It was Taleen then, by some trick! No. This woman was far too short, too tiny, to be the princess. The heavily muffled figure that stood watching him was barely five feet tall. She wore a heavy cloak of fur, trimmed with a finer and more glossy fur that he thought was ermine, or possibly sea otter. Her dark blonde hair was caught up high and held with a single long golden pin. Her coronet was of gold and figured with dragons rampant. A white veil, secured to the coronet on either side, masked her face.

She spoke first. "You are Richard Blade? He who came to this place with the Princess Taleen?" Blade did not miss the tinge of spite as she spoke Taleen's name.

He bowed. "I am that Richard Blade, my lady." He waited. He was out of his depth, knew it, and so must let her take the lead.

He could not penetrate the white veil, but knew that she was seeing very well. She eyed him up and down, making no effort to disguise the scrutiny that she might have given an animal, or a slave in the market place. Again he caught the waft of *chypre*. A perfume that only the well born could afford. Later he was to learn that the use of *chypre* was forbidden to all but a few, on pain of death.

Her voice was husky, sure and incisive, yet pitched nearly as low as a man's. She raised a white hand, on which rings sparkled, and pointed to the guttering torch. "Stand over there. I would see you better."

Blade did as he was bade. He did not like her tone. He had a premonition that, were he ever to see her face, he would not like it either. He moved into the light without speaking.

Again the long scrutiny. Blade, without seeming to, studied her as closely. Though she might be tiny, she filled the cloak well. He thought that she breathed harder now than when she entered, and the breasts beneath the cloak were full enough.

"Taleen spoke truth in one thing," she said at last. "You are a magnificent animal! Truly a brute of a man. Have you a head to go with it, Blade? Can you think? Or are you merely another bed warrior?"

Blade nearly scowled. Yet he kept his temper and

bowed again, careful not to appear obsequious. "I have been known to think, my lady." Then, before he could bite it back, "As to being a bed warrior—would you care to challenge me, my lady?"

One small foot, clad in a pale leather sandal, began to pat the earthen floor. Yet he thought she smiled behind the veil.

"You are a saucy rogue! Taleen spoke the truth again. Take down your breeches, Blade."

Complete poise, in any situation, is given to few men. Blade was one of that few. Yet even he hesitated for a moment. But only for a moment—then he loosened his ragged scarecrow's breeches and stepped out of them. He prayed now that he would not begin to react to the scent of her and the nearness of her femaleness, and so make a further show of himself. This was all very infra dig, and he thought again that in doing as the Albians did one had to do some damned nutty things!

The woman moved closer to him. One of the jeweled hands moved and for a moment he thought she would touch him, but she contented herself by looking. She walked completely around him. There was no doubt that she breathed faster now. He began to guess, a little, at the secret. Nymphomania in Alb was much the same as nymphomania in London.

As she moved away she traced fingers lightly over the small of his back. Blade shivered. And, as he had feared, began to react.

Her laugh, muffled by the veil, was husky. "A veritable ox. Put on your breeches, Blade. Pleasure postponed is pleasure prolonged."

She stood watching as he pulled on his breeches and adjusted them. She was holding the fur cloak tightly about her.

"Taleen says you are a wizard, Blade. This is true?"

He played it straight and for all it was worth. For the moment he was lost, understanding nothing, yet he sensed that there was deadly purpose in this strange visitation. The smell of intrigue, and of danger, was as palpable in the hut as the stink of the wavering torch.

He bowed again, very slightly this time. "It is true, my lady. You are in need of a wizard?" He let the sarcasm ring clear.

She let it pass. Her hand moved again, a sparkling white moth in the dim light. "Yes, Blade. I need a wizard. But I also need a warrior. You are a fighter, or so Taleen tells me." Again a wisp of spite clung to the princess' name.

"I have killed my share of men." It was true. No need to mention that he had dealt in more sophisticated death, in another life, a different cosmic dimension. She would have named him madman, raving. And death was still death—name it how you liked, purvey it as you would. Hot and bloody. Cold and final. The end result was the same.

For a moment there was silence in the hut. The torch sparked and stank. Dank mist sank through the roof hole and lay in ghostly strata near the ceiling. From somewhere in the town came a sudden roar of laughter and the chiming clash of swords. She watched him through the veil.

At last she spoke. "There is none to hear us, Blade. If trouble comes of this I will be believed, not you, and I will see that you are flayed alive, inch by inch. I will speak my heart, with no mincing of words, no lies, no Dru language of many meanings or sometimes none at all. You will listen, Blade, and you will heed well, and then you will forget that I have spoken so. It is action I require of you, not words. All this is understood?"

He inclined his head. This was indeed a night for mystery.

She moved a step closer. The sensual odor of *chypre* enveloped him.

"There is little time, Blade, so I will be as brief as may be and have you still understand me. Long ago, when I

65

was but a maiden, the Drus prophesied to me that I would one day rule Alb. The old high priestess, long dead now, bespoke me in private and said that I would marry a king. Which I did. I was also told that one day a stranger would come—his visage and manner were not foretold—but he would be a warrior, in great repute with ladies, and through him I would come to rule Alb."

Blade was listening with great attention, every sense attuned. It was all mumbo-jumbo, no doubt a stock Dru prophecy designed to flatter, and yet here he was. With the Lady Alwyth, Queen of Alb.

She sensed his thought and from behind the veil came a spate of mirthless laughter. "I also doubted, even then when I was a callow virgin. The Drus are great liars and twist words as a smith twists iron. Yet I did not forget. And you *are* here, Blade. Who can gainsay it?"

Blade nodded in silence. Who indeed could gainsay it! Not he. Not since Lord Leighton and his infernal, and erratic, computer.

"I will ease your mind about the Princess Taleen, who I think is so much taken with you," she went on. The spitefulness was back. "She came at once to me and, though we hate each other, tried to cozen me that I speak to the king and get you a place at the War Council. As brazen as any camp whore, she was. I listened, saying but little, and so learned much about you. Is it true, Blade, that she came on you sleeping naked in the forest?"

"It is true. I was carried by magic from my own land, where I am a wizard, and by a miscalculation I was unclothed."

He watched her narrowly, trying to judge reaction behind the veil.

"That is as may be," she said calmly. "I do not believe it, but it is of no moment. As soon as Taleen was empty of words I realized that my time had come, that perhaps the old Dru did not lie for profit and favor. I had a potion made and gave it to Taleen in broth. It stimulates the swooning sickness, and she lies so now."

Blade scowled. "You have harmed her? Or intend to?"

A quick negation of the white hand, jewels glinting. "I have not harmed her. She merely sleeps, and so being harmless will not be harmed. I am not fool enough to risk the wrath of her father, Voth of the North. And she is cousin to my husband, Lycanto. He is a fool, a drunkard and a weakling who seeks to dip his limp sword into every female he can find, yet an affront to his own blood would rouse him. I play not that game. Instead I shall be sly and send Taleen back to her father, with ample escort, and so gain credit with Voth for saving her from the evil Beata."

"Which I did," growled Blade.

The white veil moved as she nodded. "Which you did. And for which I will be credited." She was yet closer to him, the scent of her stronger, her white hands fluttering near his nakedness.

"A small matter, Blade. Suffice that we get Taleen out of the way with no blame to us. Forget her. I have arranged that you sit on the War Council this night!"

He did not show his surprise. He nodded gravely. "To what purpose, my lady? I know *my* purpose, my reasons for asking Taleen to arrange this, but what purpose of *yours* that I sit on this Council?"

"For diverse reasons." She ticked them off on bejeweled fingers. "That you come to know Lycanto and his warriors, most especially his chiefs and captains, for it is with them that you must deal when he is dead."

A hard smile crooked the corner of Blade's firm mouth. "He is going to die, then?" His feigned surprise sounded nearly genuine.

Impatience now, for the first time. "Taleen said you were a fool in some things, yet not a fool in many. Be not a fool now! Why think you I am here, skulking like a thief in dark night? What manner of wizard are you that cannot see what is in my mind?"

67

He turned brusque. "You are right, my lady. I would be a poor wizard indeed if I could not read you. You wish me to slay Lycanto?"

A careless shrug. "Or have him slain. It is all one to me. I do not know how wizards do these things, but it would be better if the blame lies not on you."

His little bow was mocking. "And certainly not on you, eh, my lady?"

"Certainly not on me." She glanced around the rude hut with disdain. "I leave you soon, and when I go from this pigsty I leave all knowledge of what was spoken here. I will mind my wifely affairs and wait for news that Lycanto is dead. How you arrange it is nothing to me. Perhaps you *cannot* arrange it, and it is you who will be killed, and this too matters not to me. It will mean that you are a poor wizard and not the stranger prophesied to me by the old Dru. I have done all I can—I have procured you a place at the Council, where for a little time you will sit as a peer and be listened to. There is danger, grave danger. For you. You will be tested, well tested, for if Lycanto is a fool most of his chiefs are not. But if you succeed, Blade, if you win, there will be reward enough."

"And this reward?"

"Great enough, Blade, for a man who now has nothing and who stands to win everything. Enough for a beggar who can die at the whim of any drunken man at arms and no penalty to pay, save it be a paltry few scills in murder tax. You will rule with me, Blade, if you prove the man for it. In bed as in battle, and the proving lies on you. You see I do not lie or give false promises. There is no need for such, with you."

He nodded. So be it. It was as much as he could hope for in the circumstances. He would play her game minute by minute, hour by hour, and at the same time play his own game. He must tread a prickly path, and no help for it.

He took a step toward her. They were very near now,

and her scent was cloying and tantalizing in his nostrils. Taleen had aroused him and he had fought it back; the Lady Alwyth, with her doll's figure and scent, her veil and its aura of mystery, most of all the murder in her heart, aroused a cold and careless lust in him. She sought to use him as weapon. Very well, he would use her as receptacle to cool his lust. At once. Here. Now. Swiftly and brutally.

He reached for the veil. "I would see your face, my lady."

Blade was accustomed to success in these matters, yet not greatly surprised when, with a single lithe movement, she eluded his grasp and stepped away. Her hands went to where the veil was secured to the golden coronet. Her question was filled with mockery.

"You are sure, Blade! Quite sure that you would see my face? I warn you—it is a thing to think on."

So aroused was he now that he gave no thought to anything but the taking of her, as swiftly and fiercely as possible. He moved toward her and again she skipped away, still mocking him.

She was laughing. "I am half beautiful, Blade. Riddle me that. And say again that you wish to see my face. For then I will show it, which will cool you instantly and cheat me of that monster." She was gazing at the front of his thin breeches where the physcial manifestation of his lust was plainly writ.

He did not, in that tumescent moment, give a damn what lurked behind the veil. The words, unthought on, came automatically from his lips and it was not until later that he realized the implication. He was more than merely in Alb now. He was Albian!

He leaped at her. "I would see," he said hoarsely. "By Thunor, I *will* see! And I will have you. Here and now."

She halted him with a hand against his massive chest. Her fingers curled in his dark chest hair.

"Then see, Blade." She whisked away the veil.

Blade could not repress his exclamation. He took a step back and stared. He had seen sights to turn the stomach before, but never anything like this. It was horror. Horror made double by contrast.

The Lady Alwyth was a female Janus, two faced, the schism explicit in exact middle from forehead to chin. One half-face was lovely of skin and contour, the nose high arched and patrician, chin firm, eye blue and sparkling, brow pale and unlined.

The single blue eye watched him. In a tone of mockery and venom she said, "How think you now, Blade? Do you cool?"

The other half of her face was no face at all. Where flesh had been there was now a raw red cicatrix, the fiberous tissue drawn into spiderwebbing scars that reached below her chin and around to her ear. The eye was still there, an eye that glared milky white and ulcerous beneath the maimed lid.

Blade took a deep breath. He was still in rut, but she had been right. The true urge was gone. Instinct warned that he tread as carefully as ever in his life. For his life. A wrong move now and she would see him dead, nor care that it wrecked all her plans.

Lady Alwyth turned so that only her unscathed profile was visible. She was lovely so, and Blade felt pity. And as pity is the death of love, or lust, so he felt himself begin to droop as desire fled.

She raised a hand to touch the side of her face away from him. "A gift from my King husband. Long ago, at childhood play. I was a maiden captured by sea robbers, and tortured by them. Then something—I do not now remember—something drew the other children away and left Lycanto alone with me. But recently I had quarreled with him and spat in his face. We had a fire against the cold that day and he took a brand—but you have seen it. Lycanto's revenge. He was eight years then, I but six."

He understood, then, the hate that welled in her like

70

poison in a cup. Understood her spite for the beautiful Taleen.

He could not feign ardor now, and was too wise to try. To show his pity, or revulsion, was death. In a cold, matter-of-fact voice he said, "It is true that half your beauty is ruined, my lady. But only half. You are fortunate in that, for how many women are beautiful in *any* fashion?"

"Too many," she said darkly. "A truth that does not please me." He knew she spoke of the Princess Taleen— and in the same moment knew she lied when she spoke of returning Taleen unharmed to her father. She would find a way to destroy Taleen.

She turned full face to him again. That blighted milky orb glinted in the gloom. The torch was burning low and the smoke was thickening.

Her husky voice was silken smooth, she spider wise, as she looked at him. "You still desire me, Blade? And I warn you—nothing but truth."

He met her good eye without flinching. "I am a man, my lady. I desire you."

"You will do my bidding, then? Find a clever way of killing Lycanto, so no blame attaches to us?"

"I will." He intended it as a lie, but how to be sure? He might very well have to carry it out.

"Then see another part of your prize." She threw open the fur cloak. Beneath it she was naked.

Her minikin body was as flawless as her face was imperfect. She was built in absolute proportion, on a miniscule scale, with a blonde's pale cream skin. Her firm pointed breasts were painted blue and tipped with scarlet. (Blade had already noted that some of the warriors painted themselves, and did not yet know that only married women could do likewise.)

The Lady Alwyth stood on tiptoe and preened for him. Her waist was tiny, and his big hands would have fitted well around it, but when he sought to embrace her—he was again ready—she moved away like a wraith. Blade did not pursue, but stood glowering, calling himself a simpleton and yet raging to get into her.

She stood wide legged now, her head thrown back and her beautiful half-face turned to him. She caressed her blue painted breasts with her jeweled fingers and watched him with narrowed eyes. As he gazed more intently he saw that her lush small body was marked blue in other parts—there was a sort of runic tatooing under each breast.

Her words were barely audible. "You desire me now, Blade?"

His lower brain in command, Blade said fiercely, "I desire you, my lady. Here and now."

She laughed and closed the fur cloak. "That is good. Desire me enough, Blade, do as I have spoken, and you shall have me. And doubt me not—I am a prize worth having."

She was gone, so swiftly that Blade, nearly ill with unappeased lust, his loins aching, stared at the shadows as though she might be hidden there. Her scent lingered in the hut, and but for that he might have thought it all a dream, a fantasy wrought by some potion in his beer.

It was the man Sylvo who brought him back to harsh reality. He entered and pointed his spear at Blade, his lunatic face creased in a leer.

"You have friends above the salt, master. By Thunor you have! The word comes that you are wanted at the king's great house. Gossip has it that you sit at the War Council, though this I do not believe. More likely they mean to have some sport with you before you are hanged or skinned."

Sylvo, bursting with this news, and his wits a bit fuddled by it, for once grew careless. The spear point drooped.

Blade moved like a great serpent. Before the man could breathe again he had him in a full nelson, crunching the misshapen face down into the scrawny chest. Sylvo groaned and dropped his spear. He fumbled for the dirk at his belt and Blade, loosing one hand, nearly broke the man's wrist with a downward slash.

"Now," Blade said softly, "now, Sylvo, who rules in this hut?"

"You, master! You rule." Sylvo was choking, yet he tried to kick back at Blade.

Blade, wide straddled, lifted the man as easily as he might a babe in arms. He turned the man and changed his grip, his left hand about the scrawny neck. Sylvo's tongue lolled and began to turn color, and his eyes popped even as they begged.

Blade drew back his mighty right fist. "I would teach you manners, my man. This is a lesson, nothing more. In future you will know how to speak to your betters."

He deliberately muffled the blow, for he did not wish to maim or kill, yet it was a buffet that might have floored a largish horse. Sylvo went sprawling across the floor to end up against a wall, his little eyes glazed.

Blade prodded him with a foot and grinned. "Get up, man! Escort me to the house of Lycanto."

Chapter 5

Matters went badly from the beginning.

Blade was enjoined to silence, under penalty of immediate death, and so deprived of his only weapon. He was seated in a crude, barrel-shaped chair, with the light of a flaring torch in his face, and harshly told to keep his peace. He dared not defy this—his position being so weak—so he made do with his eyes and brain, straining to use both to best advantage.

The Council Room was large, with an earthen floor strewn with rushes and sand, and leather hanging on the walls. It was well lit and stank of fish oil. A fire, like an enormous red cat, drowsed in a huge fireplace before which slept massive hounds of much the same breed as the one he had slain in defense of Taleen.

There were ten other men in the room, of whom Blade recognized only Cunobar the Gray. The man ignored him.

The ten sat grouped around a long table set on trestles. In a corner, opposite Blade, and coughing now and again from the smoke, sat a white robed Dru so heavily cowled that she seemed headless. She was an amanuensis, with aging vein-traced hands that were yet nimble enough with brush and dye pot. She wrote on large squares of pressed

74

birch bark and Blade, watching her hands move, guessed it to be a runic script.

Lycanto, King of Alb and husband to the Lady Alwyth, sat at the head of the table with Cunobar to his right and a thickset bald warrior to his left. All ignored Blade, while talking of him as if he were some strange animal, something to pique mild curiosity, but not to be taken too seriously.

"He says he is a wizard. I say he is more likely witch, or warlock, which is not at all the same thing. At very best I call him spy, sent by Redbeard, and so he should suffer a spy's death. Flaying."

The speaker, a burly man to Lycanto's left, stroked his bald head with a badly scarred hand and did not glance at Blade.

"And yet," said Cunobar, "the Lady Taleen speaks for him. She names him wizard and also vows that he saved her from Beata's men—and from a fierce hound."

A grizzled man at the lower end of the table spoke up. "Then what is the question? Why make so large a thing of what is simple enough? There is an ordeal, one we all know. Put him to it."

Blade was intent on Lycanto, the King, for in the end his fate would lie on Lycanto's whim. What he saw was not reassuring.

He judged Lycanto to be in his forties, a lanky man with drooping blond moustaches that did little to conceal a receding chin. His light blue eyes, inflamed now by copious amounts of beer, were too narrow set, his nose too long and thin. A single droplet kept appearing at the end of that thin nose, and Lycanto repeatedly wiped it away. He paid no more attention to Blade than did the others.

Only Lycanto's chair had a back, and arm rests carved in the form of dragons, and only he wore a metal helmet on which was engraved a crown. He lolled on his throne, indolent and sullen, drinking constantly from a great horn in a stand before him. His fingers, clean enough and spatulate in shape, drummed incessantly on the table. Blade thought the King's mind strayed, and he wondered if it were to the Lady Alwyth and the things she did in dark, dank mist.

Now Lycanto spoke. His voice was reedy, high pitched, with an oddly girlish tremor to it.

"There is more to this than meets your eye, Bartho." He was addressing the last speaker. "Were it not for the Lady Taleen it would be simple enough. We could put him to the ordeal, or turn him over to the Drus, and who would care? But it is not that easy. The Lady Taleen *has* vouched for him and—"

The bald burly man, who Blade already knew to be an enemy, broke in with a derisive laugh. "A maid! A simple maid, even though she be cousin to you, Lycanto. What does she know? A maid can be cozened by any likely rogue who comes along. And I give him that—he stands well. He is no doubt a great one with maids, a thing which he knows and uses well to his advantage. I say kill him and have done!"

Lycanto had stiffened in his chair. He glared at the bald man with bloodshot eyes. "I will not have you interrupt me, Horsa! See to it, that it does not happen again. Or do you forget who is king here?"

Blade, watching with fascination—yet not forgetting that his own head was the subject—marked the expression of sullen contempt on the face of the man called Horsa. No great respect for the king there!

Lycanto went on speaking. "I say once more that it is not easy, this matter. Not only does the Lady Taleen vouch for him, but she is cousin to me, and more important she is daughter to King Voth of the North. Voth of Voth! I dare not offend Voth. You all know that. He is powerful and a great warrior, though aging now."

He paused and looked around smiling wryly, his thick lips still moist from beer. "If none of you can help me I must turn him over to the Drus. They will have an answer."

"Thunor take the Drus!" It was the man Horsa again. He scowled and banged on the table with a huge fist. "And Thunor take Voth as well. I fear not Voth. Nor the Drus. Why take a chance on a maid's word, Lycanto? Kill the rogue. If we are wrong, and he is no spy or warlock, then it is unfortunate but still no great matter. If I am right, and he *is* a spy, then we are rid of him. In any case, I vote we send his head to Redbeard, and have our own spies mark his reaction. So it might be proven one way or the other."

Blade winced inwardly. It was not a system of justice for which he cared too much.

It was Cunobar who came to Blade's aid, a thing Blade was not to understand for many a day.

Cunobar's gray hair—again Blade thought it belied his age—glinted in the torches. He stood up and pointed a finger at Blade, at which all at the table turned and appeared to see the big stranger for the first time.

"I also thought him spy at first glance," said Cunobar. "And I saw him first, before any of you. I saw and I taxed the Lady Taleen that he might be spy. She denied it. If she could be here she would deny it now——"

"No doubt," growled the man Horsa. "I tell you she is bewitched of him. Who knows but that he plants his lies on her tongue?"

Cunobar held up a hand. "As may be," he went on smoothly, "but the Lady Taleen cannot be here—as against tribal law—and we all know she suffers from the swooning sickness."

"Another thing I do not understand," muttered Horsa. He shot a malignant glance at the King. "The wench was hearty enough when she came to Sarum Vil—and a glass later she is sick and swooning. How explain that to Voth, Lycanto? He will ask, make no doubt of it!"

The King paled, then reddened, but kept his tongue. He

77

reached for his beer horn and drank heavily. There was a grumbling at the lower end of the table. Blade brightened and felt his chances increased. All was not well in Alb. There was weakness, dissension, and therein lay his opportunity. He must grasp it firmly, quickly, when the moment came.

Cunobar waved a placating hand. His voice, as silken smooth as the steel gray hair, filled the chamber. Blade listened with growing wonder. Why was Cunobar now advocate to him? The man had been surly and suspicious enough before. Again there could be only one answer—Taleen.

"If we bicker among ourselves," said the graying man, "nothing will ever come of it. This matter must be settled, and quickly, for the time water drips swiftly and Redbeard is on the march. We should be marching to meet him, yet we linger here on the fate of a single stranger.

"There is no need for this. It is all so simple, if we but see it so. I agree with Lycanto that we cannot afford to anger Voth of the North. So we do *not* anger him. I also agree that the Lady Taleen is his cousin, and that she be so treated. Yet we do not have to regard her word as straight from Thunor himself. There is no problem, my Lords! We have ancient law and in that law the answer is plain—we must give this stranger trial by single combat, so he stand or fall on it. Neither the lady, nor her father Voth, can find reason against that. Did not Voth himself proclaim, long ago, that no man is above the law? Can he then quarrel with his own words? Can his daughter?"

Cunobar the Gray paused and looked around the table. Lycanto was listening intently, nodding in approval. Horsa stared down at the table, his broad red face expressionless. The others muttered and whispered among themselves.

Cunobar was looking directly at Blade. There was a message in the glance, Blade would have sworn to it, yet one that he could not yet read.

Cunobar said, "You all know our law. The man challenged has the right to pick the man he will fight." His eyes met Blade's again, then moved to the man Horsa with a bare flicker of expression that might have masked a sneer.

"I vote," said Cunobar, "that we give this man Blade the right to prove himself in single combat. I say let him speak now and take free choice of the warrior he will fight to death. I ask for fists."

Eight clenched fists shot upward. Lycanto did not vote. Horsa sat scowling for a moment, then reluctantly raised his fist.

"If you will all have it so, so must I. Yet it goes against me. We do not know this man. He may be serf, peasant, catiff or runaway slave—though I still think him a spy—and there is no constraint that nobleman fight with one of low birth. I vote yes—but I think no."

Cunobar laughed and pointed at Blade again. "Look well at him. Does he have the look of a servant? Slave? I say not. Spy, maybe. Low born, no. But let him speak and judge for yourselves—you all know what the Drus tell us when they grow impatient with our ignorance. A man is fashioned of his words. If he speaks as a slave I will take back my vote and let him be flayed without a murmur."

Cunobar had had audience with Taleen since their parting. That was certain. Even more certain was that Taleen had done all she could. As had Cunobar the Gray, for whatever reasons. Now it was up to Blade. But they had given him a weapon—his tongue.

Lycanto looked long at Blade before he said, "You can speak now, stranger. By vote we grant this boon and we will listen with patience. But words will not save your life. You must fight one of us to the death. Pick that man as you will."

Blade stood up. He swelled his chest and stood as tall as possible. Cunobar had tossed the cue deftly. These

79

Albs loved words, and war, and he guessed that lies and bragging were condoned as long as the words were sweet and firm enough. He would give them that. He stalked to the fireplace and wheeled to face the table, his arms crossed and his head high, the fire casting his shadow long on the floor. The Dru selected a fresh square of bark and dipped her pen in the dye pot, and for a moment Blade caught the gleam of intelligent old eyes from the depths of the cowl.

Blade looked them up and down with scorn. A mastiff growled and Lycanto silenced the beast with a kick.

"I am a stranger," Blade began, "and I know little of your ways. What little I know tells me that you are brave men—and a pack of fools!"

Uproar. Curses. Horsa began to struggle to his feet. "You dare, rogue? In this Council you dare—"

Lycanto was silent, but looked amused. Cunobar waved a hand for silence. "Peace, Horsa. We bade him speak— so let him speak as he likes. The reckoning will come."

Horsa sat down. "That it will," he growled.

Blade curled his lip in contempt of them. "If I were this Getorix, this one you call Redbeard, I would have your heads on poles this moment. You sit and bleat like old women while he improves each hour. One of you says kill me, the stranger, while another says do not kill me lest the Lady Taleen and her father be wrathful. So you do nothing. You talk. You let me talk. While the water runs and Redbeard marches!"

Blade pointed a finger at Lycanto. "You are the biggest fool here, King! You rule and yet you do not rule. You allow insolence to go unpunished. Not only in this room, but in all the town. I have seen and heard how your men drink and gamble and wench when they should be preparing for war. And you bury your nose in a beer horn and do nothing. Sarum Vil is a shambles, your army is a rabble, and if I were Redbeard I would laugh and deal with you as though you were maids and not warriors. But that

80

might be difficult. I admit it. You and your rabble, King, would not even make good raping. I doubt that Redbeard has an army of perverts. So he will merely hang you, or cut off your heads, and content his men with your women.

"You have heard that I am a wizard. It is true. I come from a far land, of which you know nothing, and there is no time to tell you now. But I am a wizard—if being wizard means that I use my brains for something other than to stuff my skull box.

"I can show you tricks of war that Redbeard never heard of. I can show you skills and organization that *you* have never heard of. I can do all these things, making victory over Redbeard certain, and I *will* do them. After I kill this man I choose to face in single combat. But I say this, King, that this fight is a waste of precious time and you are bound to lose a good man. But you must have it, I see that, and so I say let us begin now. No more fools chatter—get on with it. I choose the man called Horsa. And I ask Cunobar the Gray as second and companion at arms, or however you call these things."

Silence. All were staring at him. Blade took a step toward Horsa and spat at the man's feet. "I say I choose you to kill! Unless your blood is white—in which case I will choose another."

Horsa came up with a roar, pounding on the table with both fists, his broad red face contorted in rage. "Spy! Slave and whoremonger! Father of lice—son of a whore who coupled with a goat! You dare speak me so? I, Horsa, champion of all the Albs. Thunor strike me if I do not eat your liver this night."

Blade smiled coldly, having achieved his first purpose of baiting the man into near senseless anger. "If you fight half as well as you talk, Horsa, I am a dead man." He laughed and spat again.

The big hall was in tumult. Only the Dru was silent, rapidly stroking away with her brush, and Blade found

81

time to wonder, even in the midst of such chaos, who would read of this strange and unlikely encounter.

Lycanto at last got order by pounding on the table with his beer horn. All sat down again but Horsa, who remained standing and glaring at Blade, a line of white froth visible around his mouth. Blade realized that Horsa had gone berserk, and that it would be no easy matter to kill him.

Lycanto had to raise his voice almost to a scream to be heard over the din. He shouted at Blade, but there was a new, and reluctant, respect in his tone and glance.

"You have made your choice, stranger. So shall it be. Now, this night, you will fight Horsa. But I should tell you this—" Lycanto's weak mouth smirked beneath drooping moustaches. "Horsa spoke truth. He *is* champion of all Albs. He is Horsa the Skull Maker. He has made more widows than Thunor himself."

"*And* consoled them," said a voice from somewhere along the table. "A pity this stranger has no widow to be. Poor Horsa must go to the whores afterward, like any common knave."

A great roar of laughter went up. A score of good-natured gibes were flung at Horsa, who at last grinned sourly and sat down without another glance at Blade.

Lycanto pounded again with his beer horn for order. For the time Blade was ignored again. As he listened, with wonder and some amusement, he realized that this was not only a fight, but festival as well. They were a feckless lot, these Albs, and meant to have their fun. Deeming Blade as good as dead, Lycanto was ordering great quantities of food and beer to be readied. Blade allowed his burgeoning plan to emerge a little further into the light— the more they ate and caroused, the heavier they drank, the better for what he had in mind.

At last relative silence fell again. Horsa said, "As the rogue challenges me I have choice of place. Not so, Lycanto?"

The King's nod was perfunctory. "We all know that, Horsa. What choose you?"

Horsa was on his feet again. He looked at Blade with contempt. He was calmer now. "I choose the fire ring. Let it be prepared. I would see how nimbly this bastard dances when his feet begin to burn."

Lycanto gave an order and a man at arms hurriedly left the hall.

Cunobar the Gray now stood and held up a hand. The King nodded and the talk died away again.

Cunobar looked disdain at Blade, and his smile was something mingled of mirth and malice, leavened with the smugness of a man who has accomplished precisely what he intended. Blade, who had never counted the man as friend, and was puzzled by his seeming advocacy, began to understand. Cunobar was pleased with himself, and the why of it was plain enough. Cunobar wanted either Blade or Horsa dead. Or both. At the moment Blade could not fathom the reasons, nor did they matter. Cunobar could only win.

Cunobar nodded curtly in Blade's direction. "The stranger asks that I serve as companion at arms, as second to see fair play. This I cannot do. You will know the reasons, so I do not explain. I was right, I am right, in that he stands and talks like no slave I have ever seen. It is fair that he be given this chance. Yet there is no guarantee that he is a gentleman—and I will serve no other. Yet he must have a companion at arms, to abide by our law. Who among you will serve him?"

Dead silence. None looked at Blade, who laughed and strode, arms akimbo, to the foot of the table. He did not force his laughter. He was genuinely amused and his deep voice tolled in the chamber like a dark toned bell.

"So be it! I see that you gentlemen are too fastidious to serve a ragged stranger. This speaks ill of your hospitality, of which you are so proud, but I will let it pass. By your leave, then, I will choose my own man. His name is

Sylvo. He who stood watch over me in that miserable hut."

There was muttering, followed by questions among themselves.

"Sylvo? Who is he?"

"I have heard the name, and nothing good, but I cannot recall."

"Sylvo? I too have heard that name. Is he freeman or slave? Serf? Peasant?"

A thin-shanked man with a fringe of reddish hair stood up. He had a sour mouth that matched his expression.

"He is one of mine, this Sylvo. I wish he were not. He is a very cock pimp and a brawler, a drunkard and wencher, and as ugly as Thunor's ass. Yet he is brave enough, and fights well—though he steals too much—and were it not for this I would have hanged him long ago."

He looked at Blade. "If you would have such a rascal serve you I give my leave. Watch he does not steal your single pair of breeches."

There was a roar of laughter. Blade bowed in mockery to the assemblage. Lycanto made a sign and men of arms escorted him from the hall and back to the dismal hut.

As he was leaving Horsa shouted after him: "Count your cods, stranger. I vow you'll be short when you count them next in Thunor's dungeon."

Left alone, though he knew the hut well guarded, Blade paced impatiently until Sylvo appeared. The man was slightly tipsy, his mouth smeared with some whore's lip salve, but his beady little eyes were alive with intelligence and excitement.

"Ar, master! You have set them on their ears and every tongue in Sarum Vil to wagging. One thing is certain— there will be a great crowd to see you die. None will want to miss it."

Blade regarded him with a cold stare. "I die? You are a prophet, then, as well as an ugly rogue?"

Sylvo stroked the hairs on his chin, the beer fast leaving

him. He eyed Blade's massive frame with speculation. "Nay, master. I am no prophet. And now I think on it mayhap it is Horsa whose cods will end in the fire. I hope so, master, for I like you well—I have forgiven you the blow, for I deserved it—and I have no love for Horsa. He had me whipped once for not bowing low enough. Me, a freeman!"

Blade laughed and clapped a hand on the man's shoulder. "Then you will serve me in this?"

Sylvo fell to one knee. "I will serve you, master. Gladly. I am but a scurvy fellow, a sneaksby cull, and a slipgibbet. But for luck—for sometimes Thunor favors rogues—I would be hanged or flayed long since. Yet there is something about you, master—a thing I do not understand—that makes me feel like a man and as good as any. Ar, I will serve you well—even though you have a fist like Thunor's lightning bolts."

Blade scowled at him. "Good. Then get off your knees. Never again do that. Speak always to me on eye level, and look straight at me. I am master, and you are man, yet I will be as fair with you as you with me. See to it. And now listen carefully—hear what more I require of you and see if your courage still holds."

Blade spoke rapidly, firmly, nearly whispering, making sure that Sylvo understood every point. As the man listened, his squint increased and the harelip more pronounced as his jaw dropped. He took off his helmet and raked at a scurfy bald skull with filthy nails.

When Blade finished speaking Sylvo said: "Ar, master, you are determined on the death of both of us—it will be flaying sure enough. Hanging if we are lucky. We cannot do it—they will be after us like a pack of bitch hounds after a hare."

"I think not," Blade said coolly. "You forget—after I kill Horsa I will have rank and status. They will be drinking and eating themselves into stupor. It may go easier than you think, Sylvo. Just be sure you do your part well. Now, once again, what is it you are to do?"

Sylvo grinned. "What I had often thought to do before, master, but lacked courage. I go to the house of Queen Alwyth, and I enter and find a likely wench to rape and—and this part I do not like, master."

Blade frowned. "You will do it! You *pretend* to rape. Make no mistake there, Sylvo, or you will feel my hand again. You will merely pretend to rape this maid—be sure she is a servant—and you will perhaps tear her clothes a bit. Frighten her. Let her scream. The louder the better, for I want all the household to flock to her. You may hide your face if you choose. That is up to you."

Sylvo squinted horribly and his harelip twitched. "I will mask my beauty, master, never fear for that. The penalty for rape is boiling alive and I am no capon. But what if aught goes amiss? If the Lady Alwyth has drugged your lady perhaps she has hidden her well. I can linger for a few moments only, lest I am murdered by outraged females."

"I will be quick," Blade promised. "And I doubt that Lady Alwyth has hidden Taleen. She must keep to the story of the swooning sickness. I will get the lady—and meet you at the stables. See to it the horses are ready."

Sylvo made the sign across his breast that Blade had noted before with Taleen. "Thunor protect us! Stealing horses is another crime on my conscience, and even worse it is punished by the chopping off of arms and legs, with the stumps then tarred and the trunk sewn into a pack of serpents. I am ugly enough now, master. If we fail—"

Blade grinned. "On your conscience, Sylvo?"

The man grinned back. "A manner of speaking, master."

Two men of arms, accompanied by a sub-chief, entered the hut.

The sub-chief, ignoring Sylvo, spoke to Blade. "The fire

ring is prepared, stranger. You will come with us to the armory to select your weapons. At once."

Blade indicated Sylvo. "He also. He serves for me."

"As you wish. Only hasten. Horsa is impatient."

As they were conducted through the dank, fog-wreathed night Blade whispered to Sylvo. "This man Horsa—in what manner does he fight? What weapon will he use?"

"With a great bronze axe, master. He will have a shield, too, but since he always attacks he will not use it skillfully. But with the bronze axe he is a fiend. He calls his axe Aesculp—smasher of skulls. Well named. It is long hafted and double bitted and I myself could not lift it. I doubt you can match him in axe play, master."

It so happened that Richard Blade, in his former persona, had been very proficient with a battle axe. Ancient weaponry, the study and use thereof, had been a serious hobby with him. He had been a member of the Medieval Club and, where other men boxed, or played tennis or handball to keep in shape, Blade spent many an afternoon in simulated combat with lance and broadsword, axe and mace, long bow and arbalest.

But he would be a fool indeed to play Horsa's game. In the armory he selected a stout buckler of bronze and leather, with a shiny convex boss that might partially deflect a blow. The sword he chose was nearly as tall as Sylvo, with a two-handed hilt. It was of thin iron, pointed and edged with bronze, and immensely heavy. Yet Blade swung it with ease.

He could hear the crowd in the town now, squalling thirstily for his blood. Blade smiled thinly. That could change. He knew something of mobs. Let him blood Horsa first and they would change their tune. It was blood they wanted, blood to go with their beer and frolic, and whose blood did not greatly matter.

The sub-chief was chafing and cursing, yet Blade insisted that a new edge be put on the great sword. Let Horsa wait—and begin to wonder. Every moment of delay worked for Blade.

There was a great stone, and water and fish oil, and Blade carefully, with deliberate stalling, keened the edge himself. At last he was satisfied and they left the armory.

All of Sarum Vil was thronged about the open square, so close packed that for once there was no room for reckless chariot drivers. With Blade and Sylvo in their center the men-at-arms fought their way through the pushing, shoving, shouting mob. Some shouted vilification at Blade, some encouragement, and a drunken woman tried to hand him a pan of beer. Sylvo was well cursed, and gave as good as he took.

They came at last to the circle of fire. Faggots and peat had been lain roundabout and flamed with fish oil so the ring glowed cruelly crimson and leaped high, a great gaping eye staring from hell up to the dank and mist shrouded sky. Men continually heaped faggots and peats, and poured oil, so that the fire roared and hissed, in sinister whisper, and leaped as high as Blade's waist.

Lycanto's throne had been carried from the great hall. He sat on it now, beer horn in his hand, talking with the gathered chiefs and captains. They all turned to stare as Blade appeared. Behind the throne, well back in the shadows, he saw a robed and heavily cowled woman amid a gaggle of other women. The Lady Alwyth?

A thunderous howl roared from the pressing mob. Blade nodded in reluctant admiration as Horsa vaulted the flames and strode to the center of the ring. There was a rich barbarity in the scene that Blade could not but appreciate.

Horsa scorned a helmet, since Blade had none, and his bald head glinted in the flames. His legs were bare, but for cross-gaitering, and he wore a rich cloak of scarlet caught at the throat by a golden clasp. On his left arm was a small round shield, and in his right hand, which was badly scarred by an old wound, he swung a huge bronze axe.

Horsa smirked at the screaming crowd, then swung the axe several times about his head. Blade, studying the weapon more than the man, saw that it had perfect balance, was long hafted enough to reach an awesome distance, and both edges gleamed bright as razors newly ground.

I must go to the point, Blade thought. It is doubtful this one understands point, but I must be careful in learning that. Swing with him at first, match him blows that cut only air, then when the time is ripe go to the point.

Horsa took off the scarlet cloak and flung it away. He was naked to the waist, his barrel chest covered with thick dark hair. He was a shorter man than Blade, and not so prettily muscled, yet Blade knew the man's strength would match his own.

Horsa, leaning on his axe, scowled across the ring of fire at Blade. "You called my blood white, stranger. What of yours? You have thought of urgent business elsewhere, mayhap? You would be off to report to your master, Redbeard? That may not be. I have claim on your cods—which I will cut off and cast into the fire."

Blade ignored the gibe. The crowd screamed and laughed. King Lycanto made an impatient sign.

Blade turned to Sylvo. "Remember well what I have said. Timing is important. When I have killed Horsa I will make claim for privacy, for food and rest, and so will be able to come to you. I will be near, and when I hear the screams I will go in to fetch Taleen. You will know what to do then?"

Sylvo grimaced. "Run, master!"

Blade patted his shoulder. "Good. Serve me well in this, Sylvo, and you will not be sorry."

The man's squint was rueful. "I am already sorry, master, but too late for that now. Look—Horsa mocks you again!"

89

Blade vaulted the fire and stalked toward Horsa. He saluted Lycanto with his sword, but kept his eye on Horsa, which was well. With a snarl the man leaped and the great bronze axe caught the firelight, mirrored it, flashing, as it slashed at Blade's head in a glittering circle. The axe sang a threnody of blood and death.

Sylvo, squinting and open mouthed, whispered a promise to Thunor.

"Grant my master the victory, Thunor, and I make firm promise that I will not thieve for a year! I swear it. On my misbegotten soul I swear it!"

Chapter 6

Horsa attacked with unrelenting fury. At first Blade could do nothing but parry and retreat as the great bronze axe beat a ringing tattoo on the broadsword. Flames nipped at Blade's backside and he sidled first to left, then to right, somehow fending off a killing blow and at the same time evading the fire.

Sylvo was right about Horsa's manner of fighting. He bore in constantly, disdaining use of shield, and a dozen times already had been open to a thrust, had Blade been able to deliver it. Blade could not. Harried and driven constantly back and to either side, it was all he could do to turn aside the vicious glittering axe. Time after time the keen axe blade missed his bare head by less than an inch; once a lock of his dark hair was clipped and floated downward.

The mob, already sensing a kill, howled like the blood-thirsty hydra it was. There was much reference to Blade's cods and Horsa was constantly bade to cut them off and toss them into the fires.

Horsa grinned evilly and, in a sudden crouch, changed his tactics and lowered the arc of the scything axe, striking at Blade's groin. Blade had an opportunity for a thrust and might have killed Horsa then and there, but he was hesitant—the chance coming so quickly—and contented himself with swinging the heavy sword at the man's neck. Only his point touched flesh, opening a trivial gash below Horsa's chin. He skipped nimbly back from danger, muttering obscenities at Blade, then came on again with renewed rage.

Blade, continually backed against the ringing flames, by now had some minor burns, trivial as yet, but holding grim promise if he slipped but once, made one mistake.

He had thought to tire Horsa—it was incredible that the man could persist so long in such frenzy—yet the other showed no signs of fatigue. He drove Blade around and around the fire ring, the giant axe singing and whistling bloody disaster while Blade feinted and slipped and dodged and fended as best he could. Every ringing blow of the axe against the sword was like a monstrous hammer beating on an anvil, sending shuddering vibrations through the hilt to sting Blade's hands. Twice he nearly had the sword torn from his grasp, a misfortune that would have given him a choice of deaths—Horsa's axe, the fire, or the swords beyond. Lycanto had given orders and the mob had been driven back a little way, and a circle of armed men stood there with weapons drawn and pointed. If one of the combatants turned craven and dashed through the flames it would be only to die on the swords. This had been promised as a duel to the death, and Lycanto meant to make it so.

The long minutes passed. Still Horsa did not tire, though once he rested his axe and wiped his streaming forehead with his arm, the while taunting Blade.

"Come and fight, spy! Cowardly bastard and son of a dung-eating mother! Come and have it over with—you skip nimbly enough, I vow that, but you cannot escape Aesculp forever. Her edge will feel your cods yet."

Blade, needing all his wind, did not answer. Instead he

leaped in and swung a mighty, and awkward, two-handed stroke at Horsa. He had not gone to the point yet, and wished to lull the man. So, when Horsa skillfully eluded the blow, Blade pretended to stumble and make a bad recovery. Horsa bellowed with laughter and leaped to attack again.

But this time, Blade noticed, Horsa was using both hands to swing the bronze axe. The man had flung away his shield, contemptuous of all protection, and began to batter Blade backward with two-handed swinging strokes, back and forehand, that again sent Blade perilously near the flames.

Now Horsa grunted with each stroke. Sweat spattered from his thick chest hair. He had newly painted himself for the fight and the blue dye ran, losing all design of rune or symbol, mixing with blood from the neck wound to make a purplish red lavage. Horsa, constantly wiping sweat from his face now, gradually acquired a demon visage.

Blade still retreated, yet with every passing moment his confidence increased. Horsa was tiring at last. Still Blade marveled at the man—they had been fighting for nearly half an hour.

The mob had fallen silent, with only an occasional gibe, and that at Horsa. Nothing so pleases the common folk as the fall of a great hero and, while they did not yet really believe it, or cry out openly for Blade, yet the undercurrent was there.

Sylvo, muttering to himself, offered to increase his abstinence from thievery to a full two years.

Blade was in little better shape than Horsa by now. He was arm weary and his lungs pained, sweat blinded him at times, and his back was sorely scorched, yet he judged himself in better shape than Horsa. Yet he was so near exhaustion that he decided it must be done now, quickly, or not at all.

Horsa swung a mighty blow which Blade ducked under. Horsa stumbled for the first time, and went sprawling. The bronze axe flew from his hand and Blade leaped to plant his foot on the haft. Horsa, on his knees six feet from his weapon, stared at Blade with narrowed eyes that reflected only surprise. And Blade knew then that fear was not in the man.

The throng gasped in unison, a single great indrawn breath, then waited for the end. Blade stooped quickly and picked up the huge bronze axe. It hefted sweetly in his hand, a thing of perfect balance.

Horsa stood up and faced Blade, waiting. His face, a hideous mask of blue dye and blood, was set in resignation. His eyes rolled skyward and he began to sing in a coarse low voice, ignoring Blade as he chanted his death song to Thunor.

Blade did not want it so. To gain status, to become legend, the end of an epic struggle must itself be epic. He did not miss his opportunity. There was superb contempt in his voice and gesture as he flung the axe at Horsa's feet.

"Take back your toy, man! I would not have it said that I slew an unarmed foe. Nothing shall taint my killing of you."

The words were aptly chosen for his purpose. Shamed, outraged, Horsa seized his axe and ran at Blade with a berserk bellowing that clamored in the dank night. He implored Thunor as he slashed at Blade, the double-bitted bronze whispering past Blade's ear.

At last Blade went to the point. He went into a long lunge, for the moment daring to use the huge sword with one hand, and put the iron six inches into Horsa's left shoulder.

The crowd found its voice again and screamed. Horsa bellowed, more in rage than pain, and nearly decapitated Blade with a backswing. Blade had been off balance after the lunge and very nearly paid for it with his life.

Recovering, he managed to swing Horsa around so that

for the first time the man was backed into the fire. Blade grinned maliciously through the sweat that soaked his face and black stubble.

"I trust the fire is warm enough for you on such a chilly night, Horsa. A taste, man, of things in store for you." He thrust again, Horsa was slow in parrying with his axe, and Blade slashed him near the midriff.

Horsa was within inches of the roaring flame now and had to stand his ground. He breathed in tortured sobs and his eyes were wild, yet he fought on. Each time he sought to move away, to right or left, Blade herded him back with a sword that licked in and out like a serpent's fangs. Horsa was bleeding badly now and a smell of roasting flesh hung in the misty air.

The axe gleamed in firelight as Horsa swung again. It was a faltering stroke and Blade fended it easily, then went in for the kill. Two handed now, the massive sword before him like a lance, he leaped in and thrust with all his waning strength at Horsa's chest.

Horsa stepped backward into the flames. He stood rooted there, fire curling about his thick legs, blackening them, the hair scorching and the flesh beginning to char and curl from the bone. Horsa did not show pain as he slowly burned to death. He struck again at Blade and once more began to chant.

Sickened now, the joy of battle ebbing—his mind and heart staggered by such display of courage—Blade sought to end it in swift mercy. He thrust at Horsa's heart, missed, and with a backhand stroke he lopped off the man's right hand.

The hand, still gripping the bronze axe, fell into the flames. Horsa, wrapped in fire now, calmly bent and picked up the axe with his left hand. Blood spurted in a scarlet fountain from his severed right wrist. Horsa was hairless now, blackened all about his body, and the fire biting deeper into his flesh and bone with every moment. And still he fought on.

With a last great bellow of rage and defiance Horsa leaped from the fire and tried to grapple with Blade, seeking to enfold his victorious enemy in the flames that were consuming him.

Blade, sweating, cold, stricken and in a fever to have it over, held out the sword and let Horsa run on it. Horsa died, flinging the bronze axe at Blade in last defiance.

The mob, which had been in tumult, was again silent. Blade ignored the body. He could not mutilate so brave a foe, though Sylvo had told him it was the custom to cut off the testicles of a fallen adversary and burn them. Sometimes they were eaten by the winner, so that he might come by new courage and strength.

Blade picked up the bronze axe and brandished it over his head. He shouted. "As victor I claim this axe. Aesculp it was called and Aesculp it shall remain. Horsa was a brave man and a mighty warrior. I also claim his cloak and with pride will I wear it."

He picked up the heavy scarlet cloak and flung it around his big shoulders, securing the golden clasp. Then, regal in the firelight, he turned to face Lycanto and the entourage of nobles. Some smiled at him now, others were still sour. Lycanto himself fondled a beer horn and looked thoughtful.

Blade made his way through the flame circle, scattered by willing feet, and approached the throne. He saluted with the great axe. Now came a time of shrewd lies, cunningly told. He must create an image, build an edifice, that had no base in reality. By the time they realized they had been duped he must be far away, on the road to Voth, and with Princess Taleen at his side.

Sylvo had coached him well for this moment and Blade forgot nothing. He pressed his advantage.

"I have slain Horsa in fair and single combat. This is admitted?"

Lycanto nodded sulkily and stared into his beer horn.

The men around him fidgeted and whispered, some avoiding Blade's eye, and it was Cunobar who at last spoke up. But his glance was hard and there was disappointment in his tone, and Blade wondered again at the man's enmity.

"It is admitted," said Cunobar the Gray.

Blade made a slight bow to the King. "Then, by your law, I inherit all that was Horsa's. His house, his weapons, his livestock and wives and serfs, whatever may have been his property is now my property. This also is admitted?"

It was Lycanto who answered. "It is admitted. But you think wrongly about wives—an Alb is permitted but one wife. And Horsa had none, so you are cheated there. But all else is yours—as in our law. But also in law you are vassal to me, and must fight when I bid, for me and around me, and all you hold comes of my favor. This is admitted by *you?*"

Blade bowed again, a bit lower this time. "It is admitted by me, King. But I beg leave to speak of all these things another time. I am weary now, and I hunger and thirst greatly, and I want only to retire to my new home and rest. You grant this?"

As he spoke Blade searched the crowd for some sight of Sylvo. There should be none if the man was carrying out orders. At this moment he should be making arrangements at the stables.

No sign of Sylvo. They were taking the body of Horsa away, borne on a rude litter. No one, not even those who carried it, paid any attention to the charred and maimed body. Horsa was dead. Long live the victor. Grimly Blade conquered his nausea and put away all thought of the civilization he had known. He was in Alb.

Bowing a last time, with no servility at all, he swung the heavy axe to his shoulder and turned away. "I have lost that rascal man of mine already. Doubtless he is too busy cutting purses to serve me. Will someone guide me to my new house?"

There was a titter among the nobles but no one came forth. Blade grinned and bantered at them. "Must I seek it out for myself? There is a risk, and one I would not face. I might get into the wrong house and so have to fight again, and that I cannot do until tomorrow. I crave sleep."

Again it was Cunobar who came to his aid. And again Blade wondered why.

"I will show you the way," Cunobar said. "And crave pardon for such lack of courtesy from my peers." He smiled around coldly. "They all wagered heavily on Horsa, and so are all poorer men now. It sours their dispositions. Follow me, Blade, and I will show you to your newly won house."

They pushed through the moiling throng, with Cunobar leading and cuffing away the rabble seeking a closer view of Blade. Torches flared in the mist and Blade reckoned he still had several hours of darkness. He would need them.

He followed Cunobar into a narrow alley, deep with mud underfoot and stinking of dung and garbage.

Blade said: "They all bet against me? How did you wager, Lord Cunobar?"

Cunobar glanced back and the smile was as false as if painted. "I wagered on both of you. For the sport of it, not money. It is a thing that pleases me now and then. I cannot lose."

Blade laughed curtly. "That is true enough. Yet he that will not risk cannot win."

Cunobar did not answer.

They passed a side street, as narrow and muddy as the one they trod. Nearby, fronting this street, was a large wooden house with many flaring torches hung near it. Blade nodded toward it and said, "A place of consequence? Who lives there?"

"Lycanto's Queen, the Lady Alwyth. And all her women. I will warn you now, and you do well to heed.

Go not near that house. Certainly do not enter—this is forbidden by law and punished by death. Only Lycanto can enter—and he only with the queen's permission."

Blade smothered his grin. Poor Sylvo. He was going to stick his ugly nose into a bear's den. And so was Blade.

Chapter 7

Blade lay in shadow, on soft sward in an open glen, cushioned and half concealed by bracken and pink-tipped heather. The glen was bathed in a greenish cathedral light, save where a single ray of sun struck downward through the trees.

She stood in the golden beam, clad all in white, scarlet girdled and deep cowled, and she carried the golden sword before her as if in offering. Blade could not see her eyes, yet knew they regarded him with a strange and burning intensity that set his blood to coursing. He was conscious of a tremendous sexual stirring in himself.

It was the Dru High Priestess, she who had sacrificed the girl in the oak glade, and Blade spoke her name as though he had always known it.

"Drusilla! Come to me."

She nodded slowly, thrust the golden sword into earth and threw back her cowl. Blade could not breathe. Slowly, her hands outstretched to him, she approached and the beam of sun moved with her. Her hair floated in argent tendrils around a cream-skinned, heart-shaped face with a scarlet glistening mouth and eyes as lambent gold as the sword itself. The white robe did not mask, but revealed, and as she rippled toward him Blade saw her breasts dance, each to a separate tune, and her thighs and buttocks moved in a liquid flow.

She halted before him, one hand plucking at the front of her robe. A single loop and button held the garment in place.

"How know you my name?" Her voice held the chime of faery bells, yet with a deeper and mocking note.

Ravished by desire, lusting for her, Blade held out a hand and blurted, "I do not know how—I just knew it. But this is not a time for talk. Come lie with me, Drusilla."

Her amber eyes devoured him, and her hand toyed with the fastening of her robe, yet she shook her head and said, "Not so, Blade. Here is not a time or place. Yet I will not altogether deny you. Do you desire a taste of Paradise, Blade, a view of treasures you may one day win? Speak and it shall be so."

Blade groaned. "I thirst and you offer me promises. You are cruel, Drusilla!"

Her smile was edged with mockery and he thought her teeth suddenly grown long, and while she was still lovely it was now the beauty of the beast. She knelt beside him, unfastening her robe, and gave him sight and touch of the blue-veined breasts, brown tipped and wide of aureole, white as milk and firm as marble, and as cold to his touch.

The line came unbidden into his mind—*la belle dame sans merci*—and both words and language were familiar, yet he did not grasp their meaning. He caressed her breasts with his fingers, wondering why they were so cold, and she leaned closer to him. The golden eyes were half closed and she moaned as she said: "Suckle me, Blade. My breasts are heavy with milk of bloody sin. Suckle me, drink my milk, and half my sins are yours. It will make a lighter burden for both of us."

Her teat was in his mouth, cold and firm, yet he did not suckle. A great fear was on him, and at the same time a

101

great lust, and his loins betrayed him and he groaned and writhed in spasm—

"Master! Master—wake up! Your cursed moaning is like a beacon—they will be on us within the hour. Wake up, master. And shut up—if you value our skins."

Richard Blade rolled over and stared up at Sylvo. Here was no verdant grotto, no succubus High Priestess. Here was a hideaway in the fens, a narrow ledge of mud above water, screened by high growing reeds and capped by a gray and sunless sky. Marsh birds made dun arrows overhead and nearby the three horses cropped discontentedly at rank sedge and salt grass.

Blade rubbed sleep from his eyes and combed back his hair with fingers that were uncommonly dirty. Things had gone well enough, the diversion had worked and he had snatched Taleen from the queen's house without hindrance, yet what followed had been such a hurly-burly and helter-skelter of frantic improvisation that he had very nearly despaired.

Yet they won free of Sarum Vil—Blade killed two men of arms in the doing, with Sylvo leaving his best knife in the belly of a third—and the man had somehow followed marsh paths in the dark and fog to get them this far. It was a miracle for which Blade was duly grateful.

He fingered his curling dark stubble and stood up. "I was having a nightmare," Blade said a bit sheepishly. "I was loud?"

Sylvo, squatting on his haunches, squinted and twisted his harelip into a grimace. "Loud enough to wake the dead, master. Which we shall soon be if there are searchers nearby. Ar, had there been a moon I would have thought you struck by it! Who is Drusilla, master? It has a familiar ring, yet I cannot place it."

Blade waded off into the ankle deep water to relieve himself. Here a screen of rushes hid him from the still sleeping Princess Taleen.

"I do not know," he said sternly. "A phantom in a

dream, no more, no less. Who can know of dreams? And who cares! How is the Princess? Not yet awakened?"

Sylvo shook his head. "Nothing changed, master. She sleeps like a babe, and yet no healthy babe ever slept so deep. We must wake her, master, or I fear she will never wake this side of Frigga's domain."

Blade went to where Taleen slept beneath the scarlet cloak that had been Horsa's. Her long auburn hair was all in knots and tangles, her face was pinched and wan, and there were crescent purple bruises beneath her eyes. Sweat glinted on her brow. Blade, kneeling used a corner of the cloak to wipe it away. He damned the Lady Alwyth and himself for his need for sleep. Had he only noted this earlier—

Sylvo, testing the edge of his second best dirk with a thumb, said: "I could make her a posset, master." He gazed around him at the desolate fens. "There is no lack of noxious matter for the making of it. It will make her vomit, ar, how it will make her vomit, and so will she rid her belly of the sleeping poison. There is naught to lose, for I think she is dying now."

Blade glared at him. "You are a physician, then? How do I know you will not poison her further?"

Sylvo was already busy. He went to the horses and came back with a small bronze pot. Without looking at Blade he said, "When I was sure you were winning, master, I made a swift trip to Horsa's house to collect a few things. It was not thieving, as Thunor knows, because I knew it would soon belong to you. And as your man I had right to it."

"I know," Blade said dryly. "In the few minutes I spent in the house I could see it had been looted. More of that later. What of this posset?"

Sylvo dipped water into the pot and added a small quantity of mud. Into this he shredded some rotting leaves and sprinkled them with a brown powder that he produced from a fine new purse on his belt. Then he began to

103

search the ground and rank foliage about them, dirk in hand. Blade watched with the faint beginnings of nausea.

"Aha," cried Sylvo. He jabbed with his dirk at the ground and came up with a toad wriggling on the point. He tossed it into the pot and cut it to shreds. To this he added a few worms, well slashed, and then stirred the whole vigorously.

Sylvo grinned at Blade. "I am famous for this posset, master. In all of Alb none can make worse. I swear it would make a horse empty itself."

"I have a good mind," Blade said, "to try it on you first."

He thought Sylvo paled beneath the grime that caked him. "Nay, master! Do not waste it. There is not much, and anyway I am not the one who lies dying of the swooning sickness. Come, master, hold the lady's mouth open while I pour it down her."

Blade wiped sweat from her again, then cradled her head in his lap as Sylvo tipped the pot. Taleen choked, strangled, swallowed and then choked again.

"A moment," Blade commanded. "Let her breathe."

Sylvo objected, frowning. "She must have it all, master, to make her sicker. Hold her up a bit, so it goes easier down her gullet."

They got the last drop of the horrible concoction down Taleen's throat. She had been pale before, now her complexion grew more livid and was tinged with green. She rolled over suddenly and began to retch.

Sylvo leaped back. "It works, master! I told you it would. In a moment now there will be such a puking as you have never seen."

It was true. Blade held her while she vomited, with great moans and many cries for death, her slim body twisting and writhing in his arms. When at last she opened her eyes it was to stare at him in wonderment and fear.

"You? Blade! How are you come here, and I? What is this—"

104

He stood her upright and let her hang limp over his arm while he pressed her belly gently. "You have been sick, Taleen. Now you are going to be well—that's it! Throw it all up. Everything. Get it all out of you."

She dangled, her arms hanging, her hair about her face, in a great torture of gasping and retching. "I die, Blade! Let me do so, then. Frigga take me this minute! I am sick to my death! Frigga curse you, Blade, if you do not let me die this instant."

Sylvo, a little distance off, regarded his handiwork with something akin to awe. "Did I not tell you, master? She is the sickest lady I have ever had privilege to watch in all my years of sinning."

Taleen, regal even in her agony, raised her head to stare at the man. "Who is this ugly cheater of hangmen? How dare he speak so? Do you allow such insolence, Blade? Teach him manners, or I shall—" And she went into another paroxysm of retching.

"Make the horses ready," Blade ordered. "We had best quit this place as soon as the lady can ride."

Sylvo looked uneasy. "Darkness would serve us best, master."

Blade frowned at him. "Do as I say! I think it safe. If there was pursuit it was short and half-hearted. Lycanto and his Albs still have Redbeard to worry over—that will take precedence over us. You can take us northward through these marshes?"

"Ar, master, that I can. I know the fens as I know my own hand. Some twenty kils north of here we strike into the forest again."

Blade nodded, well pleased. "Good. Lycanto must march east, or south, to meet Redbeard. He can spare no men to seek us. It may be that the lady will see her father again after all."

He turned again to Taleen, who was clinging weakly to a stunted marsh tree and looking a trifle less pale.

105

"You heard? We are heading north toward Voth. Are you fit to ride?"

Her brown eyes snapped at him. She was fast recovering. "I heard, Blade. I was poisoned, not deafened! But how can I ride?" She gazed down at her short linen tunic, the same she had worn when they met. It was rumpled now, and not very clean, but that was not the problem. Blade, when he heard what the problem *was*, had trouble restraining a curse.

"My kirtle is too short," she complained. "If I stride a horse I will show everything to that low-born fellow of yours. I cannot ride, Blade."

He glared, but kept his voice low. "You will ride, Taleen! I vow that. And hear another thing, and mark it—we both owe much to that low-born fellow. I will have no more of this talk—his name is Sylvo and you will address him so. He knows his place and he will keep it. See that you do—and keep a civil tongue in that pretty head. You are a princess, I know, but I rule here and now, and shall do so until I give you into your father's hands. This is well understood?"

Her chin was up and her brown eyes dangerous, yet he thought her on the verge of tears. She was, as the dead Horsa had said, only a maid after all.

Sylvo, whose ears were as long as his nose, had missed nothing of this. Now he called Blade aside and whispered to him. Blade grinned and clapped him on the back.

"I hope your Thunor forgives you for thieving, man. I do. Fetch the things at once—and my thanks. I would not have thought of it."

Sylvo rolled his beady eyes. "I have had vast experience with women, master. Their brain does not work like a man's. Simple things go best with them."

Blade cuffed him toward the horses again. "Get the things and spare me the advice. We must get started."

Sylvo came back with a collection of oddments that brought reluctant thanks from Taleen. There was a wooden comb—she set about her tangled locks at once—and a polished bronze mirror and a sewing kit with bone needles and both wool and linen thread.

Blade pointed to her dress, where it limned the shapely thighs. "A few stitches and you will have breeches. Your modesty will be preserved and you can ride. Hurry. I have a great yearning to find this Voth of Voth, your father, and be rid of you."

She turned her back on him. "You are as insolent as ever, I see. I also hope we come soon to Voth, so I can have you properly whipped. And your mangy servant with you."

Blade grinned at her rigid back. She was no longer a sick girl. The genuine, the real Taleen, was back.

All that day they rode the misty fens with only an occasional glimpse of the sun. Sylvo rode point, for only he could take them safely through the treacherous bogs and quicksands, while Blade, the great bronze axe resting on the pommel, brought up the rear.

Taleen, wearing the scarlet cloak against the chill, rode between them and for the most part in silence. Blade noticed that once she had taken the few stitches necessary to transform her tunic into breeches, she did not appear to mind disclosing her tanned legs nearly to the hip. Women were wayward creatures in any time, place—or dimension!

Blade grew more uncomfortable as the day wore on. His buttocks had been well scorched and the chafing of the wooden saddle did not improve matters. During a halt to rest themselves and to blow the horses and let them drink the brackish water, Blade mentioned this discomfort to Sylvo.

The man laid a finger alongside his nose, blinked, then went to where his horse was drinking. Blade followed him, Taleen having discreetly withdrawn behind a tall screen of reeds for reasons of her own.

For the first time Blade paid close attention to the bulging saddlebags borne by Sylvo's horse. They were crude, of unworked hide, and so fully packed that they would not latch. Blade, who was wearing a new shirt and breeches, and a vest of light mail, all taken from Horsa's domicile, watched Sylvo as he rummaged in the saddle bags.

"You spent some time in Horsa's place, then? More than I. I had barely time to take what is on my back."

Sylvo kept digging into the saddle bags. "None so long, master. I am an experienced thief, you are not. Ar, that makes the difference. A man of my quality knows what to look for, and where to look for it. A gentleman would not know of such matters."

Blade stroked his chin, hiding a grin with a hand. "There was a dead man in the kitchen, with his throat well slit. As a gentleman I know nothing of it. Do you?"

Sylvo came up with a small parcel wrapped in oiled skin and tied with leather thongs. "I know of it, master. He was a kitchen knave, a servant, of no consequence. He disputed my right there."

"As well he might," Blade said dryly. "Considering that at the time I had not yet killed Horsa."

Sylvo avoided Blade's eye. He indicated the parcel. "Here is a wondrous soothing ointment, master. By your leave I will spread some on you. It has magic powers, or so I have heard, and was made by Ogarth the Dwarf, who also cast the great bronze axe for Horsa."

Blade was staring at the new purse on Sylvo's belt. It was bulging at the sides. He prodded the purse with a finger.

"You found other things as well? Smaller things, but of greater value, that fit easier into a purse?"

"Only some trinkets, master. Poor things they are, too. Horsa had the taste of a barbarian whore. Now, master, shall we apply this magic to your burns?"

Blade let it pass. Taleen had reappeared and was standing by her horse, gazing disconsolately at the vast fens stretching northward. Blade and Sylvo vanished behind the reeds.

Blade, dropping his breeches, found a relatively dry spot and stretched on his belly. Sylvo rubbed a dark sweet-smelling ointment on the scorched flesh.

"Ar, master, you took a burning indeed. I could not have stood it—I would have run, or begged for mercy."

"And found none."

"Ar, that is Thunor's truth."

"And if I am scorched," Blade said grimly, "it was not so bad as Horsa took." He thought of Horsa standing in the flames, burning alive and still fighting, and shook his head. "You did not see it, Sylvo, for you were too busy thieving, but that Horsa was a man!"

The servant did not answer and after a moment Blade glanced up at him. There was an odd, and thoughtful, expression on Sylvo's seamed and scapegrace face as he applied the ointment in even strokes.

Blade watched three ants dragging a dead fly toward a tiny mound.

Sylvo said: "Ar, master. Horsa was a man. Yet you slew him, so that you are a better man. And at times I wonder vastly at the nature of things—"

Already Blade's pain was vanishing. He stifled a yawn, confessing himself still weary, yet knew there was no rest, safety or peace, until he had come to Voth and delivered the girl. There he might expect thanks, along with reward and rest, and a chance to puzzle out this new life of his.

So it was without much real interest that he said: "The nature of what things, man?"

Sylvo spread more ointment. "This thing, master. Putting ointment on your arse! It is a magnificent arse, I admit, and I admire it, but it's really only an arse after all. My own arse is skinny and ill favored, though prettier than my face, but it is as much an arse as yours in the end—I do not pun, master.

"So why the difference, master, in our stations? In the

109

nature of things, in true things that count, our arses are much similar. Then why are you master and I man? It is a matter I think on from time to time."

Blade smiled and cuffed him with a good-natured backhand. "Then think on your own time, man, when I have no use for you. Thunor forbid that I have found a philosopher instead of a man and companion at arms. If you voiced such thoughts around Sarum Vil I do not wonder they gave you a dog's name." He stood and pulled up his breeches. "Thank you, Sylvo. I will ride easier now."

"Master."

Blade turned back, slightly vexed. "What now? More philosophy?"

"No, master. This." Sylvo extended the bulging purse to Blade. "I am a liar, master."

Blade kept a straight face. "That I knew already. What else?"

"Look you in the purse, master. You will see. It was a great temptation. I have always been a poor man, and this time I thought to find my fortune. But you have been good to me and have treated me as a man and now I cannot lie to you. Take it all, master, and beat me afterward."

Blade tumbled out the contents of the purse. There were scores of coins, large and small, iron and bronze, and a small leather bag with a drawstring.

"More than twenty mancus," said Sylvo. He sounded pained. "Enough for three farms, and cattle and horses, and as many servants as I could beat. A wife also—if I could find one to take me."

Blade emptied the contents of the leather bag into his broad palm. There were twenty matched black pearls, as shining dark as the Devil's heart. Blade extended his palm to let Sylvo see. Faint sunlight broke through just then and the pearls glowed in tenebrous splendor.

"What of these? How came Horsa by such wealth?"

But Sylvo was not impressed by the pearls. He shrugged.

110

"I know little of such things, though I have seen them before. They are found on the far shore of the Narrow Sea and it is said that the sea raiders value them over all other things. No doubt Horsa took them as loot from a dead enemy. Am I to be beaten, master?"

Blade tucked the little bag of pearls into the waistband of his breeches. The money he scooped back into the purse and tossed to Sylvo. "You will not be beaten. I do not beat honest men, though with you it is sometimes a near thing. The money is yours, the pearls mine. Now come—I would reach the forest before the sun goes."

There was yet an hour of light when they left the fens and came into the forest once more. By that time Taleen's mood had changed, she being as mercurial as any weathercock, and during the last hour in the fens Blade rode at her side while they exchanged stories. Blade held back nothing, even to the bargain Lady Alwyth had sought to make with him.

Taleen's lustrous eyes sparked with anger, but her tone was grave. "So you have scorned her, Blade, and because of her face she will deem it worse than that—as betrayal. She will not forgive. And she has long had a reputation for dark deeds. I pray Frigga that this Getorix routs Lycanto and puts all Albs to the sword, even though we be cousins. A sword in her heart is all that will quell the evil in Alwyth."

Her face flushed and she used words that might have made Sylvo blanch. "A fine fool she made of me! I admit it. I should have known not to match wiles with her, but I was weary and hungry and thirsty and off guard. She listened to all I said of you—and I' spoke well, Blade, and praised you too much, because of the danger. I made you out a great deal more than you are."

He nodded, unsmiling. "My thanks, princess. I know you meant it well."

She shot him a suspicious glance, then continued. "So when she did offer me a broth I took it without thought."

She made a face. "Fool! I remember nothing until I came back to sickness in the fens."

Blade looked ahead. The fens were ending and the dark arching forest, with caverns of shadows and dusky twilight, lay just ahead. A path led plainly from the fens into tall oaks and beeches and thick trunked yew wearing garlands of vine.

"Forget the Lady Alwyth," advised Blade. "Her fate will overtake her without our help. Neither she nor Lycanto can harm us here, but there may be other dangers. Know you anything of this country, Taleen? How far to the north lies Voth?"

She frowned. "I know little enough, never having traveled this way. What of that low fellow of yours? He has gotten us through the fens without mishap—cannot he do likewise in the forest?"

Blade shook his head. "No. I asked. Sylvo is a fensman and also knows something of the sea, but he will be as lost in the forest as ourselves. Which," he added cheerfully to hearten her, "will not be so lost if we have the sun. I am woodsman enough for that."

"The Drus know of such things," said Taleen. She shot him a sidelong glance and he knew her thinking. As for himself, he had not thought recently of the sacrifice in the glade. Rather had his mind, when he let it range, been full of the strange and compelling, the passionate, dream of the woman called Drusilla. Drusilla! Dru? Odd he had not marked it before. But what matter—it was all fantasy, a phantom play conjured in his unconscious mind.

"The Drus," Taleen went on, "can tell direction by stars, and how lichen grows on a tree, or by the set of the moon."

"Forget the Drus also," Blade said harshly. "They cannot harm us any more than can Alwyth. I am more interested in what Sylvo can find to put in that pot of his—I am starving again."

Taleen smiled again and laughed. "I too. It seems we

are always hungry, Blade! If that rapscallion of yours can find us food I may begin to forgive him his looks."

When they reached a suitable clearing Blade called a halt. Sylvo, after cutting some vines for snares, went in search of a hare or two for their dinner. They had twice seen deer since entering the forest, but the axe was no weapon for deer and Sylvo had only his knife.

Taleen gathered faggots and Blade struck a fire with flints, using an iron striker Sylvo had given him. As twilight thickened around the merry little blaze, and Taleen warmed her hands, Blade thought he heard a sound in the forest. Seizing the bronze axe he strode to the edge of the clearing and stood listening. It could have been anything—a deer or some other animal, or merely Sylvo falling over a root. But it did not come again and Blade did not like the silence. No birds sang and the rustling of small creatures had ceased.

Taleen joined him, huddling close. "What is it, Blade? Your man does not return—does it take so long to catch hares?"

He put a hand over her mouth, his lips to her ear. She had lost the odor of *chypre* now and smelled only of sweet girlish flesh.

"Stay here and keep quiet," said Blade. "I will go look for Sylvo."

"No! I will not stay in this place alone. I will come with you."

"Quietly, then, and not too close. If there is danger I must have room to swing my axe."

He had no chance to use the great axe. He and Taleen were not fifty yards into the trees, along a faint path, when the finely woven nets fell from above and enmeshed them. There was a sudden great shouting and men leaped from the trees and from bushes fringing the path.

Blade, his stalwart frame netted like any fish, could not free the axe for action. He heard Taleen scream once— "Beata's men! We are taken!"

113

He butted and bellowed and made a rare fight of it while he could. He got his hands through the net and knocked heads together, swinging his massive fists like maces, sending half a dozen of his attackers sprawling. At the last, standing like one of the forest oaks, choking a man black-faced with either hand, Blade went down before a dozen men. He took three with him and kept pummeling them until a spear butt crashed down on his head.

At the very last, before the darkness, he heard a man scream a command: "Do not kill the big one! Queen Beata wants him alive."

Chapter 8

Blade awoke in an oubliette. The slimy stone floor was covered with dank straw in which things crawled. A wick, guttering in a pannikin of fish oil, gave the only light. He was chained, hand and foot, to a ring bolt set into a wall. He itched intolerably and there was a great soreness at the back of his head. For a moment he lost control, slipped the habit of self-discipline built up over the years, and raged at the chains, tugging at them with fierce oaths and swinging and slamming them about.

"No use, master," said a voice from a dim corner. "We are well taken. The evil Queen Beata has us, and even the Lady Alwyth is merciful by comparison. I have been thinking hard, master, and my thought is that we are in a great deal of trouble!" There was a great rattling of chains as Sylvo shifted his malformed bones.

Blade, forcing calm on himself, squatted in the filthy straw. "What of the Princess Taleen?"

He could not see the man's shrug, but heard the chains rattle again.

"Safe enough, master. At least not yet harmed, as I saw. Beata holds her for ransom from Voth, as before—I remember your telling of it—and so we are back to the

115

beginning. Or the lady is. What happens to us may be another matter—and not one on which I like to think."

Blade quietly tested one of the chains, his huge sinews cracking with the effort. The chain held.

"Keep your heart up," said Blade. "I will somehow get us out of this." At the moment he could not have said how.

Sylvo's tone grew more cheerful. "So you will, master. I was forgetting that you are something of a wizard."

Blade, testing the chains again, scowled in the gloom. It was going to take a little more than wizardry to get them out of this. He began to question Sylvo; the basis of all effort, of all successful action, is knowledge.

"What is this place and how came we here?"

"A great castle called Craghead. On the Western Sea. As to coming here—I walked, the Lady Taleen rode, and you were carried on a litter. You were well drugged to keep you sleeping, master, as Beata's men were in fear of you."

That accounted for his slight headache. He remembered the spear butt crashing down and fingered the wound on his head, swollen and sticky through the thick hair.

"They had nets in the trees," Blade mused. "I wonder how—at just that place and time?"

"Ar, master. I wondered also. I was taken like a minnow and stifled without a cry. But I think I have it—the Lady Alwyth must have sent word to Beata. They are in league, no doubt. King Lycanto would never have done it—he and the Queen are enemies."

It was possible. Indeed it was probable. Lady Alwyth ran deep, was an intriguer by nature, and Blade had spurned her. Taleen was hated for her beauty, if nothing else, and Alwyth would have many tendrils to her web. She and Queen Beata may have been conspiring for years. Blade dismissed the thought. He must think of what would serve him now.

"Tell me of this Queen Beata, Sylvo. What manner of woman is she?"

Sylvo told him and Blade felt the prickles rise on his neck as he listened. Yet he doubted not a word. Such things *were* in this strange dimension he now inhabited. As real as life—or death.

"And that is all I know," Sylvo concluded. "She is a bawd, if the stories can be believed, and likes women as well as men in bed. Children also—it is said that she murders these afterwards so they cannot carry tales—and I myself have seen her cruelty to those who serve her. Most of the men lack an ear, the left one, and many of her women have their left breast cut off. As we entered the castle I saw men hanging on iron hooks on the walls, and was told they were the guards who let the Lady Taleen escape. One was still wriggling, poor bastard."

"What is her age?"

Chains rattled as Sylvo moved. "Who knows that? Some say fifty, some say five hundred. If she is a witch, as is also said, I doubt not that the last figure could be possible. All say she is beautiful, but none is allowed close to her and so it may be artifice. Women are full of tricks, even witches, and—"

A trapdoor opened in the ceiling and a face stared down at them.

"You—he who is called Richard Blade—you are wanted by the Queen at once. No tricks, now, or you will be slain on the instant."

A ladder was lowered into the oubliette and armed men swarmed down it. They wore the same loose breeches and cross-gaitering of the Albs, but their mailed coats were longer and heavier and their helmets flatter. The helmets bore the blazon of a unicorn instead of the Albian dragon.

None of them had a left ear.

They unchained Blade and pushed him to the ladder. Sylvo set up a squalling. "I lack water here. And food! Will you let a man starve and thirst? The place is also

117

lousy and you have rats—in all as stinking a dungeon as I have ever seen."

Some of the men laughed. One walked over to Sylvo and kicked him into silence. "I'll wot," the man said, "that you know whereof you speak and have known many prisons. Now shut that ugly mouth or you die before the time set."

Blade was prodded up the ladder. None of the men approached him too closely. As he went through the trapdoor he heard Sylvo call after him.

"Be of cheer, master, and remember that you are a wizard."

The castle called Craghead was vast. Blade was conducted down endless long corridors floored with rushes, ill lit by torches in sconces. They ascended score after score of stairs, the stone hollowed by centuries of wear, and crossed bristling battlements where Blade caught the tang of salt and heard the sullen mutter of surf far below in the mist. It was dark, without stars or moon, and the roiling bank of mist below was like cloud seen from above.

They came to a round, tall thrusting tower, the pinnacle of Craghead. Then more stairs and Blade was pushed into a chamber and a great ironbound door slammed behind him. He heard a heavy bar fall. He was alone.

And yet not alone. He sensed it from the first. He made no sign that he suspected a watcher as he strolled about the chamber, his mien calm and his handsome face impassive. If Queen Beata wished to play cat and mouse it was all right with him. He was thinking now, planning again, and he judged it a good omen that he and Sylvo had not been immediately executed.

The chamber, really a series of rooms with connecting doors, was furnished sumptuously. He had seen nothing like it in Alb. There were skins on the flagstoned floor— one of a bear that must have stood ten feet tall when alive—and flat couches covered with hide. He saw no windows. The rooms were warm enough, and the stone

118

floors warmest of all. He guessed at thermal ducts that were heated from below.

In a corner was a large table laden with cold meats and white bread—another thing he had not seen in Alb—and bronze and pewter vessels containing beer and wine. Blade ate, but was careful not to drink. He was going to need all his wits about him.

He covertly examined the wall hangings, of pale leather richly worked with golden thread, mostly in cabals that he did not understand. There was one large and central hanging depicting a unicorn and, as he watched in seeming unconcern, he saw the flicker of an eye. The watcher! He had no doubt it was Queen Beata.

Blade, his mouth full, and with a joint of meat in his right hand, bowed extravagantly to the unicorn: "I thank you for the food, good queen. It is excellent and I am hungry. Might I request that some be sent to my man now languishing in your dungeon?"

The eye glittered. Then came a muffled laugh, and a voice as husky and deep as many a man's.

"I have heard true of you, Blade. An upstart rogue of great impudence. Neither did Alwyth lie about your face and figure—both are as fair as she wrote. Tell me, Blade, are you the man you look to be? For I warn you fairly, your life depends on it."

There was a chill beneath the huskiness that sent the prickles up his spine again. He did not know the manner of it, but grasped the substance—he was on trial again.

With another bow he answered, "If I am a rogue, your Majesty, at least I am a modest one. As to being a man—I lay claim to that also. How *much* a man I cannot say until I know the hazards I face."

Again the muffled laugh. "You mince words like a Dru! I do not like that. But in other aspects you please me and you shall have a chance to prove yourself. I shall put you to the sweetest ordeal of all, Blade, and if you win I may be persuaded to spare your life."

119

He did not bow again. Hands on hips, he stared straight at the unicorn. "And that of my man, Queen? And the Princess Taleen shall go free to her father?"

Silence. Then, in a voice as cold as the mist enshrouding the battlements: "You try too far, Blade! A little impudence is like salt, I relish it, but you dare to bargain with me? So soon—as though you had rights here!"

He had begun with boldness and with boldness he must continue. He stared at the flickering eye and answered in a voice as cold as her own. "I only ask, my queen. A man is no man who does not seek to aid his friends."

"Enough! You will be prepared for my coming. I advise you to spend some of that time in learning how to leash your tongue."

The eye vanished.

There was a rippling of leather as a door opened behind another wall hanging and four maidens came into the room. They wore only gauzy pants, cut full and falling to the knee, and secured by a single amber button. Their hair was cut short, in mannish style, and each lacked a left breast. Where the breast had been each carried a saucer-shaped red scar. The sanguinary badge of Beata's service. Blade marveled that the men and women would serve such a cruel mistress, and for an instant his memory flickered into life and he could remember another place, another world, in which such things were not tolerated. And yet that world, as much as he could recall of it, had been bad enough. Then the mists closed in again and memory vanished.

The maidens were all young and fair, discounting the mammary scars, and they went about their tasks with efficiency and absolute silence. They did not look directly at Blade, nor converse among themselves. He guessed at the reason for this and, while the others stared in stricken horror, he gently seized a shapely blonde girl and pried her mouth open. Her tongue had been cut out.

They filled a large bronze tub with foamy warm water

120

and bathed him. He was dried on towels of fine linen, perfumed with *chypre* and dressed in saffron-dyed linen breeches and a long tunic. He was given soft leather sandals that laced to his knees. His beard was combed out and his thick dark hair combed into place.

When they had finished he was allowed to see the results in a bronze mirror and could not repress a grimace of disgust at the finery he was wearing. Yet this was Queen Beata's game and he must play by her rules. By this time he had a shrewd idea of what the game would be, and he was determined to best her at it. In his past life he had been a sensual man, highly sexed, and hardly let a day pass without gratification. Now he was more than ready. He had had enough of blood and iron for the nonce, and of vixens like Lady Alwyth and malicious kittens like Taleen.

The maidens left and Blade strode the chambers alone, a hard smile on his face. He would give this cruel queen a bit more than she bargained for, and so might ensure his future. He knew, better than most men, what women are born knowing, that sex is a weapon.

There was movement behind the unicorn wall hanging. Blade, at his ease on one of the couches, regarded the hanging with equanimity. Let the bitch come. He was more than ready for her.

The hanging parted in the center and Queen Beata stepped forth. She wore a simple black robe that clung to her supple figure. The robe was girdled with a scarlet cord and though it was opaque it concealed nothing, clinging like oil to her breasts and buttocks and thighs. Her face was long and deathly pale, with a scarlet slash of mouth and a high arching nose, and her upswept hair, dark and tinged with silver, was so intricately coifed that Blade guessed at once that it was a wig.

There had been a dozen large candles in the room before; the maidens, on leaving, had taken all but one. In this tiny spear of unwavering light she approached him.

121

Blade stood up and bowed slightly, with a touch of insolence. Instinct told him that servility was not the ploy.

"Your Majesty, you are beautiful."

It was, in a certain sense, the truth. She was not young—even in the dim candlelight he saw the finespun wrinkles around her mouth and the throat creases, and what the wig concealed he did not know—yet she had beauty. Or the relic of beauty. He was in no position, or mood, to make fine distinctions.

For a moment she regarded him without speaking. The almond shaped eyes, as shiny black as lacquer, glinted through narrowed lids that had been painted blue. She examined every inch of him before she spoke.

"You will approach me, Blade, on your knees. It is the custom here—all who seek my favor must tender to me that homage. Do so now."

It occurred to Blade that he was not so much seeking her favors, as having them thrust on him, yet he complied. He slid off the couch and to his knees, with what grace he could muster, and sidled toward her.

Queen Beata's robe fell open. Blade, glancing up, saw that the body, if not the face, was young. Her breasts were firm pale goblets, her belly flat and unwrinkled, her hips trimly flowed into legs that were slim as any girl's. Her body scent was cloying, thick with woman smell and *chypre*.

"Good," Beata said, her voice cold and mocking, yet excited. He wondered which pleased her the most—to kill a man and hang him on hooks, or to have him sexually. Both? "You have made homage and so will live a little time. I will confess that I am glad of it, for you are a man such as I have never seen before this night. Come now, Blade, to the couch, and prove me that you *are* a man and not a phantom, not a tunic and breeches stuffed with muscles that are useless to a woman."

At the couch she bade him lie just so. She adjusted his brawny limbed body to her exact liking. Then she disrobed him, lingering over each part of his nakedness with her lips and fingers. She was still wearing the black robe and when he reached for one of her breasts she slapped his hand aside.

"I decide, Blade, when it is time for that! You will obey. That is all I require of you. That you obey and be instantly ready when I have need of you."

Blade, who at the moment was very much instantly ready, still thought it a tall order. Every man has his limitations. The situation might have been amusing, take away the grim reality. His life, and that of Sylvo, and possibly the Princess Taleen, hung on his ability to perform for the lady. He had an instant of panic during which he feared that the tension, the pressure of the moment, might in itself cause him to fail. He fought off the idea. It would be irony indeed to die of that.

The queen took the dominant position. She kept silent and would not let him speak. She kissed his mouth, avidly and wetly, her tongue sharp and probing, while her hands roamed over his big body. Her pleasure was at first tactile, she could not seem to have enough of his flesh; then her pleasure switched and became oral. She suckled him lightly, teasing and biting, then put that aside to straddle him and permit him to thrust himself into her. She moaned at last—the first amorous sound she had uttered—and fell into rhythm with him. Blade, watching her face contort—the mouth writhing and the eyes wild, the sinews taut and stringy in her throat—knew that this was an old woman. At the moment it did not matter.

She began to talk, the words gasping and jolting out of her straining mouth as she rode him down to climax.

"You-do-well-Blade! That is good. No! Keep you silent. Only I speak—Ah, sweet Frigga, you do well! Do not stop. Never stop until I command or you die on the morning. Many have pleased me this far, only to fail at last and so die of it. Ahhhhhh, Blade! Blade! Frigga take me if I am not beswooned of you!"

123

The queen, trembling and thrashing about, collapsed atop him and murmured: "Ah, Blade, that was fine for first encounter. You did not spend?"

So tumultuous was his breathing that he could not speak and shook his head. He had been on the verge a dozen times and had fought it back. A fine pass, he thought bitterly, when a man's life depends on his ability to last.

Beata placed herself so her breasts were against his lips. "Caress me, Blade. I will have more of you, and soon. Meantime, for such fine first service, I will grant you any small favor you may ask."

At such close vantage, as she lay on him with eyes closed and face limned in candle ray, he saw how heavily she painted. The wig had slipped a bit, was askew a trifle, but he could not make out the color beneath it.

"I have given you large satisfaction," he said boldly, "yet you offer me only a small favor. Is this worthy of a great queen?"

The blue painted eyelids twitched. "You are still too impudent, Blade, and still do not understand your position. Grant that you are a great stallion, with a bear bone such as I have never known, yet it gains you nothing special. You are alive, man! Alive! Yet you do not seem grateful."

He must go very cannily now, but he thought boldness was still the ploy.

"Only a small man is satisfied with small things," he said. "I am not a small man and I do not accept small favors. I would have the life of my man, and the safety of the Lady Taleen."

With her eyes closed she traced her fingers over his cheek. The nails were long and blue painted. "You please me, Blade, you greatly please me. It may be that Frigga has sent me a true man at last. Yet how can I know? The test is over the long journey, not a single trip. And there is much you do not understand—were I not cruel and ruthless, and without pity in my heart, I could not rule here in Craghead. My people are so, and expect me to be so, and if I weaken I am done. I cannot grant what you ask me, Blade. Not in total. Yet there may be a chance if you are man enough."

When he would have questioned her further she bade him be silent and closed his mouth with her own. She laved his body with her tongue and searched him inch by inch with her fingers. She bade him watch while she titillated herself and then sought his body for final pleasure. She demanded copulation in grotesque positions that Blade, for all his experience, had only guessed at heretofore. She suckled him to massive climax, swallowing his seed greedily, then produced a water clock from behind an arras and gave him a quarter hour to regain his readiness. Blade made it.

She doubled the scarlet girdle, whipped him lightly with it and at last permitted Blade to mount her, the first time he had been granted the dominant position.

Blade forgot his exhaustion and rammed into her like any wild beast in heat. For the better part of an hour he strove on her, while she uttered little screams and moans and begged for more, refusing to let him go. He knew her demented and himself in little different case. To probe her belly, to hurt her, to split her raw and bleeding, became his sole aim in life.

Her lithe young-old body was bathed in sweat. Blade hammered away. It was a sexual saturnalia he had not known before, and knew he would not know again, nor wanted to, but for the moment he was as much a senseless creature as she.

In a rare moment of sanity, looking into her contorted face, he saw that her teeth were false, cunningly contrived of some animal bone. Her wig fell away and her head was clipped and bare, with gray stubble showing.

In the end it was she who cried quits, as Blade had sworn she would. She arched high, screamed once in piercing crescendo, and went lax under him. She pushed him away.

"Go now, Blade. Go at once." She kept her eyes closed. "I will not look on you again now, for I am surfeit, and I know my own moods. If you were an ordinary man I would have you killed now. So go—quickly! Your wants will be seen to."

Blade stood over her, fighting back nausea, his brawny legs trembling with weariness and something of self-disgust. Her wig had tumbled to the floor beside the couch and in the fading candle gleam she was a bald-pated hag with a painted skull for face.

And yet he dared. "My man? And the Princess Taleen? Surely I have earned their safety this night."

She turned her face from him, ready for sleep, and he heard her whisper.

"I cannot grant you that, Blade. My people must have a show. They want blood and entertainment. It is how I rule them. But you *have* earned the right to try. This very day you shall be given the opportunity to save them and yourself. This much I promise. Now go—before I forget how you have pleasured me and have you killed!"

There was movement behind the leather hangings and two of the maidens entered. One of them picked up the black robe and spread it over the sleeping Queen. Then, without looking at Blade directly, they conducted him to the door by which he had entered and turned him over to armed men.

He was not returned to the oubliette where Sylvo waited—if he still lived—but was taken to a large chamber hewn out of the living stone. He was given food and drink and there was a pile of skins in a corner for sleeping. The guards left him and he heard a great bar slotted into place.

One small barred window overlooked the battlements. Blade, weary to the marrow, stared through the bars and wondered what the day would bring. For day had come, gray, dank and misty, with the surf moaning like a lost soul in the fog below. Around him the castle was coming awake, with the familiar sounds of dawn and a great clanking of iron and bronze as the guard was changed.

He thought of Taleen, wondering where she was kept and how she fared. It was not likely she would come to harm—not if Beata planned to ransom her back to King Voth of the North—and yet there was no surety of this. Beata and Voth were brother and sister and there is no hatred so fierce and unrelenting as blood hate.

Blade's smile was faint as he turned from the window. He would not have harm come to Taleen. She was an irksome child—yet not so much child that she did not at times tempt his flesh—and he would be glad to see the last of her. Yet she figured large in his plans. In a way he was holding Taleen to ransom as much as was the queen—for through the princess, Blade meant to earn the good will of Voth and so come to some status and independence in this new world in which he must live. As live he would. As live he must! He vowed it fiercely. Then, being a practical man and having need of his strength for whatever new ordeal lay ahead that day, he threw his body atop the pile of skins and was fast asleep in a minute.

Chapter 9

Before the slaughter Blade was given leave to speak briefly with Taleen and Sylvo. Both were tied to stakes in the great inner court of Craghead castle, where a madding and blood-thirsty throng of Queen Beata's subjects had assembled to see the fun. The Queen was generous on these days, and in these matters: long tables laden with viands were waiting, and there was an abundance of wine and beer for all. The day was dark and dank, with a cold sea mist sweeping in to cloak the castle and muffle sounds.

The sea fog did not succeed in muffling the ferocious snarls of the caged bears.

"Thunor save us now!" said Sylvo. It was the first time Blade had seen the man show real fear. Sylvo, trussed to his stake with cord, was spattered with the straw and dung of the oubliette, and his squint and harelip brought him little sympathy from the crowd. He had a criminal hang-dog look—even Blade could not gainsay this—and so was cruelly baited. Even so, and despite his fear, the man was alert and bright of eye as he whispered to Blade.

"I know, master, that if Thunor saves us it must be with your aid. So listen you well—there is a chance if you can kill one of the bears quickly. At once. They eat each other, these beasts, and if you can strike one down the other may fall upon him and so give you time. And time, master, is what you must have. You see how the stakes are placed? This is not accident, master. The Queen Beata—may Thunor drive a spear through her evil heart—has given you a grievous choice, master."

This was truth. The stakes had been placed some fifty feet apart, so that Blade could defend only one of them at a time. He must make a choice between Sylvo and Princess Taleen.

Blade, as he listened to Sylvo, swung the mighty bronze axe in his right hand and looked to where Beata sat on a wooden throne beneath a canopy. He tried to fathom her thinking. She was not a fool, and he did not think her likely to sacrifice Taleen merely to please the mob and without profit to herself. Sylvo, on the other hand, was of no importance at all and his death might provide entertainment enough.

Another thing made Blade wonder—there was a squad of archers drawn up near each stake, behind crude barriers, and at the moment one of the queen's officers was giving them orders. Blade thought he could guess at those orders. He was to be given a chance to defend himself, and Sylvo and Taleen, from the bears. If he could do it, so much the better. The populace would have their show and the only loss would be three slain bears.

Queen Beata was gambling that Blade would elect to defend Taleen, thus leaving Sylvo to be torn to bits. This, or so Blade reckoned now, would satisfy the blood lust of the people and Beata could call it off when she would, and save Blade and the princess for other things—Blade for her perverted pleasures, Taleen for ransom and power over her hated brother Voth.

So the archers were placed as safeguards, to take over and slay the bears in case matters got out of hand. Blade's grin was hard. He would nearly have wagered Aesculp, the bronze axe they had returned to him, that he had figured the matter correctly.

But as he clapped Sylvo on the shoulder now and spoke encouragement, both he and the servant knew the truth: if it came down to the bone of the matter Blade would have to save Taleen and let Sylvo die.

Sylvo signified his understanding with a wink of his better eye. "I know you will do your best, master, but I am nothing beside the lady. We both know that. But by Thunor's cods do not forget that you are a wizard—and make the most of it."

Blade smote him again on the shoulder, very gently, and left him. There was nothing more to say.

A silence fell on the crowd as Blade walked to Taleen's stake. They had not seen a man like this before, and the silence gave way to a low buzzing as if they realized they would not see his like again.

Blade strode with a supreme confidence that belied his inner thoughts. He made a brave figure as he twirled the great axe as easily as any toothpick, the keen bronze glinting in the dull light. His hair had grown long, and his beard thick, and he used a riband begged of the guards to keep his hair back away from his eyes. He was stripped to breeches and cross-gaitering, barefoot to get a better grip on the muddy earth, and as he moved the great muscles of his shoulders and chest rippled beneath his swarthy skin.

The bears, in wheeled cages near the throne of Beata, exploded into a new frenzy of horrendous growls as if they scented and identified their enemy.

Princess Taleen stood proudly, her head high and her brown eyes sparkling with defiance, as Blade approached. Her tunic had been ripped away to her waist and her small breasts, girlish yet full enough, thrust as defiantly as the firm chin. Cold had hardened her nipples into firm brown buttons.

Blade, though he knew her to be ambivalent and wayward, and his longing to be rid of her was real enough,

130

could not but admire her now. She might be terrified of Drus, or of dark forest shadows, but there was no trace of fear in the face of a very real and horrible death. Or perhaps she had fathomed the Queen's plan, as had Blade.

Not so. Taleen was first to speak.

"She means to have my death, Blade. As she means to spare you for her filthy pleasure. See that you make her pay for it! I ask this, Blade. Nay—I beg it. I beg—I who am a true born princess of Voth."

He stopped several feet away from her. Beata was watching and he did not want to show concern too plainly. Blade spoke what was in his heart.

"You are a brave lass, Taleen. Continue so. I will do as best I can, and I think you not in as much danger as appears. Beata sports with you and me. It is poor Sylvo she means to die. I am sure of it."

Taleen's smooth brow creased in thought, her luminous brown eyes calm and intent on Blade as she pondered this.

"Then save your man," she commanded. "He is a scurvy pick-purse who has cheated the hangman too often, but he is your man and you owe it him. Yet I think you wrong—Beata means to have my death, one way or the other. I am not a fool, Blade, nor the child you think, and I can see a thing that is plain before my face. So I command it—if it lies between the two of us you will save your man. Then revenge me!"

He smiled at her and winked so that only she saw. "I will save the two of you," he said. And knew it to be a brave boast that might well come back to haunt him.

The crowd grew restless again and Blade was summoned to the throne.

Queen Beata this noon was resplendent in saffron robes that went ill with her complexion, heavily painted though she was. Her wig was freshly cleaned and curled. She studied Blade with narrow dark eyes and leaned to tap him on one stalwart shoulder. Her smile was thick with scarlet lip salve and behind it the animal bone teeth glint-ed dull white.

Her whisper was sibilant. "I have been thinking on the matter, Blade, and I would have you live. Defend the girl and let your man die. I have given orders. But you must make a brave show of it—these stupid peasants of mine must have blood and entertainment today. Go now and do well. I will come to you again tonight." He could not mis-take the message in those jaded eyes.

Blade raised Aesculp in salute to her. "I am ready, Queen. Bring on your bears."

He turned and ran back to the spot he had selected, midway between the two stakes. The bear cages were wheeled forward through a gap in the temporary barrier.

The keepers unwittingly played Blade's game. They had not been warned and Blade's thinking was right. They uncaged the bears one at a time, thus granting him a pre-cious minute or two.

The first bear came shambling out of the cage, rearing and snarling, froth dripping from two enormous saber fangs in the upper lip. The creature was ten feet tall as it stood on its hind legs and sniffed about, all the while emit-ting horrible noises from a massive chest. It was thick furred, tipped with silver, and the little eyes were canny and feral as it spotted Taleen and waddled toward her. Blade had killed grizzlies in his other life, and this beast was like enough, though as a babe is to a full grown man.

Blade swung the bronze axe in a glittering circle around his head and charged the bear, shouting a deep voiced and wordless war cry to attract its attention.

"Hooaaaaaaaahhhh—hoooaaaaahhhh—"

The bear scented woman flesh and ignored Blade. Blade plunged in to the attack, seeing another bear just coming out of its cage.

He swung Aesculp, a mighty blow that buried the blade in the animal's thick chest. The enraged bear wheeled and cuffed at the man with two inch claws that could disembowel at a stroke. Blade ducked in under the blow and tugged at the bronze axe trapped deep in fur and flesh.

The bear sought to embrace Blade, to crush the man, and at the same time to bury the saber teeth in his flesh. Blade tugged the axe free and skipped nimbly back from danger, as yet untouched. He saw the second bear making for Sylvo. Time was very short, for Sylvo was the one meant to die.

The first bear, forgetting the girl in its rage, came after Blade. It must be done quickly. Blade whirled the axe to gain power, then leaped in again with a fierce cry. He had swung too high before and this was his last chance if Sylvo was to be saved.

His blow was true and terrible. He felt the haft spring in his hand as the bronze slashed through skullbone and into the brain of the bear. The animal, slavering blood and foam, came on as it died on its feet. Blade turned and ran. The second bear was just rearing over Sylvo. As Blade ran he heard the man cry out in terror, a matter Blade could understand, for the second bear was bigger and more ferocious looking than the first. As Blade darted in to the attack he saw the last bear leave the cage and shamble toward the girl. Despair clutched at his heart. There was no more time.

The bear, unaware of Blade, slapped at Sylvo's head with terrible claws. Blade, in the last possible instant, swung the axe and slashed off the paw. The bear bellowed in rage and surprise and turned on Blade, red arterial blood spurting six feet from the stump. Blade, caught in the scarlet spray, was covered from head to foot. His face a lurid mask, the taste of the beast's blood hot and salty in his mouth, Blade leaped in with a great scream of defiance.

"Hoaaaaaahhhhhhhhh."

The bronze axe glinted around, shining and deadly. He put every ounce of his tremendous power into the blow, yet did not quite decapitate the animal. The head fell sideways, held still by tough muscle and fur flesh, the neck shooting out new torrents of blood while the near headless thing walked and groped toward Blade.

Blade wheeled once more toward the girl. His heart leaped and he gave a mighty shout. His plan, rather Sylvo's, had worked. The last bear had stopped to sniff at its dead companion, then had bitten into the corpse, and now was crouched and preparing to eat.

It was a stupid animal and paid no need to Blade as he ran on it from behind. He brained it with one blow from Aesculp, then retreated slowly to stand once more before Taleen. He was a gruesome sight and knew it, bespattered with bear blood as he was, yet he did not mistake the look in her eyes. That it might change in the next moment did not matter—in her glance now there was adoration and a full offering of herself. A blind man would have seen it.

Blade, in the heat and excitement of the moment, was pleased with her and with himself. Yet such a look in a woman's eyes meant trouble, if that woman was Taleen, Princess of Voth. Capricious child, simple maid as the dead Horsa named her, arrogant princess. All three the same woman, with now a fourth added—a woman who saw Blade as a gallant and bloodied savior.

The moment sped away. There was new and more immediate trouble. The mob had been cheated and did not like it. A great caterwauling went up, drowning out those few who shouted for Blade's prowess.

"Kill them! Slay them all!"

"More bears. Bring more bears!"

"Flay them alive—only save the woman! Give the woman to us."

"Three fine bears lost, and to what purpose? This man Blade is a fiend—prick his carcass with arrows!"

So it went as the mob surged out of control against the barriers. Blade moved close to Taleen and began to cut her free with the axe blade. Surprisingly, no one paid him

134

any attention. The courtyard was a maelstrom of rage and defiance as the throng swayed this way and that, a mindless thing bent on trampling itself to death. Queen Beata, pale with rage, was standing and shouting orders at her officers. A squad of archers suddenly wheeled and sent a volley into the mob. Nothing daunted by this, the screaming rabble charged across the barriers in earnest, overturning tables and spilling food and wine, hurling stones and handfuls of mud at the archers.

Blade had Taleen free at last and, keeping a secure grip on her arm, ran to Sylvo. The man had not been so fortunate. A stray arrow had lodged in the stake, near his head, and some lout had pulled it out of the wood and was jabbing it at Sylvo's face, all the while screaming in inarticulate fury.

Blade laid the broad side of Aesculp alongside the oaf's head, none too gently, then slashed at Sylvo's bonds as the melee raged around them. More archers and men at arms had moved in now, as Beata began to get matters under control, and the mob surged back in sullen defeat.

Sylvo was muttering in excitement. "Hurry, master! There is a postern—I marked it when we were brought here. If we can gain it, and run fast enough, there is a chance."

Blade chopped the last cord free, then glanced around. His heart sank. A squad of archers and men at arms was headed his way. Beata had no intention of losing her profit—or her pleasure.

For an instant Blade's heart struggled against his head. Good sense bade him wait and fight another day, seek a better opportunity. The odds were too long against him now. And nothing had really changed—he could still pleasure the queen and Taleen would still be held to ransom. He might even be able to beg Sylvo's life.

Yet Blade wanted to fight. He leaped in front of Taleen and Sylvo and brandished the axe high. Upon seeing this the squad captain gave an order and the file of archers

135

halted and went to one knee, their bows half drawn and a score of arrows aimed at Blade.

Sylvo cried out. "No, master! They are too many. Yield to them."

"Not so," said Taleen. She came to Blade, though he sought to push her back, and so clung, her two small hands entwining his great bicep.

Her face was flushed and her voice shrill and high. "Fight, Blade. We will die here and now! At least we shall cheat that bitch-whore! Fight, Blade. I will die with you!"

The horns sounded then. Savage, cruel, menacing in the dank mist, the horns sounded doom and disaster for Craghead. There came a great shouting, a feral surf of barbarian voices breaking against the castle walls. And the horns squalled on and on and on.

For a moment, suspended in terror, the mob and soldiers in the vast inner court were silent. Rage died on the instant, to be replaced by fear. Men ran, women screamed and forgotten babies wailed. Blade, watching the captain of archers, saw him mouth an order. The file of archers reversed and faced the ramparts. Blade, the girl and Sylvo were forgotten.

Where had been frenzy before was now absolute chaos. A single outcry went up and hung over the courtyard like a palpable blazon.

"REDBEARD!"

Chapter 10

It was Sylvo who saw him first. The man clutched at Blade's arm and pointed. "See, master! Yonder by the great tower. Thunor protect us now, for that is surely Getorix. He who is called Redbeard."

Taleen still gripped Blade's arm and he could feel her trembling. Her courage had run out. She was ashen and sad-faced as she said, "It is over now, Blade. Nothing can save us. It is the arch-fiend and even Frigga cannot prevail against such evil."

They were ignored for the moment, in no immediate peril, and Blade gripped the haft of Aesculp and stared up at the great tower where last night he had done such yeoman service. In that instant he began to plan ahead—new dangers meant new techniques of survival. One thought was salient over all: in what was coming there would be no margin for error. None at all.

The man who stood by the tower was seven feet tall and built to proportion. He wore a helmet that had a noseguard, came low behind to protect the neck, and was topped by a long golden spike. A rich purple cloak flowed from the Gargantuan shoulders. The man stood with arms crossed on his chest as his raiders swarmed about him, and he did not appear to be armed. Now and then he bellowed a command in stentorian tones, but for the most part he watched in silence as his men raped the castle of Craghead.

But it was his beard that most marked the man. It flowed to his waist, a pennon of flame, and it was plaited in two parts and tied with gay colored ribbons. Blade, in reluctant admiration, and seeking desperately for clues to his planning, noticed that Getorix now and then toyed with his plaited beard, adjusting a ribbon just so. And this in the heat of battle. Vanity!

Blade saw her then, for just a moment, and something sweet and sick, and at the same time cold, leaped in his heart. It was only a brief shimmer of white that could have been illusion, but was not. A moment's flurry of pale robes, a beech tree's slimness, a glint of silver hair beneath a cowl. Drusilla! She so named in his weird dream. She had been phantom then but was not phantom now—unless he was mad—and she vanished in a fraction of a second.

The tableau broke and time swept on and Redbeard was alone near the tower, shouting his orders. The ramparts had been won by this time, the Unicorn standards of Beata trampled, and the dead were piling high with each passing moment. Blade had never really doubted—Craghead was doomed.

Sylvo tugged at his sleeve again. "Why do we linger, master? The postern I know—there is still a chance, though it grows less every second we dally."

They had retreated—Blade so engrossed that he was not aware—into a niche formed by two great buttresses supporting the wall. It was a *cul de sac* and a fit place to die with their backs to the wall, had Blade so chosen. He did not so choose. He had made his decision.

He turned on Sylvo in haste. "What do these raiders, and this Getorix called Redbeard, value above all else in life? Quickly now!"

138

Sylvo, poor man, stared at his master as though he thought him demented. Taleen awoke from her apathy to say, "What matters *that*, Blade? We are all dead."

He frowned through the bear blood now caking on his face and beard. "Perhaps not. Well, Sylvo? Think, man, and answer as if your life hangs on it—for it does."

Sylvo squinted horribly. A spear flew past his head and he ducked.

"Courage, master! That is the greatest of matters to the sea robbers. Courage and feats of battle. It is all they care about—to be a great warrior is to be everything. But *we* are not sea robbers, master, and they scorn anyone not of their cutthroat tribe. And they take no prisoners, but for women." He did not look at Taleen.

The girl said: "You will kill me, Blade, when the time comes." She touched the broad edge of Aesculp. "My skull is fragile—one small blow will do it."

Blade ordered them both behind him, back against the rampart wall. "Keep there," he said, "and keep you quiet. No words. None! And you, Sylvo, make no effort to help me. Or you, Taleen. You will spoil everything if you do. I am playing a desperate game for all of us, but I must do it alone. You must be alert, both of you, and follow me as this play progresses. I will have no time to explain, you must delve it for yourselves, and be not astounded at the great lies I am going to tell. If you must speak—though it is best you keep shut mouths—you will support me in every lie I tell. Now I begin. You two crouch back there and look afraid."

Sylvo's harelip writhed in an attempted smile. "That is not a hard part to play, master. Ar, I can do it most convincing."

Blade turned his back on them. The alcove formed by the buttresses was some eight feet across where he stood, and narrowed behind him. With his arm extended, and swinging the bronze axe by the very end, he could cover

139

nearly six feet. If he were nimble enough afoot, and his luck ran well, he should be able to do it.

So Richard Blade, a towering and bloody apparition, leaned on the handle of the bronze axe and surveyed the waning battle before him. On his face he carefully fashioned an expression of boredom and utter scorn, while his eyes missed nothing, no significant detail, of the carnage.

A few of Queen Beata's men still fought on, though most had long since thrown down their arms and cried for quarter. It was rarely given, most of the quitters being butchered on the spot, but Blade did note a few sullen prisoners huddled together under guard. Of the queen there was no sign, and he judged her already taken, or slain, or fleeing by some secret passage. Blade had no care for that.

The courtyard, keep, ramparts and the stairs were thick with corpses. Some still moved and twitched, and were being dispatched as quickly as the raiders could get to it. The victors appeared more concerned, at the moment, with rape and drinking than in following up victory. Not twenty feet from Blade a buxom young woman lay naked and silent, a sword at her throat, while man after man dropped his loot, raped her, picked up his loot and staggered away to be replaced by the next. Not far from the young woman a boy was being sexually attacked by a huge warrior who, laughing uproariously at the youth's screams and struggles, kept cuffing him into position again.

A great deal of the wine and beer swept from the tables had been in corked jugs and bottles of fired clay and had not been spilt. It was now being guzzled as fast as possible. Blade glanced up at the tower and saw Redbeard conversing with two men, both of whom wore purple cloaks also, and had helmet spikes of silver instead of gold. They were big men—and as dwarfs beside Redbeard.

Redbeard gave an order and one of the men, with an odd, open-handed salute, turned and stalked away. There was no sign of the slim, silver haired Dru—if indeed she had ever been there. Blade at the moment was not so sure. Battle, and blood, did eerie things to a man's senses.

At last he was noticed, just as he was about to call out to seek attention. The alcove he guarded was small, the day dreary and dark—the mist even now changing to rain—and it was not so strange that the three had escaped notice until now. But now, as Blade stepped forward one pace and whirled the axe over his head, now the reckoning was due.

First notice came from the group around the naked woman nearby. They had given up raping her, so she must be dead, and now some ten of them came at Blade in a casual fashion that was nonetheless businesslike. One of them, a short burly man, noticed Blade's warlike demeanor, his villainous aspect, and stopped short. With an open mouth he stared at Blade. The others clotted behind him.

Blade, hideous with the gouted bear blood, spun Aesculp in a glittering circle and gibed at them.

"You hesitate, men of Redbeard? Why is this—I am but one man! Do you have second thoughts, then?" Blade grinned malevolently through his mask of blood and pointed with his axe to the naked dead woman.

"I promise I will not die as easily as that one. You will find the raping of me harder! But I can see you prefer women and children to fighting men, and are a coward's spawn. Go, then, and find a man to do your work—if there is a man among you!"

A great shout of rage went up from the raiders, so fierce that it attracted the attention of Redbeard. From a corner of his eye Blade saw the huge chieftain turn and stare down into the courtyard. This had been Blade's aim and he was pleased. Near silence fell on the courtyard now, a relative hush as the other sea robbers left off looting and raping and gravitated to the group facing Blade.

Blade did not waste the opportunity. His voice rang

loud and clear over the voices, the shuffle of many feet and clangor of armed and mailed men.

"I know you worship courage, men of Redbeard. To die in battle is a great and good thing to you. So I give you opportunity. Who will come and die first? Who will make a legend today? Whose name will be sung by the skalds for years to come?"

The bronze axe sang as he whirled it over his head. "Come forward and die a hero's death. Aesculp is impatient."

Behind him he heard Sylvo mutter: "Thunor's balls! He has gone mad. They will flay us and have our livers for dinner!"

One of the raiders fitted an arrow to his bowstring and raised the weapon. Another man struck it down. "Fool! Kill him so and we are all marked coward as he proclaims. Why spoil a good fight? Rejoice that at least one of the whore queen's men is a warrior. It has been a poor battle until now, and this our chance to better it. Who goes first?"

A great clamor went up as a dozen of them vied for first chance at Blade. When the choice was made after bitter argument and a hush fell again, Blade spoke. Redbeard, his arms crossed and a tolerant smile on his face, was watching from the tower.

"I am no whelp of Beata's," Blade shouted. "I am a prince in my own land, and a wizard. Also a great warrior. I came to Craghead to fight for the lives of this maid, and for my servant, they who stand behind me. I had won, and we would be gone now but for your coming. So I must fight again! That this will be a pleasure I will not deny, for I ever enjoy killing scum, but I will have it understood that I was no man of Queen Beata's. But enough of talk—who dies first?"

The man chosen stepped forward. He was a swarthy fellow, short in the legs but with massive chest and shoulders. He wore untanned boots, ragged breeches with cross-gaitering, and a wolf skin did service as a tunic. His hair was straw colored, his eyes a cold blue beneath a helmet that bore the insignia of two serpents entwined on the haft of an axe.

The raiders fell back to form a semi-circle about the alcove. They raised a great outcry as their man approached Blade cautiously.

"Wulfa! Wulfa!"

"Let him hear your axe sing, Wulfa. I wager he will not like the tune."

The man carried a small leather and wood buckler, bossed with an iron spike. His axe was shorter in haft than Aesculp, with a single biting edge of iron, the second edge having been ground down to a long sharp spike that still bore traces of the blood of a recent victim.

The man sprang at Blade and feinted a blow with his axe. Blade, not fooled, shifted position slightly and laughed. "You hesitate, Wulfa? What does that name mean in your language—coward?"

The raiders snarled as one man and the semi-circle closed in a step or two. "Have done with him, Wulfa! Cut out his lying tongue."

Wulfa, darting cold blue hate at Blade, feinted again and thrust the spiked buckler at Blade's naked chest. Blade, making sure the axe swing was a feint, chopped viciously with Aesculp and hewed the buckler from the man's forearm and hand. Two of his fingers went with it. Blade leaped back in defensive posture.

Wulfa cast a glance at his two fingers lying in the mud, then spat in disgust and leaped in to attack again, no feinting this time. The man reversed the axe haft in his hand and swung the pointed edge at Blade's skull. Blade countered with Aesculp and a fierce clanging filled the courtyard as the axes met again and again. Sparks glittered in the murky air as axe slammed on axe and the din and clamor grew.

Wulfa sought to draw Blade out, away from the alcove,

143

but Blade would have none of it. With a snarl of baffled rage the raider leaped in again, swinging mightily. He slipped in the mud underfoot. Blade, instead of fending off the blow, let it pass over his head, then countered with a smashing backhand blow with the bronze axe. It bit into the man's neck at the base, just at the collar bone, and so great was the force that the axe cleft nearly down to the navel. Wulfa screamed and fell away as Blade pulled out the axe.

Two men ran forward to seize the dying Wulfa by the heels and drag him away. Blade leaned on Aesculp and smiled at them.

"Who comes next?"

There was no shouting now. They eyed Blade warily and whispered among themselves. Some glanced nervously to where Redbeard still watched by the tower.

Blade mocked them through the gore that covered him, Wulfa's blood having been added to that of the bears.

"I was right, then? You have no stomach for a man? But I give you this—you are great rapers of women and children."

The second opponent was as large as Blade, dark bearded and bareheaded, fighting with a sword and dirk. Blade, tiring now and not daring to show it, began a slow silent count to ten. At nine he struck and the man's head flew off and rolled into a puddle, the eyes still staring in amazement at his fellow raiders.

Blade was arm weary, yet he swung Aesculp like a stick of pinewood. "The next? Do not hang back, warriors. There is no fame in living—so come and die."

He gambled with the third man and killed him at the second pass. The bronze axe tore out the man's throat and his head fell back on a slender skein of flesh to lie grotesquely between his shoulders.

Blade, though hard put to breathe, brandished the axe at them. "Aesculp is thirsty today. Who will offer his blood next?"

The muttering was sullen now. For a moment none stepped forward. The rain had increased and was washing some of the blood from Blade's face and body. Behind him Taleen and Sylvo crouched in silence, as he had bid them, and for this much he was grateful. He could not fight forever; if he was to win his gamble it must be soon.

The raiders sent up a new shout.

"Jarl—Jarl—Jarl—Jarl!"

The man who stepped out to face Blade was of only medium height but his arms were as solid and packed with muscle as Blade's own. His hairy legs were thick and very badly bowed. He wore a purple cloak and a helmet with a silver spike, and Blade had seen him before. He was one of the two officers who had been talking to Redbeard.

The man called Jarl faced Blade with an enigmatic smile. He was smooth shaven—a rare thing among the sea robbers—with wide-set gray eyes that sparkled with intelligence. Beneath the purple cloak he wore a corselet of leather and bronze, and over this a shirt of light mail. Instead of the ubiquitous breeches this man wore a kilt of heavy plaid cloth that came high on his sturdy legs.

He saluted Blade with a broadsword very like the one Blade had used to kill Horsa, and though his tone was sombre enough there was a strain of merriment just beneath. The voice was a light tenor and, in his former life, Blade would have marked it as that of an educated man.

"It appears," said the man called Jarl, "that these dogs of mine have had a belly full of you, sire. I cannot say that I blame them, for you fight like a fiend. Perhaps you are a fiend, but that is no matter to me. You must die all the same. This I truly regret, sire, for I admire the way you handle that axe."

Blade scowled at him, knowing this to be the real test. This man had mettle that Blade had not faced before.

"Come and meet Aesculp," Blade taunted. "I doubt you will admire her so much then."

Jarl stroked his smooth chin. "You could yield, man. I like not to kill you and that is whole truth. Yield in honor and take your chances."

Blade scowled again. "I might yield, but not to promises. I am a prince in my own land and I will be treated as such. I also demand safety for my servant and the maid."

Jarl's gray eyes narrowd. "You demand?" It was spoken very softly.

"I demand!" And Blade swung the bronze axe again.

He thought Jarl's regret to be genuine. The man raised the great sword and advanced on Blade. "I am sorry for that," he said. "I have not the authority to grant demands to any unwise enough to make them. Only Getorix can do that, he who is called Redbeard, and the only answer *he* makes to demands is death! I wish you were wiser, man. I would have you fight with us and not against us. Warriors like you are not easily come by."

"Then summon Redbeard," said Blade boldly. "Such a bargain is possible, for I would as lief have my life as any man, and I know I cannot kill you all. But if only Redbeard commands—only Redbeard can bargain! I will not treat with underlings."

"We shall see," said Jarl softly, "who is underling. Defend yourself, man."

Jarl went immediately to the point, wasting no time on clumsy broad strokes, and Blade barely parried the first thrust. Nausea rose in his throat and his heart was leaden. He was bone weary and this man was a swordsman. For a moment a mindless cold fear clutched at him, then he shook it off. A man had to die sometime.

Again Jarl's sword licked in like a striking serpent. Blade took a minor scratch on the forearm. The circle of raiders set up a gleeful howl. "Jarl—Jarl—Jarl!"

Jarl's smile was merry, though with a hint of melancholy. "If I must kill a brave man," he muttered softly, "I would know his name. How are you called?"

"I am Blade," panted Blade. "Prince Blade of London!" The lie came smoothly out of nowhere, with no effort on his part. He leaped at Jarl, summoning a final surge of strength, and drove the man backward. The bronze axe grew increasingly heavier and sweat dewed on Blade's face and ran stinging into his eyes, while his lungs labored painfully.

When the voice came it was like a brazen trumpet filling the courtyard. It clangored and hung long in the sudden silence.

"Hold!" It was Redbeard, shouting from the ramparts. Jarl dropped his point immediately and stepped back. A murmur of disappointment came from the watching sea robbers.

Redbeard, hands cupped to his mouth, shouted again. "I say hold! You, Jarl, offer the man his life and honor. That of his companions also. Such a warrior must not be slain meanly. But he owes me for the death of three of mine and I will have him pay in kind. See to it, Jarl. You speak in my name."

Blade stared up at the rampart. Redbeard, hands on hips now, stared back at him. The distance was great, yet Blade felt the impact of those feral eyes over the flaming beard.

"You, stranger, listen to Jarl. His word is mine." Redbeard turned away to attend another officer, and his last words were flung over his shoulder.

"Take my offer or refuse it, stranger. The choice is yours. I will not make it again."

Redbeard disappeared into the tower. Jarl half raised his sword and looked at Blade. "So, Blade? What is it to be?"

There was loud grumbling from the onlookers. One man called out, "Kill him, Jarl. We will all lie and say he refused mercy!"

147

Another man pointed to the bodies of the three Blade had slain. "Who pays for those?"

Jarl gave them a contemptuous glance. "Quiet, you dogs. You all heard Redbeard. The next man to speak so loses his booty."

The threat had great effect, much more than any to life or limb. They grew silent.

Jarl looked again at Blade. "You will yield?"

From the alcove Sylvo said: "Yield, master. The bargain is a good one. We still have our heads—which is more than I expected. And the Drus have a saying—while a man breathes he has hope."

Blade glanced at Taleen. "And you, princess?"

There was adoration in the glance she gave him. "As you say, Prince Blade. I will live with you, or die with you. It is your choice."

Blade turned back to Jarl. Their eyes met and held steady for a moment. Then Blade flung the great bronze axe at the other man's feet. "I yield," said Blade, "and hold you to the terms your Redbeard spoke."

Jarl picked up the axe and handed it back to Blade, but not before he had hefted it and swung it a few times. "A marvelously fine weapon," he said as he gave it to Blade. And added, "A pity in a way, Blade. Now we will never know who is master between us two."

Blade received Aesculp back with a curt nod. Utter weariness was closing on him and he struggled to keep it secret.

"And yet," Jarl said, "who can know? Perhaps another time, Blade? But Thunor will decide that, not us."

Blade managed a smile. "I would have quarters for myself and my companions, Jarl. Food and drink and fresh clothing. Water for bathing, for we are all filthy. Tell your Redbeard that I will attend him whenever he is ready."

Again Jarl's smile was enigmatic. "That will not be until dark, I think. Our chief has duties to attend to—a division of booty, and the raping and punishment of the whore queen. But tonight at the great victory feast you will meet Redbeard, never doubt it. Now come with me."

Jarl bowed slightly, standing aside, as Blade, Taleen and Sylvo filed through the hostile and hard-eyed ranks of the sea raiders.

Chapter 11

The first half of Blade's strategy having come to fruition, he began that very night to complete the second half. Yet he made haste slowly, cannily, feeling his way. He walked the thin edge of disaster—one slip and there would be no second chance.

He was given a fine chamber overlooking a sea still hidden in mist. The fogs were prevalent this time of year, Jarl explained, and so Redbeard had only feinted at Penvey, to the south, to draw Lycanto and his Albians to the attack. Spies had been circulated about Alb to spread the rumor that Penvey was to be attacked. But Alb was a poor kingdom, hardly worth looting, and as soon as Lycanto was committed, and on the march, Redbeard's sleek long ships of war had prowled north and west, like ghosts in the gray fog, and achieved complete surprise at Craghead.

"Few sentries had been posted," Jarl said, "and those we throttled silently at their posts. They were too busy watching you fight bears, Blade. I could have taken Craghead with a dozen men."

Blade slept the afternoon away, with Sylvo snoring on a pile of skins in a corner. When the man awoke Blade night had come. The skies were clearing and there was a faint promise of a moon. The same wind that was blowing the mists away fluttered the snake standard of Getorix from Craghead's highest pinnacle. Sounds of drunken revelry were coming from Queen Beata's great dining hall.

A scalding hot bath was prepared and Blade lolled in it until Sylvo's frets drove him out. The man dried him on a fine linen towel and combed his hair and beard, chattering all the while. Blade, while enduring the ministrations, eyed Sylvo with speculation. He had never seen the man so on edge.

"A messenger came," Sylvo rattled on. "You are bidden to the feast this night, to sit at the table of Getorix. The one named Jarl will come for you at the ninth glass. Your burns, master, are much improved. I told you that salve was magic."

Blade, nodding, about to speak, was silenced by a new flood of words.

"It is said that Beata is well raped—first by Redbeard himself and then half his men—and is to be hanged in an iron cage to die. Ar, I think that for once she has had her fill of men. Those of her men who cried quarter are to be executed tomorrow, but the women and children are to be sold into slavery to the land across the Narrow Sea. Ar, master, I think we have done well enough to come off with our skins, thanks to the way you fought. Now if you will only mind your ways, and we all play our parts skillfully enough, we may live long enough to enjoy—"

Blade hid his smile. So that was it. Sylvo, half guessing at Blade's future plans, was nervous. Not without cause, Blade admitted. He was a bit nervous himself. Yet he meant to carry the plan through.

He smote his fist into his palm to interrupt Sylvo. "What of Princess Taleen?"

The man squinted at him and his harelip twitched. "The princess, master? She fares well enough—as well as we do. She has been taken in charge by the kyries and they see to her needs."

151

"Kyries? What are they?"

Sylvo smacked his lips and winked. "Women, master. Stout, buxom, blonde women who go about bare titted and see to the needs of fighting men. In Alb they would be called whores and camp followers—which I suppose they are—but I think they are more than that. I have heard that they sometimes fight alongside the men. They tend the wounded and fix the food and bear wine and beer to the thirsty—and do other things as well, you will understand!"

Sylvo rolled his eyes suggestively and smacked his lips again. "Some of the kyries have beauty, master. Sturdy and plump and well made for a strong man. I—"

"You," Blade said harshly, "will stay away from kyries. As you will also stay clear of wine and beer. I have made a plan and when it comes to the crux I may have need of you, sudden and desperate need, and I will have you sober. In any case it will be unhealthy for you to go sniffing around these kyries—you will end up shorter by a head. This is understood?"

Sylvo looked worried again, but nodded vigorously. "It is well understood, master, and also wise. I had the same thoughts myself, not being a complete fool, and though one of the kyries has already taken a fancy to me I paid her no attention. Ar, master, it is not myself that I worry about."

Blade was donning the clothing laid out for him. There was a kilt instead of breeches, a fine tunic with a leather corselet to go over it, under-breeches and high-lacing sandals. There was no helmet, a thing that Blade understood. He had not yet been accepted as an equal by the corsairs, even though he had earned the right in battle. Yet he was not discontent. Aesculp, her bronze clean and shining, stood in a corner.

Blade finished dressing, deliberately prolonging the silence while Sylvo mumbled and fidgeted.

Then: "You mean that it is *me* you worry about? You will explain that remark, Sylvo!"

The man still fidgeted but his squint eyes met Blade's squarely. "Ar, master, I will. You have treated me like a man, not a dog, and as a man I will speak. I fear that you will go too far—that is the plain truth of it. I know not your plans, nor want to, but I am frightened all the same. I have come to know you well, master, and I know how you dare things that would scare even Thunor. And since my fate is linked with yours, master—I would not have it else—I beseech you to go gently and with caution. This Getorix, called Redbeard, is a great warrior, though also a murderous one, and those who serve him well are rewarded well. Have done, master. Leave off! This is our chance to live and to make our fortunes."

Blade fetched him a buffet between the shoulders that nearly drove Sylvo to his knees. He grinned hugely at the man. "You have cast your fortunes with mine in this matter, Sylvo. If things go well I will make you a prince."

Sylvo, withdrawing a discreet pace or two, and rubbing his shoulder, smiled wryly. "Ar, master, even as you made yourself a prince of London? Wherever that is."

"Mind your tongue," said Blade. "I will keep my promise—I will make you a prince, though you will make a sorry one enough."

"And if things go badly, master?"

"You will share my fate," Blade told him grimly. "Whatever it may be. Now enough of this prattle—have you still the black pearls?"

"I have, master. Redbeard's men did not think me worth searching." Sylvo fumbled in the waistband of his ragged breeches and brought out the leathern pouch. He handed it to Blade.

"I thank you," Blade said. "More for your skill in picking pockets than for the pearls. You are a most excellent thief."

When the nets had fallen and Blade had gone down under the blows of a dozen of Queen Beata's men he had been immediately searched and the black pearls taken. Later, in the oubliette, Sylvo explained.

"I was searched by the same bastard that took your pearls, master. Whilst he took my purse I took the pearls from him. Later I also recovered my money, but planted the purse on one of them. They fell out about it, each accusing the other of thieving, and nearly fought. It was something to watch."

Blade spilled the luminous black pearls into his palm. He selected the largest and tucked it into a fold of his tunic. "You say these sea robbers value pearls?"

"Ar, master. So I have heard."

"We will see." He handed the pouch back to Sylvo. "Keep it well concealed. We may have need of these others."

Jarl came and escorted Blade to the great hall. As they crossed the courtyard the sounds of wassail smote their ears, a moving squall of furious noise.

"Getorix lets his dogs off the leash tonight," Jarl explained. "They have fought well and have been much at sea. Take care, Blade, that you do not fall foul of them, for you are not loved by the commonality. You slew three of their brethren today."

"In fair fight, Jarl. Are they children, to nurse grudges?"

A block had been set up in the courtyard and Blade halted by it now, professing an interest he did not feel. It was a talk with Jarl he wanted.

Jarl, who was brave tonight in a new cloak and a golden chain about his broad shoulders, watched as Blade picked up a headsman's axe from the block and hefted it.

"For the morning," he said. "Getorix means to give them the blood they cry for. Which in part answers your question —yes, they are children and as sulky and unpredictable as such. They must be so treated. Even Getorix himself, at times, is not so much—"

Jarl broke off abruptly and looked away. Blade waited.

Had Jarl been about to say that Getorix himself was childish and unpredictable? That would be an important thing to know.

Jarl shuffled impatiently in the mud. He was wearing high boots of soft leather. There was a sliver of moon and the faint rays pricked glints from the headsman's axe.

"We'd best go," Jarl said brusquely. "Getorix does not like to be kept waiting."

Blade placed the axe on the block and turned away. "You call him Getorix at times. Others call him Redbeard. Why is this?"

Jarl shrugged. "I call him what I like. I am his brother-in-law, married to his own sister, Perdita, and I have certain privilege. Which you do not have, Blade!"

They had halted at the entrance to the great hall. Jarl, ignoring the two guards who stood nearby, big men in horned helmets and armed with shields and spears, stared hard at Blade.

"I have a liking for you, Blade. Getorix does not like anyone, but he admires courage and skill in battle, and more important, he needs good officers. These scoundrels of ours fight well, but they must also be well led. I have had talk with Getorix since I saw you last, and he means to make you a captain. On trial, of course. But take some advice—your status is not yet such as gives you the right to ask questions. For myself, I do not care, but Getorix hates and distrusts questions and those who ask them. He wants only obedience and shut mouths. You do well to remember that."

Blade bowed slightly and touched his fingers to his forehead, a gesture he had seen them use.

"My thanks, Jarl. I think we are going to be friends. And yet I will dare one more question."

Jarl was watching the guards who, bored with their own company, and forbidden to drink or wench this night, had drawn nearer. A new burst of drunken laughter came from the great hall.

Jarl frowned. "Then be brief, in Thunor's name! Those swine will finish the beer and wine before we are seated, and I have a great thirst."

Blade kept his voice low. "When you first attacked, and I saw this Redbeard for the first time, I would have sworn there was a woman with him. A woman wearing a white robe such as the Drus wear. A silver-haired woman. Did I dream, Jarl? Did my eyes trick me?"

The man took a step away from Blade. His smooth shaven, not unhandsome face was set in a grim scowl, the gray eyes narrowed and unfriendly.

"You see too much, Blade. You ask too much. I beg you a last time—have done of it! Else we cannot be friends, and I would have it that we are. Now come."

Blade smiled at him. "Then she *was* there! She is here— a woman of the Dru order and who is called Drusilla?" Was it possible, this last? He had never been a believer in the validity of dreams.

Jarl appeared to have lost interest. He only shrugged and strolled through the entrance, leaving Blade to follow. Yet Blade caught the words plainly enough.

"Drusilla is a title, not a name. It means leader of all the Drus. As for such a woman, Blade, I cannot speak either way. I know nothing of it! Nor will I hear of it again. Now come—and mind your manners and your tongue, or our friendship will be of short life."

He followed him, convinced that Jarl was lying. Blade knew he had to walk carefully here—there were bogs underfoot—yet he could not rid himself of the dream, nor of the reality of a lovely silver-haired woman, a golden sword and a writhing victim. He would have been hard put to define the reality—the sword in the forest glade or his dream. He only knew that the silver-haired Dru haunted him and would not be put away.

Entering the great hall shocked Blade back to reality fast enough. There was a blast of noise and wavering torchlight and the smell of some two hundred unwashed sea raiders. Men drank and quarreled, laughed and sang, slept in spilled wine or spilled it gleefully over the head of a neighbor. Dogs were everywhere, snatching at bones, snarling and fighting among themselves and sometimes snapping at an unwary ankle or hand.

Long tables set on trestles groaned with food and drink. Huge tubs of wine were set about conveniently, and Blade caught his first glimpse of the kyries as they bore foaming tankards and horns of beer to their men. They were all big women, these kyries, and as bare breasted as Sylvo had sworn. Such a flopping and jouncing of bare pink flesh Blade had never seen, nor such a wriggling of large shapely buttocks in thin linen pants. All of them were bare legged and barefoot, and other than the thin pants wore only a leather helmet with metal horns under which they tucked a mass of blonde or red hair. Most were blue eyed and had pale skins beneath and rosy cheeks. All were buxom enough, if not fat, and it was evident that Redbeard's raiders liked them so. There was a great deal of laying on of hands as the beer was served, a great clapping of plump buttocks and squeezing of breasts, and now and then a warrior would take greater liberties and receive a clout on the ear for his daring. Yet Blade noted that now and again one of the men would leave with a woman, be gone a short time, and come back to laughter and grinning jibes from his companions.

Jarl, a bit to Blade's surprise, regarded the women with something of disgust. As they were met and escorted by a serving man who wore an iron collar bearing the snake blazon of Getorix, Jarl said: "They call them war maidens. Whores would be a fairer name. Yet Getorix vows they serve a purpose and will not get rid of them."

They were seated at a small table at some distance from where Redbeard sat on Beata's throne. This was another surprise. Blade looked to where Redbeard, his flaming head as tall as the throne itself, spoke with his officers gathered about a table just below him. Redbeard, if he

157

had marked their entry, made no sign. He quaffed now and again at a horn of beer and listened moodily to the chatter of his captains. He wore a vast scarlet cloak that muffled even his enormous body, and on his head was a simple crown of gold with the serpents entwining round-about. His beard was plaited as before and gay with ribbons from chin to waist. Now and again he would pick up one of the plaits, or both, and swing it idly or adjust a ribbon.

It was, thought Blade, as good a time as any to begin his campaign. So he began with Jarl, who was not the real target. He noted that Jarl had already emptied a large flagon of wine and was on his second, and judged that he had found a weakness in this man who, by his manner and speech, was so different from the other sea robbers.

Feigning sulkiness, Blade said: "I had not thought to sit alone. And you? Are we outcasts, then, not good enough to sup and drink with the great man who puts ribbons in his beard like any maid?" He made sure that Jarl did not miss the sneer in his voice.

Jarl, if he was in truth a drunkard, had not yet had enough wine to cushion the shock of what he heard. He stared at Blade, his mouth open, and put down his tankard with a thump that spilled wine.

"What ails you, Blade? Keep your voice down, in Thunor's name! Else you ruin yourself and those with you. Patience, man! There is more here than you understand."

Blade raised his voice. "That is true. I thought I had won a warrior's status. Why am I not treated so?"

Jarl, disdaining his cup, gulped wine from the flagon and looked uneasily at Blade. Neither Redbeard nor his officers seemed aware of the dissension.

"Patience," enjoined Jarl. "You do not understand our customs, Blade. You have been honored—I, Jarl, have been appointed to keep you close company, to be brother in arms and companion to you, and to teach you our ways until your period of trial is over. In Thunor's name, Blade, forbear these manners or we will be enemies again. I would not have it so, because I have come to like you, man."

And now Blade, liking Jarl and desperately needing a friend, forced himself to be perverse. He was being ignored, and had to prick a quarrel with Jarl that he might force one on Redbeard.

He scowled at Jarl. "I am not sure I want the liking of a man who wears skirts." He glanced down at his own kilt. "And sends them to his friends."

Jarl's hand trembled as he picked up his wine cup. "You are ignorant, man, and I will overlook that. Where I come from the kilt is honorable dress."

"That may be," Blade conceded with ill grace. "Though I have only your word for it."

Jarl leaned over the table, his face gone livid. "By the beard of Thunor, Blade, do not push too far! I am appointed friend to you, but I will not suffer—"

Blade, watching Redbeard from the corner of his eye, saw the huge man looking at them now. There was a hush about the throne as the officers followed their leader's glance and fell silent.

Blade raised his voice. "That is another thing," he sneered. "I do not understand your easy use of Thunor. Have you no gods of your own, that you must borrow from the Albs?"

Jarl smiled and for a moment the tension eased. "Gods are all one to us," said Jarl. "We borrow freely, I admit, and when we conquer a people we also conquer their gods." He leaned close to Blade again. "I, personally, have no gods. Gods are for simple people, who need them. I do not." He smiled and touched Blade's hand. "Come, drink! We will forget all that has been said. And tread you carefully—later you will understand why I say this."

Blade felt a pang. Jarl was trying so hard to stay his

159

friend! Yet Blade had to push on, using Jarl as a fulcrum to move the quarrel to Redbeard. It must be done now, tonight, in full view of this cut-throat assemblage. The gauntlet must be hurled at Redbeard in such a manner that he could not ignore it, nor settle the matter quietly with a furtive knife in Blade's ribs. His only chance hinged on open defiance that involved Redbeard's honor and courage.

So he pondered Jarl now with a skeptic's smile. "I have wondered about you, Jarl, and why you are so determined to be a friend to me. What will you gain from it? I note that you are much above this rabble"—Blade waved a hand toward the crowded tables—"and I think you are something of a philosopher. I'll wager that you can read and rune, as they certainly cannot, and if my thinking is right you are also treasurer and scribe to this oaf named Redbeard. And you are married to his sister? Is that how you cull favor?"

The last words, loudly spoken, carried easily to the throne and the group around it. Redbeard stood up, towering like a colossus. He glared at Blade and Jarl and gestured.

"Bring the man called Blade to me."

Jarl gulped wine and would not meet Blade's eye. He was in the first stage of drunkenness now, still his words were concise and a clue to his keen brain.

"I have done!" Jarl said. "You have your wish, man. I never thought your quarrel was with me—now you have it with Redbeard and I wish you well of it. Thunor protect you now. Aye, you will need him—and as many other gods as you can summon."

Another of Redbeard's captains, splendid in purple cloak and silver spiked helmet, tapped Blade's arm. "You heard our chief. Obey, man!"

Blade went toward the throne, walking easily and with a hint of swagger that belied the queasiness in his belly. So far, so good. He had pushed it to the breaking point, had maneuvered Getorix, and himself, into a position from which there was no retreat.

But this, Blade thought as he strode to the throne, was extrapolation in his own mind. It was not *yet* so—though he meant to clinch and confirm it with the words he held in store. He could still, by guile and grace of tongue, eschew the quarrel. Back out.

Redbeard, all seven feet of him, grew like a mountain in stature as Blade drew near. Blade, as human as any, felt a roil of fear in his guts. Had he pressed too far? Could he bring it off? For one breath only he faltered, then filled his lungs and shook off the cold manacle of doubt. He had come so far—he could not settle for less than his heart's desire.

The sea raiders, taking their cue from the throne, had left off eating and drinking and roistering. A hush fell over the vast hall, broken only by a muted squeal as some war maiden was pinched. All eyes followed Blade as he reached the throne and stopped, confronting Redbeard.

Getorix remained standing. Blade did not bow. Their stares locked and held and in that moment, with no words spoken, each knew the truth of it. Craghead could not harbor them both.

Redbeard's eyes were small and as frosty hard as blue agates. He dawdled with a ribbon as he looked Blade up and down, and when he spoke his voice was harsh, though low in pitch.

"You quarrel with Jarl, stranger?"

Blade, hands on hips and with narrowed eyes, stared back at the huge man. "Not so, Redbeard. My quarrel is with you."

A sound of indrawn breath ran like a wind through the silent hall.

Redbeard nodded and toyed with his plaited beard. "So? And why is this, stranger? I think you have been well enough treated."

Blade, his mind racing, began to worry. Would Redbeard, realizing how he had been manipulated into this confrontation, temporize and somehow wriggle out of a quarrel here and now? And settle matters later, in private, when Blade would not have even the slim chance he had now?

To forestall this Blade crossed his Rubicon a little prematurely. He had intended to build this scene, to lead the man, and himself, into the ultimate confrontation by degrees. This he now discarded.

With no trace of sneer, with only a hint of arrogance that these freebooters would understand, Blade said: "I have been well enough treated. I thank you for that. But it is not enough! I am no underling. I am a prince of London, as I have told you. I am a leader and I must therefore lead."

Blade halted just long enough, then pointed at the throne that had been Beata's. "You sit there now, Redbeard. *I* would sit there. I do not think it large enough for two."

The small blue eyes blinked at him. The bigger man toyed with the ribbons in his beard. Then he smiled, a cruel smile that disclosed a few blackened teeth.

"You *are* a warrior, stranger. I have seen that with my own eyes. And for now—until your death—I will acknowledge you a prince of this London you quote me. Perhaps you *are* a prince—Thunor knows you speak boldly enough to be one. And you come to the point quickly, a thing I like. I am a simple man who cannot even rune. I have Jarl to do that for me, as I also have Jarl to fight for me, and he is a great warrior also. The best and bravest—even though his manner be sometimes clerkish."

"I have challenged you," said Blade. "Not Jarl."

Getorix had hands like the paws of the bears Blade had slain. He pawed again at his ribbons. He was stalling now, and enjoying himself, and Blade wondered at it. And felt sudden unease. Jarl had said it—there was something here he did not understand.

Redbeard was in no hurry. He gave Blade an icy look. "I have hanged the whore queen in a cage, naked to the weather. She will suffer many days before she dies. How is it that you do not fear the same fate? I am still ruler here."

Blade's reply was loud and clear, ringing like a trumpet call over the fascinated assembly.

"Because if you do that to me, Redbeard, you would not be ruler long. You will proclaim yourself coward and afraid of me. I have challenged you openly and fairly, by virtue of my claim to warrior status. You yourself have given me this. I do not know all your laws, but I will wager the same life I pit against yours that there is a common law saying you must meet any fair challenge to your rule."

There was a stir and a great sighing among the onlookers. Blade knew he had won that point.

Now, adding insult to injury, and with a cunning he had not known he possessed, he produced the single black pearl from his tunic. He held it up between thumb and forefinger for all to see. It was the largest of the pearls, nearly the size of a pigeon's egg, and it glimmered in the smoky light like some demon's tear.

Blade altered his voice so the sneer was unmistakable, keeping his face impassive. "I have heard that you and your people set great store by these trinkets, Redbeard. I have more. If, as I begin to believe, you are afraid to fight me—perhaps you will *sell* me your men and your kingship."

That was too much. A great roar went up from the hall, though Redbeard himself kept silent and watched Blade with malevolent small eyes. And smiled through the fiery beard like a man who knows he cannot lose.

The men were shouting now.

"Kill him, Redbeard!"

"Enough of this—show us his heart and liver!"

163

"He has right to challenge—so grant him what he seeks. Death!"

Getorix let them rant for a minute, then held up a hand for silence. When the hall was quiet again he leaned to whisper an order to an aide. The man departed swiftly, sneering at Blade as he passed.

Redbeard pointed a huge finger at Blade. "You have spoken, Prince of London, and I have listened in patience. Now hear me.

"It is I who must thank you—for you have made a difficult matter very simple. There is a woman—the Princess Taleen. She is the daughter of Voth of the North, a thing I know to be true, and she says that she is betrothed to you. That you are to marry when she is returned to Voth. This is true?"

Damn the girl! Yet this was no time to ponder her motives. As he had bid Taleen and Sylvo follow his lead, and play up to his lies, so now he must do the same. Blade nodded.

"That is true. We are to be married. What has that to do with our quarrel?" He held up the black pearl. "You evade me, Redbeard. Do you fight me—or will you sell out to me?"

Redbeard reached and took the black pearl from Blade's fingers. He examined it for a moment, then flung it into the crowd. There was a furious scramble and a dirk or two flashed.

"That for your pearl," said Redbeard. "I like not black pearls. It is a white pearl I covet, the Princess Taleen. But as you have said just now—we have our laws. As to women they are very strict. If you are indeed betrothed to the princess I cannot take her—other than over your corpse! She is a fair prize, Prince of London, and when I kill you she will belong to me. King Voth cannot go against the law, for Jarl—who knows of such matters—tells me that the same law is observed in Voth's own kingdom. So do I thank you, Prince Blade. I had wondered

164

how to take Taleen from you, for if I had you killed it would be a base thing and my men would mutter against me. The same had I challenged you over a woman betrothed to you—our laws do not smile on this sort of thing, for it gives too much power to a ruler.

"But you have made matters easier for me. Now I can kill you in good conscience, Prince, and take your woman in the same way. And she to bear witness to this—so that in future, when Voth asks questions, he may know the truth of it."

Blade followed his glance. Taleen, escorted by four of the kyries, was coming toward the throne. Blade caught his breath and for the moment was not angry with the girl. He had never seen her so lovely, so regal, and so pale. They had combed out her long auburn hair and banded it with gold. Her small feet were shod in red slippers and she wore a long manteau of yellow silk that rippled and clung alternately to her pliant girl's body as she walked. A scarlet sash made her waist impossibly tiny.

Her maiden's breasts, beneath the single garment sheathing them, were larger than he had thought and tremulous now as she caught sight of Blade. A hand went to her red moist mouth and another to the firm breasts, and she looked at him with wet brown eyes that sent their message plain—love of him and fear for him.

They had put lip salve on her and enhanced her color with paint and Blade was angered that Redbeard had had her prepared for himself. As if Blade were already dead.

Taleen held out her arms to him, and would have spoken, but the kyries bustled her past to a chair at one side of the throne. Blade turned away. She would have to watch it, though he would have spared her if he could. And there was nothing to say.

Redbeard was watching him closely. Men were clearing a space in front of the throne.

Redbeard said: "You have challenged me before all my men. I then have choice of weapons."

Blade nodded curtly. "As you will. I will use my bronze axe, Aesculp. Have it sent for."

Redbeard smiled and his beard twitched. The ribbons fluttered. "There is no need for that, Prince. I choose these."

He held up his hands. They were, Blade considered, larger than bear's paws, and would have made two of his own. And his were large.

A roar of delight went up from the men. There would be a fine strangling now. Blade sensed that they had seen it happen before. He set his will to work instantly, bidding it whip his sluggish memory into action. Once, in that other and now nearly forgotten dimension, he had been a killer with his hands. Karate? Judo? Yes, of course. He had been an expert judoka and had killed men with his hands. Could he remember the techniques?

Redbeard slipped off the scarlet robe and tossed it to an aide. He was naked to the waist. Blade's heart muscles tightened. He was himself a big man, and powerful, and he had known bigger and more powerful men, but he had never seen anything like this body before him now. It scarcely seemed human. Rather it was a statue cast in bronze—Getorix was heavily tanned by sea and sun—with every tremendous muscle chiseled by the hand of a master sculptor.

Redbeard's shoulders were wider than Blade's by half a span, and the girth of his biceps nearly twice the size. His legs were more oak trees than flesh, gnarled and corded with sinew.

Blade kept trying to remember—he flexed his right hand at his side, extending the thumb and tightening the muscles, pulling the fingers straight into a chopping edge. That was it! He ran the hand along his bare leg and felt the callouses from the tip of his little finger to his wrist. Yes. It was coming back to him now. His right hand was, literally, a flesh axe.

There was more—much more—and he must remember

166

it. Holds and throws, pressure points, nerve ganglia, every dirty trick of street fighting he had once known.

Blade doffed his leather corselet and his tunic and handed them to a man who came forward. Jarl, sitting at the table staring into his wine cup, did not look up. Blade cast a last glance at Taleen. She was sitting rigidly in the chair, her hands crossed over her breasts, staring at him with a face gone white as milk. He could see her trembling. There was a tiny stain of blood at a corner of her mouth where she had bitten her lip.

Redbeard stepped forward into the cleared space amongst the tables. It was, and Blade was remembering now, about the size of a boxing ring. Boxing? Was there any help there?

Redbeard raised his hand for silence. When it came he did not look at Blade, but at Jarl, and his words, and his mien, were kingly enough for any man. Blade was forced to admiration.

"The gods are strange," said Redbeard, "and no man knows how they decide. I, Getorix called Redbeard, have scoffed at gods and taken them were I found them, as we all do—yet I acknowledge their power. If I am to lose my life, and my kingdom, to this puny stranger"—he indicated Blade with a gesture of infinite contempt—"then it is so written and so it shall be. If I am vanquished I charge all of you to accept the Prince of London as your new ruler. You will obey him. I also charge Jarl that he be guide and mentor to this man—if he is to be king in my stead."

Blade, falling back a few steps into a posture of defense, had to admit the cleverness of the man. He was doing it well. Redbeard was leaning over backward to be fair, to build a legend that would be sung of by the skalds and, more important, would stand in his favor when the reckoning came with Voth. It was also a gesture of supreme confidence. Getorix had no thought of failure—he counted Blade as dead.

Redbeard lowered his arms and faced Blade. Blade tensed, then made himself relax as he tried to fashion a battle plan. *Savate!* The word slipped into his mind from nowhere. Foot boxing. He had once been proficient in it.

And yet Redbeard did not move toward him. He made a signal and a cupbearer came forward.

Redbeard grinned at Blade. "One last thing, Prince of London. It is a tradition with us. We must drink the death toast."

The cupbearer tipped wine into the cup and handed it to Blade. Blade stared at it. It was contrived of a skull, white as alabaster and chased with gold runes. The teeth were still intact, large and white and perfect, and they grinned at Blade as he drank.

The cupbearer filled the skull again and took it to Redbeard. The massive man held it on high, laughing, an honest mirth that filled the great hall and started echoes.

"This belonged to Thoth," said Redbeard. He drank and flung the skull at the servant.

"The last man to challenge me."

Chapter 12

Redbeard advanced on Blade, his great arms spread wide. Blade retreated slowly, feinting with his head and body, knowing that at all costs he must avoid that deadly embrace. He did not doubt that, once Redbeard had him enfolded in those arms, the man could crush him to death.

Blade had never before played the role of David. In his former life his size and strength had given him an advantage; now the roles were reversed and he was David to this Goliath called Redbeard.

Redbeard, tired of playing about, rushed at Blade and swung a sledgehammer fist. Blade ducked under the blow, feeling a rush of air, and countered with a smashing right hand to the bigger man's belly. The impact nearly broke his wrist. It was like hitting a cast iron washboard.

Blade slipped deftly away from the tables where Redbeard had nearly cornered him. Redbeard grinned and followed patiently, taunting Blade.

"What is this, Prince of London? You will not stand and fight? Yet it was you who picked this quarrel."

Blade did not answer. He was busy trying to remember—and he was going to need every bit of wind he could get. He knew one other thing—he must defeat this giant quickly or not at all. Here was a man who would not tire, as even Horsa had tired at last. Here was an enemy who could fight all night and all day. Guile, cunning, superior technique; in all these, plus speed, lay Blade's only chance. As he ran swiftly backward he saw the skull cup on a nearby table. He did not want to furnish a mate to it.

Redbeard leaped in again, pounding with both hands. One blow caught Blade on the shoulder and spun him a dozen feet. The watching raiders came to their feet in unison, screaming for the kill. Redbeard lunged after Blade, trying to grapple. Blade recovered balance just in time and stood his ground for a moment, shooting a left and right hand into the grinning bearded face. Memory and reflex served him well—Blade had not consciously planned the blows—and they were a perfect combination. Jarring left and a murderous right cross. Both landed squarely on Redbeard's chin.

Pain shivered up to Blade's shoulders. Redbeard, scowling now, annoyed with such insect bites, came on.

Blade leaped into the air, turned half to his right and kicked the giant in the face. A *savate* kick that came somewhere out of memory. His heel cut the flesh around Redbeard's right eye and a little blood trickled.

Redbeard laughed. "Thunor take me! He fights like a maid—kicking and striking puny blows. How is this, Prince? I know you to be a warrior, for I have seen it, but you do not fight like one now. Come, Prince! Best have it over. Lock arms with me like a man and let us see who is stronger."

Blade leaped again, turned, and kicked the man in the stomach. Futile. Blade went back to his fists and landed another left and several stunning rights. Redbeard stood rooted like a tree, his hands on his hips, his face bleeding into the beard, and took the blows laughing.

Blade was already beginning to feel arm weary—he had fought much of late—and he had a churning in his stomach that was worse. Panic. He could not do this thing.

The task was impossible. This was not a mortal flesh and blood creature he faced—Getorix was an automaton with bronze for flesh and iron for muscles.

Redbeard leaped in with a speed that surprised Blade and caught him off balance. The great arms, greasy with sweat now, twined around Blade's waist and began to lock behind him.

"Aha," cried Redbeard. "Now we shall hear how your bones crack." The little blue eyes glinted cold at Blade over the flaming hair.

Blade nearly died then. It was more reflex than conscious effort that saved him. Reflex and fear. Pure clammy fear—and the cunning lower brain that Lord Leighton's computer had not touched.

Blade arched backward, at the same time clawing at Redbeard's eyes and kneeing him in the groin. It was not enough. The arms closed steadily around him and Blade felt a rib go.

Blade seized one of the beribboned plaits and tugged at it with all his might, wrenching at the beard with every ounce of strength he possessed. He pulled it out of that contorted face, so close to his own, by the bloody roots.

Redbeard let out a bellow of pain and rage. For an instant his hold loosened and Blade slipped out of that terrible vise.

He flaunted the plait, half of the man's treasured beard, at his opponent, and spoke for the first time since the fight had started.

"Here are your pretty ribbons. Come and take them back!"

Redbeard charged like a berserk bull, his pride and vanity outraged, his only thought to crush and maul this upstart stranger into a pulp.

Blade moved to one side, tripped the charging man, and whipped him in the face with his own beard. The red hair, tightly coiled and plaited, a good three feet long, was as flexible as a serpent in his hand. A new memory

171

flashed into Blade's consciousness and he knew how he was going to kill Redbeard.

But quickly. It must be fast! He was weary, his chest heaving and legs trembling, while Redbeard scarcely breathed hard except for rage and chagrin.

When Blade tripped him and Redbeard went sprawling to his knees Blade had a flash of pure inspiration. The more demented with rage his opponent, the better Blade's chances.

With a look of utter contempt Blade kicked the big man squarely in the rear. A roar went up from the tables. Men were seeing what had not been dreamed of—the fabulous Getorix kicked like any common slave.

Redbeard, hurt only in his pride—and that damaged beyond repair—clambered to his feet, like a felled tree rising again, and charged back at Blade. He was insane with rage and lust to kill, his huge face swollen purple, his eyes rolling and showing the whites. He came at Blade like a battering ram.

Blade sideslipped and flicked the plait of hair into Redbeard's eyes. He make a karate axe of his right hand and chopped viciously at the man's neck as he stormed past. Nothing. Redbeard shook off the blow, wheeled and came bellowing back at Blade. Blade tripped him again and this time Redbeard fell in a long sprawl, so heavily that the hall shook on its foundations. Redbeard's massive head slammed into a large wine tub that stood nearby and for a moment he lay stunned.

It was a chance that might not come again. Blade leaped.

He was on Redbeard's back, with the plait of beard around the man's throat and twisted into a thugee cord. Redbeard, choking now, came rearing up and Blade rode him like a horse, clinging with his knees and locked legs while he used both hands to twist the plait deeper and deeper into that thick neck. Redbeard, using his hands to claw away the thing that was throttling him, could not dislodge Blade. He fought to pull the now deeply embedded hair cord from his flesh. He shook and pranced and leaped and still Blade rode him. Redbeard's mouth opened wide, his tongue lolled out, and still he clawed at the plait of har. Blade, using his last bit of strength, pulled it tighter.

His face was turning black now. Redbeard fell crashing to his knees, pawing at the strangling cord of hair, his head swaying in agony as he fought for one gasp of precious air. He remained on his knees, rocking back and forth, refusing to die, the death vibrations of his great body fully transmitted to the desperately clinging Blade.

When it was too late Redbeard used his brain. He stopped trying to wrench away the noose and his huge hands fumbled behind him for some portion of Blade that was vulnerable. His hands found Blade's ankles, one in each hand, and with a final tremendous effort the man tried to tear Blade into two pieces. Blade, convulsed with pain, fought back by tensing his muscles, resisting the unnatural strain with every bit of his own waning strength. His hands, ever twisting the hair noose deeper into Redbeard's neck, were numb and long beyond pain or feeling of any sort.

It was over. The great carcass slumped, the hands fell away from Blade, as a final tremor ran through the man Getorix, called Redbeard. He slumped out at full length near the wine tub, dead.

Richard Blade, near dead himself, left the plait coiled around the throat and staggered to his feet. Every nerve and muscle screamed for rest, for the merciful oblivion of sleep. Or death? Blade, in those frenetic last moments, was not quite sure who had won, who lived and who had died. He knew only an enormous longing to close his eyes and have done with it.

Yet the matter must be carried out to a fitting and proper conclusion. As his senses filtered back he began to understand, through the roaring in his head, that he was now king of the Sea Raiders. Redbeard was dead! He, Blade, now ruled.

He swayed over the huge corpse. Silence had fallen over the vast hall.

Blade raised a hand and in a voice that was surprisingly strong—he was amazed himself—said: "I rule now. I make Jarl my First Captain. You will obey him as you would me."

Blade looked down at the corpse of Redbeard, still not quite believing that he had killed such a man.

"Let this man be given a proper burial, as befits such a warrior. Jarl will see to it. As for all of you, who now serve me, get on with your feasting. As soon as the body has been taken to a place of honor. I—"

Blade never saw his attacker. The man, who had been sitting at a table near the wine tub, leaped at him with a high scream of hate and mourning. A long dirk flashed in the smoky light and Blade felt exquisite white agony as the metal ripped his flesh. He staggered away, blood streaming from his back, and cast frantically around for a weapon as the man came at him again.

Blade stumbled into a table and fell half across it. He turned, trying again to face his attacker, blood drenching him, as Jarl leaped into action.

Blade saw what followed through a curtain of pain and blood. Jarl, a long sword in his hand, shouting in anger, sprang at the man who had daggered Blade. The sword came around in a level, glistening circle and bit into flesh with a loud *chunk*.

Blade's attacker, headless, stood for an instant and spurted blood from the dying trunk high into the air. The dagger, stained with Blade's blood, clung to the fingers.

The head fell into the tub of wine and floated there, eyes staring, crimsoning the wine.

Blade felt himself falling into sleep. Now that he could achieve oblivion, so longed for just an instant ago, he did not want it. He was suddenly afraid of it. This was not a

174

natural sleep that stalked him, this numbness that pervaded his feet and legs and arms and was fast working toward his brain. He sought to speak and heard only a strangled cry. He was falling and felt himself caught and supported by brawny arms.

Jarl, bloody sword still in his hand, was peering at Blade. His lips moved and Blade heard the words from a great distance. They sparked a final bitterness and rebellion in him—to have come so far, to have done so much, to have defied circumstance so valiantly—and to have it end here, like this.

Jarl's voice was a muted trumpet sounding on a vagrant and fading breeze. Blade could barely hear, but what he heard told him he was dying.

"Oleg—natural son of Redbeard—his dagger poisoned—we know of no antidote, Lord Blade. But we will try—there is a Dru, she you spoke of, and it is said, it is possible that—"

Jarl's voice was gone. His face was fading. Blade smiled up at the ring of faces and wondered *why* he was smiling. He was an idiot! He had always hated death—and feared it in his secret soul—and why should he smile now that it was here at last? What would happen to Taleen and poor Sylvo?—Then everything went black.

Chapter 13

For ten days the wind blew from the northeast, stubborn and unrelenting, and scattered the ships like autumn leaves over the Western Sea.

Richard Blade, in waking dream and nightmare sleep, fancied himself in a cradle rocked by a giant's hand. His wound festered and the poison was insidious, seeking his life, held in check only by the bitter draughts given him by the silver-haired Dru, she who in his dream he had called Drusilla.

Her real name was Canace. This she told him in one of his rare lucid moments, before she administered the black cool liquid, so bitter to his tongue, that brought on the drowsy inertia, the waking dream state, that sapped his will and made his great muscles so much mush.

In the dim recesses of his brain he knew he was being drugged. He also knew the drug was combating the poison and saving his life. So, though he did not think to make the comparison, Blade at the moment was like the ship on which he lay, driven and harried, floating helpless on the tides, too weak to resist what he knew was happening to him. And—such was the sly machination of the drug— he did not *want* to resist. His mind was lulled and dormant, he welcomed his seduction as heartily as any spinster who dreads to die before experiencing the ultimate convulsion.

It could have been on the first day aboard ship, or the fifth—Blade had no track of time—that he dimly sensed what she was about. She paid him frequent visits, always with the bitter potion, careful that he never lapse back into full consciousness and will power. Blade, wandering lonely and bemused in his dream forest, welcomed her coming. The bitter drink meant an end to the pain in his back, and to the terrible cramps of his belly, and the wily potion persuaded him that he was lucid.

The cool hand on his brow. Gentle, smooth as satin fingers. The bitter drink to his lips and the cloths, wrung out in an ewer of cold water and pressed to his burning flesh. Then, for a little time, she would sit beside his rude cot and hold his hand and watch him with topaz eyes in which swam darker flecks of brown. She would toss back her white cowl, her hair a draping silver fall breaking gently on her shoulders, and Blade would marvel at her beauty and knew not, nor cared, if he was in death or life.

Her breasts were well swathed in the white robe, but Blade remembered the dream in the fens and knew those breasts—he was too weak to raise a hand to touch— would be firm and cold.

Then, from between those deep breasts, she would take the little golden medallion, worked in intaglio, of a crescent moon ensnared in a design of oak leaves. It hung from her white throat on a fine chain of gold. Her long fingers, blue nailed, toyed with the pendant and set it to swinging ever so gently to and fro while Blade watched as a cat will watch a string dangled before it.

Always she began in the same way, with the same words, her voice as low and unctuous as rich cream pouring.

"I am Drusilla, Lord Blade. That is my title, not my name. My name is Canace. I am also called Drusilla,

177

leader of all the Drus in this land and in all the lands across the seas . . ."

On the first day, at this juncture, Blade opened his mouth in an effort to speak. A cool, soft, perfumed hand closed it gently and he had not tried again. Did not *want* to speak. Wanted only to listen to that voice running on like some celestial choir, recounting his sins and forgiving them, promising him joys in future—and sealing it in the end with the greatest pleasure he had ever known. Blade, stricken and inert hulk that he was, lived for the paradise that was to come. That came every day just before she left him for the long interval of night.

On this day—Blade did not know that it was the tenth and that the storm was at last abating—she began in the same fashion. Her words were always the same, never varying, as though she meant to imprint them in Blade's mind forever. The golden medallion swayed before his eyes and he followed it listlessly. Somewhere, for the first time, a spark stirred in his mind and he was near to understanding what she was doing to him. There was a word for it. A technique called—

The effort to think was too much and Blade closed his eyes. A soft blue-nailed finger opened them and she went on intoning what had become a litany between them:

"You killed a Dru, Lord Blade. There is no proof of this, but proof is not needed when a Dru accuses. But I do not accuse, though I know you guilty. It was you who slew that aged Dru in the forest, near the sacred glade. For this your life is forfeit, after dreadful torture. None can save you, nor will any aid or shelter you, for none dare challenge the Drus.

"This is our secret, Lord Blade. Ours, and that of Princess Taleen, but she is a child and of no importance. None will *know* that you are a murderer of Drus, and you need not suffer the terrible penalty, so long as we have understanding of each other."

Blade would have closed his eyes again, but she gently

178

stroked them open. The little medallion flickered back and forth like a golden pendulum. His pain had gone now and he floated on an euphoric sea of anticipation. Soon the words would end she would do—that!

"There has been much unrest of late. In Alb, in the late Beata's kingdom, in the lands over the Narrow sea, and now in Voth. There are some who dare, for the first time, to scoff openly at the Drus. To defy them. This is an evil thing, Lord Blade, and it will be stamped out without mercy. But for this warriors are needed, men of iron and bronze, and we Drus are not warriors. Our kingdom is of the mind, of the wondrous control of minds and of the thoughts therein.

"I thought to use Getorix, he who was called Redbeard, as the warrior arm of the Drus. But you killed him, Lord Blade, and are a far better man in mind than he ever was. So you will take his place, Blade. You see that I do not always call you Lord—there will be equality with us. I will rule the minds and you, with force, will rule the bodies. You will accept this idea and when you are again well, which will be soon, you will execute my plans as I bid you. None but ourselves will know of this, nor of our personal relationship, for you will be a true believer of Dru faith, and will do what you do out of conviction. All these things you will do, Lord Blade, and you will not question nor need to understand why you do them. All I have spoken these days will be forgotten.

"You will marry Princess Taleen, if you like, because I think it fitting. Her father, King Voth, will be easier swayed thus. This is important, for Voth is important, and I wish his sanction. He respects Drus now, but he does not fear them. He must be made to fear them, and that will be part of your work in the months and years to come. For all this will not be done easily, nor quickly, and so you must understand. But it will be done!"

Always, on these last words, her voice rose in pitch and firmness. Blade, watching that lovely face, saw the scarlet mouth tighten over the perfect little bones of her teeth, and sometimes he could see the golden sword flashing down. And cared not. For when she reached this point it was almost time.

On this last day something new was added. "The seas grow calm," she said, "and the fleet is reassembling. In a day or two you will be much better, and we will come to the port of Bourne, where we will land and march overland to Voth. When that happens I shall leave you and travel alone to Voth, with my own people. But I will meet you there, in Voth's place, and it shall be as I have spoken these past days. With this difference—and this you must not forget—that our meetings will be clandestine and our speech covert. Though you are a Dru believer, and do my bidding, we must not be named together in these matters. All this you will remember, and you will act upon, and you will never speak of them."

The medallion swayed back and forth, back and forth. Blade closed his eyes, knowing she would not open them again. For now it was time.

Silence. Silence broken only by the creaking and travail of the ship's timbers as it labored easily in the lessening seas. Then, as always before, he heard her breathing change. The breath rasped in her throat, as though she could scarcely inhale, and he knew without seeing that her mouth was open.

She took one of his hands and put it between her thighs, pressing gently on it so he felt the easy tremor of long femoral muscles. She was slim legged, yet with a fullness of soft flesh that lay warm beneath the robe. She pressed her knees together harder, leaning forward, and he heard her breathing roughen as she bent close to him.

It was at such times that her words varied from the routine he had come to expect.

One day she had said: "Drus are also women!"

On another day: "How like a god you are!"

This day she muttered, so low he could barely hear, as she went to her knees beside the cot.

"Ah, Blade, if babes could be gotten so I would as lief conceive from your seed in my mouth."

Blade swam on a misty sea of pleasure. To the drug already flowing in him was added the opiate of her mouth. He could not keep from writhing and his excitement spurred her own. This was sensual witchcraft beyond his experience, and while in the throes he did not know if she were human or not. That she was the mother of all fellatrices he did not doubt, and when he could think at all it was to wonder if it had something to do with the Dru religion. For she would submit to nothing else, even had he possessed the strength.

She had been plain about it: "We Drus do only this to men. What we do among ourselves you may not know, or any man. Lie still, Lord Blade, and empty yourself of all dark spirits. They cannot harm me, for I am Drusilla!"

On this tenth day Blade, already drifting into dark limbo, had one last glimpse of her. Of Canace, called Drusilla. He knew her evil and he cared not. She had saved his life that she might use it, for her own vicious ends, and he cared not.

She smiled up at him, still on her knees, her velvety red mouth moist with his essence, and repeated what she had said once before.

"How like a god you are!"

She left, as she always did, without a backward glance.

Blade, tumbling into sleep, fought his torpid mind so that he might grasp two things—she hated being a woman and would be a man. And—a growing, though very faint spark of rebellion—she held him in thrall as much with her mouth as with her drug. If he could combat one he could—could—

The effort was too much. Blade slept.

Topside a large square sail slatted and boomed as it was hoisted up the single mast in the brisk wind. They had been running before the wind for days, under bare poles, and a great halloa went up from the sea raiders as the cloth firmed and slewed about and the rudder took firm hold. If this new wind held steady a week would see them in Bourne. Already the men spoke eagerly of new loot to come.

Jarl, though ruling them with an iron hand cunningly concealed, had been noncommital. He did not know of Blade's plans. First they would have to see if the new ruler lived or died.

At first there had been very little grumbling, thanks to the terrible storm which had menaced them all. It took all their efforts to stay afloat and it was one of Thunor's miracles that only five ships had been lost out of twenty. There having been no treasure on the lost ships, the concern for them was not great except in the case of relatives.

But the moment the storm began to fail the grumbling began. Men gave loud opinions without being asked, and certain brazen-tongued sea lawyers opined that it was stupid, as well as unprofitable, to march all the way to Voth when there was plenty of loot to be found nearer by. They could, for instance, go south to Alb and sack it after all. Not prime pickings, perhaps, but not bad and better than making the long and perilous voyage north to Bourne, a mere fishing village.

Jarl handled the complainers in his own way. He had a dozen soundly whipped, keelhauled three, and at last had to hang a man from the yardarm when he struck an officer in an argument. The grumbling went underground.

Jarl stood with the Princess Taleen on the tiny poop deck as the silver-haired Dru passed on the way to her cabin. She was cowled and did not speak or glance at them as she passed, carrying the ewer and flask she used in ministering to Blade.

Both watched her out of sight down the aft hold where the tiny cabins, hardly larger or cleaner than pigstys, were situated.

Taleen, dressed warmly for shipboard, her auburn tresses flying in the wind, looked at Jarl and frowned. They had become good friends during Blade's illness and Taleen, suspecting the truth about Jarl and women, did not mind at all and kept it to herself.

Taleen said: "I would see Blade, Jarl. You must arrange it this very night."

Jarl looked unhappy. "I think it not wise, Princess. You know the Dru's orders. No one to see Blade, and only she to minister to him. I dare not go against her."

Taleen's brown eyes flashed angrily in the sun. "Ha! You are all afraid of her. And yet you call yourself men!"

Jarl stroked his smooth chin and a smile flickered at the corner of his mouth. "Yes, Princess. We are. And you are *not* afraid of Drus?"

She would not look at him and he thought that tears lurked not far below the surface. "Yes," she admitted. "I am. I am as great a coward as any of you."

"Only when it comes to Drus," Jarl said stoutly. "You will not find us cowards else. But I, who do not even believe in the gods, confess that I find Drus terrifying. I do not understand it myself. Yet they are powerful, Princess. Very powerful. And Blade lives, does he not? Hate and fear the silver Dru as you will, she brought Blade back from death. Our physicians—I will admit they are poor enough things—had all given him up and could only pray to Thunor for him."

"And I to Frigga," Taleen scowled. "So I admit that the silver Dru saved Blade—and yet I hate and distrust her. She is much too beautiful for a Dru!"

Jarl, wiser than he knew, smiled at that and said, "And too much alone with the man you mean to marry, eh, Princess?"

Taleen gave him a scornful look. "That matters not. Drus are pledged celibate. Anyway Blade will not marry me—I only said that when I thought to help him against Redbeard. I hoped Redbeard would hold my father in fear, and would not dare—but that is over. Let us not prate of things past. I mean to see Blade, if only to tell him what I think of him for letting himself be stabbed!"

Jarl settled his silver spiked helmet in place against the wind. "Be patient, Princess. And grateful. Blade lives—she would not lie about that—and soon we will be at Bourne and beginning the march to Voth. If I can hold these surly dogs in leash that long!"

The brown eyes glittered and Jarl, unaccountably, felt uneasy.

"Patience is a thing the Drus preach," said Taleen. "When it serves their purpose. They say it to be a virtue—but I have had enough of Dru virtues. But you need not be privy to it, Jarl. I will do it alone."

She was staring at the hold where the silver Dru had vanished and Jarl did not like the look of speculation in her eyes.

184

Chapter 14

Blade was waked by a blaze of sun through an open porthole. Drusilla never did this—all their conversation had been by candle or smelly lamp—and now the buttery sun and the fresh smell of salt sea invaded the stuffy cabin like a tonic. Blade felt better than he had in days. His head was clear, his will had returned, and though he was weak and had some pain from his wound there was none of the deathly lethargy he had been prey to.

Sylvo, after opening another porthole, beamed at his master with that dreadful grimace Blade had come to recognize as a smile. The squint was there, as was the harelip, but Sylvo was gay in new clothing and had shaven the scraggy hairs from his chin.

He handed Blade an enormous wooden bowl steaming with some fragrant substance, and gave him a pewter spoon after polishing it on his sleeve.

"Brewed from the livers of wild hare, master. We went ashore for water yesterday—the storm having broached most of our casks—and I caught the creatures just that I might fashion a stew for you. Sup of it, master, and tell me what you think. Ar, I was a rare cook once on a time."

Blade tasted the stew. It was delicious and he suddenly found himself ravenous. Now that his mind was clear he could not recall the Dru ever feeding him, other than ship's biscuit and water.

Blade ladled the stew into his mouth, watching Sylvo as he did so. He had come to know the man well. Sylvo was excited, happy, and he was talking too much.

"You look marvelous well, master, considering you were so near to seeing Thunor in person. Ar, you'll never come closer to death. That was powerful poison on the dagger Oleg put into you. He was one of Redbeard's bastards and must have loved the man, for he surely tried to murder you."

Blade had a brief vision of a head floating in the wine tub, then dismissed it.

He scraped the last bit of stew into his mouth and sighed. "You are a good cook, rascal. I give you that. Now no more of this dithering—how come you here, and where is the silver-haired Dru?"

Sylvo went to a corner and came back with the scarlet cloak Blade had won from Horsa. "See, master, how fine it is now. I have cleaned it, and furbished the gold work. Also the great bronze axe—my hands ache from working on it—though I could not bring it because my hands were full of the stew and your fresh clothing and—"

Blade pushed himself up in the cot, feeling already stronger as the food nourished him and the sun and air dissipated the last lingering effects of the drug. He scowled mightily at Sylvo.

"I asked a question! Answer it—or I am not too weak to climb from this bed and give you a blow you'll remember always. Where is the Dru who has been tending me?"

Sylvo's squint increased. He fell back a few steps, still holding the scarlet cloak and a pair of clean under-breeches, and rubbed his newly shaven chin with a finger. Blade knew he was searching for a lie.

Blade roared. "Well, man! Out with it—and I want truth."

Sylvo avoided his eye. "The truth, master, is that I do not know. No one knows. The silver Dru has disappeared. She was not in her cabin this morning and her servant, a Dru of low order, came squalling to Captain Jarl in panic that her mistress had fallen overboard in the night. She would have Captain Jarl put back and search the sea."

Blade regarded him steadily. This time he could not be quite sure—he thought Sylvo to be lying, but he could not be positive.

"So? Did Jarl put back?"

"Nay, master. He did not. He said it was useless—a thing we all knew without being told—and he ordered the ship to be well searched. We found nothing, master. The silver Dru is gone. Vanished. For which, and I am bold enough to say it now that she is gone and cannot hear me, we are all offering thanks to Thunor. I myself saw Captain Jarl smiling as he prayed—and he does not even believe in Thunor. Ar, master, it is a fine thing that the Dru fell overboard. We are all happy about it."

Blade regarded his servant stonily. He was his own man again, and knowing what he did, he privately considered it just as well that the silver Dru was gone. Canace. Called Drusilla, leader of all the Drus. High Priestess with the golden sword of sacrifice. Lovely phantom of dreams, expert succuba clothed in velvet human flesh, who had planned so far and so well. Now all the dreams, and the flesh, were fathoms deep in the cold green of the Western Sea. Yes. It was just as well.

Yet Blade said: "She saved my life, Sylvo."

"Ar, master. I know that. We all do. We had given you to Thunor when she came forward, from the place Redbeard kept her hidden, and took command of matters pertaining to you. She bade Jarl do this, and Jarl do that, and Jarl did as he was told. We all did, for that matter. Because we were all in terror of her and of Dru magic. But

187

that is all over now, master, and you are well. And she is dead—well, gone at least, because some say that Drus do not die like other people."

Blade regarded him with a tolerant affection. He did like the man, thief and scrapegrace that he was, and he did not doubt his loyalty. That he had been afraid of the Dru was natural enough—even Blade, in his drug haunted dreams, had been a little afraid of her. He thought for a moment of the things she had done to him, then put the thought away. He would not know that sweet sickness again. Just as well.

"When you speak of Jarl you will speak of him as Captain Jarl," he said sternly. "That is my wish. And now, rogue, pull up the stool yonder and tell me everything that has happened while I have been sick. *Everything.* Miss no detail. I would come up to date on matters."

Sylvo took huge pleasure in the telling, embroidering matters until Blade cursed him and swore he had missed his calling—instead of a mangy cutpurse he should have been a lying skald, setting his wild tales to music on a lute.

"In detail," he groaned. "In detail, man, but not so much so! And stick to the proper time of things—you leap ahead and dart back like a hare with hounds after it. Now begin again, from the time I fell unconscious until this moment."

When Sylvo had finished Blade fell into a deep study and stared for a long time out the open port.

Finally he said: "It has been ten days?"

"More like to twelve now, master. You have been very ill."

Blade started to speak, then only nodded. Yes. He had been very ill. Only he knew how ill. And only he would ever know of what transpired—for he would never tell a living soul.

He turned on Sylvo again, warily because the rib that

Redbeard had cracked still hurt, and asked the question that he must ask.

"The silver Dru *fell* overboard?"

Sylvo shrugged and rolled his eyes. "What else, master? And none so strange—it happens often enough at sea, or so I am told. I am no seaman myself, not of deep water anyway, and I was dreadful sick for two days. It is my thought the the Dru came on deck for air—the cabins are not fit for slaves—and was swept overboard. Simple enough. But why question it, master. Let us be grateful and—"

Blade silenced him with a hand. "You say the silver Dru had a servant? Another Dru of a lesser rank?"

Sylvo looked puzzled and scratched himself. "Ar, master. That is the truth of it. Why?"

"You have too many whys," Blade said curtly. "Leave off—and go fetch me this other Dru, this servant. Unless, of course, you are afraid of her also?"

"I *am* afraid of her," Sylvo admitted, "but not so much as of the silver Dru. Her glance gave me a gallows feeling, I swear. But the Dru servant will know nothing, master. No use to talk to her. She saw nothing, heard nothing, and anyway she is in a screaming fit such as ordinary women get. I doubt you can make sense of her."

Blade stared at his man. Obviously Sylvo did not want him to talk to the servant.

"Go fetch her to me," Blade snapped. "And no more of your clack or, by Thunor, I will regain my strength on you. No—stay and help me dress."

He decided on the instant. It was time to be up and doing. Sylvo put a fresh dressing on the wound, which was healing nicely, and helped Blade into clean clothes and a corselet, then combed his hair and beard. Blade badly wanted a bath, but there was no water to spare.

Sylvo clasped the scarlet cloak about Blade's big shoulders and stood back in admiration. "There, master. You are your old self again. Lord Blade. King of the Sea Raiders!"

"And shall be," Blade muttered, "until we come safe to Voth. Then no more. Now go fetch me that servant, Sylvo. And my bronze axe as well. I want it with me when I first appear on deck."

Sylvo lingered. "Ar, master. It would be as well. They are a surly lot of brutes, these raiders, and Captain Jarl is hard set to keep them under hand. They know there is no loot in Bourne, and they cry that Voth is too far and King Voth too strong—they would turn back and loot Alb. Which is all right with me, for I am all in favor of—"

Blade, now steady on his feet, moved toward him and doubled up a great fist. "I gave you an order, man! Still you linger and defy me?" He raised his hand.

"Nay, master. I go." Sylvo backed hastily out of the door. "But I wish you would not do this—for you will rue it unless I am more fool than I think."

Blade, left alone to ponder that enigmatic remark, had still no answer when Sylvo returned with the woman in question. He pushed her into the room and fled without a word.

The woman stood quietly in the middle of the cabin, her work-worn hands clasped before her. She was thin and stoop shouldered, yet her eyes peered from the cowl at Blade with the bright alertness of a sparrow. Her robe was soiled. Blade guessed her to belong to the lowest, working order of the Drus.

She was not hysterical. One lie to Sylvo's credit. Blade, to put her at ease, motioned to a stool. She refused, saying she would stand. Her voice was flat and unmelodious and her eyes never left off searching Blade's.

"You know who I am?"

Her head inclined. "I know, Lord Blade."

"Good. I want truth from you. This is understood?"

"I have no reason to lie, Lord Blade."

"We all have reason to lie at times," he said harshly,

190

"but never mind that. Tell me, quickly and simply, of what befell your mistress—the Dru called Drusilla. The silver-haired woman who cared for me. What do you know of this?"

"Not much," said the woman. "And yet more than most." She squeezed her bony hands together and the tendons cracked.

Blade frowned and left off pacing. "I do not want riddles."

"I make none. I know more than most because I have not been asked until now. Only *you* ask, Lord Blade. For the others it is enough to believe that my mistress, the High Priestess, fell overboard. They have not dared ask."

Blade tugged at his beard, black and curling now. "So I *do* ask. What have you to tell?"

"The Drusilla did not fall overboard. One came and tapped at our door in the reaches of the night. I had just fallen to sleep, so the Drusilla answered. I woke then, but did not speak or stir, and I heard them whispering at the door. What words I did not hear, but I understood that the caller wanted the Drusilla to come on deck. There was great urgency to the whispering. So the Drusilla put on her robe and cowl and left the cabin. She did not return. And that is all I know, Lord Blade. Unless it be this bit more—my mistress did not fall overboard. She was pushed overboard by the one who came to the door and whispered. Perhaps the Drusilla was slain first. Perhaps not. But she is dead. Murdered. This I know."

Blade remembered the golden sword stabbing down at the screaming, terror-crazed serving wench of Lycanto. A deed conspired by the Lady Alwyth? But what matter now—

A sudden pang struck Blade, an electric pain slashing at his head like a lightning bolt. He staggered and clung to the wall for a moment, bemused, dazed, his head buzzing with a thousand bees. For a micro-instant he saw words

191

blazoned on his memory: *He who lives by the sword dies by the sword!*

The old Dru was staring at Blade. "You are ill, Lord Blade?"

It had gone. Blade rubbed his head and frowned. How strange. For a moment he had been nearly blind, with a tempest raging in his skull and his body light as feathers.

"It is nothing," he told her gruffly. "A headache. I have been in darkness too long and perhaps the sun— But back to our business. This one who came and whispered. You recognized the voice?"

"No."

"Was it man or woman—certainly you could tell that."

"I could not, Lord Blade. They spoke too low. I could not say, in truth, that it was a man—or a woman."

He considered her for a moment, scratching his chin. "You may go then. Do not speak of this to anyone. I will look into it in person."

"And see the guilty punished, my Lord Blade? Man— or woman?" There was no mistaking the doubt and mockery in that dry old voice.

"That is my affair," he said, turning to stare out the port. "I said I will look into it. Go."

She had been gone but a moment when there came another tapping at the door. Blade's mood was turning vile now and he had no wish for company at the moment. His "Enter" was cold and curt.

It was the Princess Taleen, her nymph body robed against the sea air. She was wearing her auburn hair long again, as when he had first seen her and killed the mastiff, and the luxuriant tresses were held back by the same simple golden band. She was buskined and the robe, which was short, revealed dimpled knees. Sea and sun had imparted a fine bronze glow to her already magnificent skin.

She bowed slightly and there was faint mockery in the deep brown eyes that were too limpid, too innocent. He did not trust her in this mood. It meant mischief. He recalled the way she had looked at him when he was in danger—with all her love shining forth.

"I have come to pay my respects," she said. "To the new ruler of the Sea Robbers. And to say that I am glad you are alive, Lord Blade. I prayed to Frigga for it."

Blade's smile was tentative. This one had as many humors as a chameleon has colors.

"*Lord* Blade? We are most formal today,"

She bowed again. "As befits a mere maid with a great lord and warrior. Even though she is the daughter of a true king, and has known the great lord and warrior when he wore a scarecrow's breeches."

Blade frowned at her, arms akimbo. "You have come to quarrel, Taleen. With me, who is just back from death. Why?"

For a moment she did not answer. She went to the cot and began to make it, smoothing the coverlet and patting the sweat-stained pillow where he had tossed for so many dark hours. Blade studied that trim behind as she bent over the cot and felt much as he had that first night by the brook, when her girlish breasts had been practically thrust into his face. That this was lust, he acknowledged. Yet it was a kind of lust he had never known before—lust with an oddly gentle strain.

"I do not come to quarrel," she said. She bustled around the tiny cabin, straightening and tidying. "I come to explain."

"Explain what, Princess?"

"Why I did not come before, to tend you in your sickness. I tried. The silver Dru would not permit it. Only once she spoke to me—to warn me away from you. I was frightened, Blade. I admit it. I, princess of Voth, did not have courage to go against her."

Blade smiled. When she called him Blade things were nearly back to normal.

"So was Jarl frightened," he said. "And I account him no coward. And all the others, from what I hear. So what of all this? She is dead and I live. Forget the rest. It is over."

He watched her narrowly.

Taleen made much of tossing a handful of litter out the port. "Yes," she agreed. "That is over. We will forget it. Tomorrow we come to Bourne and then it is only four days march to Voth. Which brings about another matter, Blade."

"Speak then." He still watched her closely, but knew now that it would not avail him. For one so young she schooled her features well. They would not betray her—if there was aught to betray.

She faced him at last, full in the rays of the sun slanting through the port, crimsoning beneath the golden patina of her skin. Her flashing eyes belied the blush.

"I lied to Redbeard when I said we were betrothed! I said it because I thought it might aid us—you. That he would then leave us alone. I did not know that he—that he wanted me for himself."

"Any man would want you," Blade said softly. "You are very lovely, Taleen. And very young, with very much to learn. I will be glad when we come at last to Voth and you are again safe and happy in the life you knew before. As for what you said to Redbeard—I thank you. I know you tried to help me. And all ended well."

Her smile was no real smile. There was a vixen in it. "I am glad you understand me, Blade. I would not have you think I would throw myself at a man, or in any manner force myself on a man. I have had suitors aplenty, thank you, without asking a stranger in scarecrow's breeches to marry me!"

Blade struggled to keep his temper. This could be an exasperating child.

He folded his arms over his massive chest and regarded her coldly. "It seems to me that you make a great deal of those breeches. Yet I—"

She did not let him finish. "And it seems to me that, at

194

least once in ten days, you might have sent for me! Or even for that gallows bird servant of yours. We were afraid. We knew nothing of your state. I nigh to perished of anxi—"

She halted abruptly and turned so that he might not see her eyes. "Now I begin to see that you were never in great peril of death! Not with a High Priestess to tend you. Did you tell her, Blade, that you killed one of her sisters that night in the wood?"

Taleen glared at him, her words dripping with spite.

"I did not tell her," he replied. "She told me. Which requires a question, Taleen. Did *you* tell her about that night—and what we saw?"

Her brown eyes widened in honest amazement. "Me tell her? You must think I am a fool as well as a child, Blade, and I am neither! I told her nothing. I said I spoke but once with her. That is the truth, I swear it on Frigga, and I told her nothing."

"And yet she knew," mused Blade.

Taleen was eyeing him with new speculation. Very softly she said: "She knew? And you live yet. I think I begin to understand, Blade. Matters I had not dreamed on, because Drus are sworn celibate. But yet—ha! I *do* understand."

"You understand nothing," he shouted harshly. She had taunted him into loss of temper and he was helpless to resist it. He took subterfuge in the weakest of excuses, and knowing it so, lost his temper even more.

"You'd best go," he told her. "My thanks for coming to inquire of my health. But I confess to feeling a bit faint just now and I would rest. If you see Jarl send him to me, please, and likewise that rascally man of mine."

"You are well consorted," she told him bitterly. "You and that squinting knave. Ay, you go well together. Like master, like man—it is well said."

A sharp pain began to materialize again in Blade's head, then vanished abruptly.

"Yet it was I who saved you from Queen Beata's dogs and men," he reminded her now. "I who came for you when you had been drugged by Lady Alwyth. I who fought bears for you at Beata's court, and later put you behind me and killed three brave men for you. I who fought and killed Redbeard for you, and like to died of a poisoned dirk, all that I might bring you safe once again to your father in Voth—"

"Lies! Liar!" she screamed. "Liar—liar! You fought to save your own life as well, and that you might bring me to Voth, as you say so piously, but only to seek and establish favor with my father. You have always meant to trade me, Blade, for favor and substance with my father, the King. Oh, you are brave enough! But you are also a great schemer and a liar—and as blind as the furred mice that flutter in twilight. You claim you are a wizard! You say you are Prince of London—wherever that is—and I admit you command well and can go grave and sage of mien when it pleases you. Yet I say you are a fool—and blind into the bargain. Blind—blind—"

Her loss of temper had restored his own. Blade gave her a sweet smile of tolerance.

"Wherefore am I so blind, then?"

Taleen picked up a stool. Blade, eyeing it, moved a step back.

"That I will not answer," she snapped. "If you cannot see it for yourself I will not tell you. But *I* am not blind! Do you think it any secret how you so near won that bitch Queen Beata over? Why you were given time, not slain at once, why you were permitted to fight bears instead of being flayed? And a false fight at that, with only that scummy servant of yours in real danger! I know, Blade, I know! Such things are not secret long. You must be a monster yourself to have gratified that red whore!"

Blade smiled at her. "That also I did for you, Taleen."

She hurled the stool at him. He ducked and it shattered against the wall.

196

At the door she hurled back a glance tipped with venom. "We left Beata in her cage, though Jarl spared the lives of her people yet alive. She was sniveling for mercy when last I saw her, crying to be killed and put out of pain. Jarl might have granted her this, but I said nay. I hope she still lives, Blade. And suffers. I wish you could have seen her, Blade. They had taken away her wig and her bald gray head was pitiful in the rain. Aye, she was a loathsome creature. I admit your taste was better with the silver Dru."

She was reminding Blade of things he did not want to remember, and he lost his temper for the second time.

"You speak of matters you know nothing about," he said coldly. "I had begun to doubt myself, but now I see that I have been right all along. You *are* a child! A willful and nasty child with the body of a woman. You need taming, and I know how it should be done, but I'll not be the one to do it. Now go, wench, before I lose all my temper and box your ears! A thing your father, king though he may be, has not done often enough. Get out!"

Halting in the door, she said: "I had always thought to have you whipped, Blade. Then I favored flaying, and I admit that hanging has entered my mind. But now I know what is best, and when we come to Voth I will see to it. There is a man, Blade, who wants me more than he wants his own life. He is to come for me. And I will go to him—if he pleasures me by killing you first!"

The door almost left its leathern hinges as she slammed out. Blade, trying to get his own irrational rage under control—it was strange how she brought out the worst in him—went to the port and stared out at the sunlit water rippling past. The ship was heeled well over and running fast before a stiff breeze. From above came the boisterous shouts of the sea robbers and the chanting of the tillerman as he conned the ship.

"A man? What man? What in Thunor's hell was she talking about?"

Sylvo, just entering with the bronze axe, stared at Blade.

"A man, master? I do not take your meaning. What man?"

Blade seized Aesculp and swung her. And knew how weak he still was. It would be days before he could fight again.

Sylvo squinted at his master. "What man do you speak of? There was no one here when I entered, master, though I passed the Princess Taleen as I came. By Thunor, she looked black as any tempest—worse than the storm that so nearly sent us to Trit's kingdom. But a man, master? I—"

"Leave off your chatter," Blade shouted. "And mind your affairs, not mine!"

He flung the bronze axe at the opposite wall, where it hung quivering for a moment, then fell to the floor with a crash. Blade looked at it with disgust.

"Think not of it, master. Your strength will come back fast, like the tide sweeping in. In a few days—"

Blade turned on him so fierce a visage that Sylvo quailed and backed away with his hands raised to shield his head.

"You have a choice," Blade thundered. "Silence or a maimed ear."

Sylvo chose silence. Blade shattered it as he left the cabin, leaving the door hanging by one hinge.

Chapter 15

And so Richard Blade came at last to the land of Voth, ruled by King Voth of the North, from the Imperial City of Voth.

The city lay pleasantly situated in a green valley, on the confluence of two wide rivers that twined down from surrounding mountains, and was sentineled by a high wall of stone and earth. All about were hill forts, cunningly placed, and before the great wall was a deep valley with a steep counterscarp, and bristling with chevaux-de-frise. There were new mass graves about, freshly dug, and a few corpses still rotted in the spikes in the vallum, evidence that another band of sea raiders had been to Voth and got more than they bargained for.

When Blade and Jarl landed in Bourne they found the town a smoking ruin full of stink. It had been well raped. Not a soul greeted them.

Jarl, after examining one of the few robber corpses, said: "This is the work of Fjordar, son of Thoth. Remember—you drank from the skull of Thoth before strangling Getorix with his own beard."

Blade, holding a cloth over his nose against the stink, nodded. "They did a thorough bit of work here, by

199

Thunor! To what end? A mere fishing village, with nothing worth looting."

Jarl, resplendent in purple cloak and gold tipped helmet—which Blade had given him the right to wear—ran a finger over his smooth chin. "Malice, nothing more. A few women slaves taken, perhaps. Fjordar is beast and madman—by comparison Redbeard had great virtues—and we are sworn enemies. He is sure to march to Voth, Lord Blade, and try his luck there. I would like to catch up with him."

Blade agreed immediately. "I think it wise, Jarl. There has been the smell of mutiny in the air of late, as palpable as this corpse stink. Your lads need a fight! Else they will fight among themselves and, in time, turn on us. It is best that we march at once."

Jarl regarded him steadily. "They are *your* men, Lord Blade. Not mine. You have the heritage of them from Redbeard—I am but second in command."

"I know," said Blade, "and it is an inheritance I do not greatly care for. But we will speak of this again—order the march to begin!"

He had not seen or spoken with Taleen again; she kept well out of sight. When Sylvo would have gossiped Blade bade him keep his ugly mouth shut. Sylvo, valuing his crooked bones, squinted and said nothing. He had never seen his master in such a dour mood.

It was three days march from Bourne to Voth and the trail they followed was plain, marked by hanged men and women, raped children, butchered cattle and smoldering villages. The complaints and grumbling among the men grew louder and more ominous. There was nothing left for them, they said. Not a slave, nor a woman, not even food that was fit for men. Fjordar was picking the bones clean as he went.

On the evening of the third day—the next morning they would see Voth—Blade called Jarl to his tent for conference. They had taken a straggler that day, one of Fjordar's men who was a coward and had deserted to loot. It took but little torture to make the man tell all he knew. Blade, watching until he was sickened, bade them end it by striking off the man's head. This brought him more dark looks and new muttering—not only were they deprived of loot, but also of their pleasure.

Blade had drawn a crude map on an ox hide, based on the intelligence gasped out by the straggler when the hot pincers tore his flesh. He and Jarl studied it now as Blade pointed with a finger.

"If that fellow spoke truth," said Blade, "this Fjordar has hidden his ships in this cove, marked so, a few kils to the north of Bourne. If he is well beaten at Voth—which you tell me is certain—he should try to regain his ships by the most direct route. You agree?"

Jarl leaned close to study the map, and Blade noticed what he had never noted before—an odor of *chypre* about the man.

"I agree," said Jarl. He traced a path with his finger. "When he has had his fill of Voth, a city that had never been taken, nor its wall even breached, he will run for his ships leaving his dead and wounded behind, for such is his custom. I told you he is more fiend than man."

Blade, in the feeble light of a smoking fish oil lamp, drew a small cross on the map near the Western Sea, using a Dru's dye and brush that Jarl had somehow come by.

"It is my thought," said Blade, "that if you were to take the men—*your* men now, for I will them freely to you—and start tonight, you could be waiting snug in ambush for Fjordar when he returns to his ships. He will be fresh from a beating, weary, and his men exhausted, and it should be an easy prize. What say you, Jarl? It solves many problems—your rascals will come by easy loot, that Fjordar has already won for them, and there will be the ships as well. No doubt stored with more treasure. I think it an opportunity not to be missed."

Jarl was not looking at the map now, but at Blade direct. A smile crinkled his lips. "You are right about one thing, Lord Blade. It solves many problems. Voth will never admit my men to his city, and I doubt I could control them in sight of so much loot and so many women. And there is the account with Fjordar to put right. Yes, I think your plan is a good one. It is best we part tonight, you to go your way and I to go mine. I will send a trumpet to wake the men—at which there will be more whining. But they'll march fast enough when I promise them Fjordar's head and all his treasure."

For a moment they watched each other in the feeble light. Blade put out his hand. "You have been a good friend to me, Jarl. I thank you for it."

Jarl's hand was sweaty, and again Blade caught a whiff of *chypre*. Jarl said: "I did what my heart said do, Lord Blade. I am sorry for none of it. But there is one other thing I would have you know of me—"

"And that is?" Blade waited.

Jarl snatched away his hand and wheeled to go. "No! It is of no importance now, and would serve no purpose. Fare you well, Lord Blade. You were a stranger and you are a stranger still—yet until I go to Thunor, whom I do not believe in, I will remember you."

So Blade came to Voth alone with Sylvo and the Princess Taleen, Taleen riding on a gray horse found in one of the looted villages and somehow spared. Taleen rode in aloof silence, without complaint, and would not speak to Blade. Poor Sylvo was harried into being an intermediary, an additional burden to him because he had by now acquired a wife. And, Blade was surprised to note, something of a pot belly. The kyrie he had chosen was feeding him well.

The woman was a buxom lass, near twice the size of Sylvo, and with a great mass of yellow hair that cascaded over massive white breasts. She walked well behind the small party, carrying Sylvo's few possessions, yet the prin-

202

cess found cause to complain. To Sylvo, for she would not so much as glance at Blade, except when his back was turned.

"Bid her cover those vast teats," Taleen snapped. "She looks like a sow in farrow. We enter the city soon and I will not be seen with such as her."

Sylvo fidgeted and squinted at the ground. "You do not understand, my princess. It is the custom of the kyries, the war maidens, to go about so. It means nothing—it will cause no trouble, I assure and—"

Taleen glared at him. "Do as I bid you, you low fellow! And at once. Do not tell me what I do not understand— else you want to hang with your master when we come to Voth."

Blade, striding along a few paces ahead, had trouble concealing his grin. Now that the spires of Voth were in sight he was in a better mood. The pains in his head came more frequently, and were more severe, but now he understood them and was not anxious. It could only mean that Lord Leighton was reaching for him with the computer, trying to recall him, sending out electronic feelers, seeking to change the molecular structure of Blade's brain back to the original state and snatch Richard Blade back to his own dimension.

Princess Taleen was rasping at Sylvo once again. "Ask your master, the great Lord Blade, if he prefers to be hanged with a golden rope before he is flayed. His rank entitles him to this honor."

Blade, trying not to laugh, swung the bronze axe in a great circle. "Tell Princess Taleen that a common rope will do. As for the flaying of me—I ask only that my poor hide be placed in her bed chamber, before the fire, and that she tread on me nightly with her dainty feet."

Sylvo stared from one to the other, scratching himself and squinting horribly, and wisely said nothing. There was an explosive sound from Taleen that could have only been choked laughter, but she would not look at Blade.

They were admitted to the city by a postern gate, after some brief parley, and soon separated. Blade and Sylvo were shown to a suite of sumptuous rooms in the great wooden palace, an enormous structure that was painted a vivid gold and scarlet and was more bespired and turreted than Craghead had been.

Sylvo's chief concern was at being separated from his kyrie. He patted his newly plump belly as he was attending to Blade's bath.

"She is a cook of cooks, master. Ar, I have never eaten so well. By Thunor, I swear it! And she has other talents, too! But it is a puzzle to me, master. She had a fine sea robber for a man, a big bastard, too, and she gave him up for me! I, who am admittedly a trifle ill formed and lacking in couth and education. How do you think of this, master?"

Blade considered his man through a foam of suds. The bronze tub was too small for him, but he was enjoying his first real bath in many a day. He kept a straight face.

"It is a puzzle to me also, Sylvo. The greatest puzzle being—why did this warrior let you take her. What happened to him?"

Sylvo busied himself scrubbing Blade's back. "There was some sort of accident, master. He was found dead. His heart had stopped."

"I'll wager that! What stopped it? Out with it, man!"

Sylvo dribbled water over him. "There was a small knife in his back, master. I know nothing more on it."

Blade repressed a smile and tried to look grim. "You are a great rascal, man, and will end on a gallows yet. And serve you right."

"No doubt," said Sylvo cheerily. "No doubt, master." Then he looked glum. "Already I doubt my wisdom in taking the kyrie—she is a marvelous cook and wondrous in bed, but I cannot beat her. I tried and she near killed me with one blow!"

Blade let out a bellow of laughter. "A fit punishment. It will teach you not to use your knife so freely."

Sylvo looked abashed, but nonetheless pleased with himself. He bent to retrieve a washing cloth that Blade had dropped from the tub. Something shiny and metallic slipped from his waistband and tumbled to the floor. It lay there, glimmering in sunlight that came aslant through an open window.

A golden medallion on a fine gold chain, with an intaglio crescent moon caught in a net of oak leaves.

Blade stepped from the tub, naked and dripping, and picked up the medallion. He held it by the chain on a finger and stared hard at Sylvo. "How came you by this?"

Sylvo, after taking a few hasty steps back, halted and met his eye squarely. "I found it, master. May Thunor strike me if I did not find it!"

"Where did you find it?" Blade, though frowning and black of visage, did not think Sylvo was lying. He thought that the truth, when he heard it, would be about as he had expected.

"On the deck, master. Where the silver Dru dropped it in the fight with—nay, master, do not make me tell it! It is over now and this serves no purpose. I have tried to keep it from you."

"I know," said Blade. "And a pitiful try, too. Any dolt could have guessed it. So I will tell *you!* There was a scuffle and the silver Dru dropped it when she was pushed overboard. That is right?"

"Yes, master. I could not sleep in my swine pen. I was on deck and they did not see me. But I saw and listened and later, when it was over, I thought I had as much right to the trinket as any."

Blade hurled the medallion at him. It was a talisman of a time he wanted to forget, of things that sickened him when he thought back on them. Not the things themselves, but the manner in which he had craved and been slave to them. His mind had been as sick as his body.

"You are right," he told Sylvo. "It is yours. So long as I never see it again. If I do I will destroy it. Now leave me. You have quarters down the corridor. Go to them and wait until I call for you."

And now Sylvo, seeing that his gossip was anticipated, and dying to tell, gave his master a sly glance. "You do not order me to tell you who pushed the silver Dru, master?"

Blade jerked a thumb at the door. "I know who pushed her. It was Princess Taleen. Get out!"

"Ar, master, that it was. A most terrible struggle it was, too. I thought—"

A step and a baleful glare. "Out!"

When the man had gone Blade paced the chamber restlessly. He had known all along, in his heart, that it was Taleen. No one else would have dared touch a Dru, much less a High Priestess. But Taleen, when the mood was on her, would dare anything.

To ease his mind of her he tried to think of King Voth. Word had been sent that Voth would give Blade an audience that evening. An audience at which—and the message had been precisely worded—Blade could expect thanks and reward for restoring Taleen to the paternal arms.

Blade sought to conjure what King Voth might be like. From what Taleen had said, now and again, and from other sources, Blade pictured an Arthurian figure cast in heroic mold. A veritable porphyrogene. Well, he would soon know. As for the thanks, and reward, they did not matter so much any more. The pains in his head had become more frequent, as bit by bit his memory of former life flowed back. Blade had a premonition that his stay in Voth would not be long. It also occurred to him that Lord Leighton, in trying to recapture him, might only succeed in killing him.

Hard on the thought came another blinding pain. This one was worse by far than any of the preceding—Blade cried aloud and clutched at his head in agony. There was a dagger in his brain. He staggered to the huge bed in a corner and collapsed into a roaring darkness.

He was awakened by a soft tapping at the door. He noted that it was dark—he had been unconscious for hours, then?—and with even more surprise he realized that he was still in Voth.

He went to the door, feeling his way across the unfamiliar chamber. "Who knocks?"

"It is Taleen, Blade. Let me in quickly." She was whispering.

She slipped through the door like a wraith in white. She carried a candle and in the dim light he saw the shimmer of her body under the single garment she wore, a pale linen kirtle that ended well above her knees and barely covered her breasts.

Blade closed the door, barred it, and turned to face her.

"There is little profit, Princess, in coming to whisper at *my* door. I am not a Dru and this is not a ship. Or perhaps you thought to push me out the window?"

The moon, sheltering behind high flying scud, now chose to show its face. Lambent bars of silver radiance spread athwart the floor. Taleen blew out her candle and came to Blade. Her eyes were wide and wild, her auburn hair all tousled, and she was as bright as the moonlight. She fell to her knees before him and clutched his legs.

"Scold me, Blade. Beat me! I have come to abase myself to you. I am evil and it is true that I killed the silver Dru. I was jealous, Blade. Murderous in jealousy. Love me, Blade! Or if you cannot, if you yet deem me a child and not for loving, then let me love you. I plead with you, Blade. Let me stay. Love me. I have asked Frigga for help and she gave it not—only saying that I must come to you and say these things. Do you understand me, Blade? I speak nothing but truth now—I have been sick with love of you since that first day!"

Saying not a word, Blade raised her to her feet and

kissed her. And knew how wrong he had been. This was no child. Her mouth was moist and hot, yet her tongue somehow innocent in its fumbling. Here was lack of experience, but great desire, a combination that set Blade's loins to raging.

Nor was there any reticence about Taleen, she now having declared herself. She kissed him back furiously, then she turned him to full moonlight and broke off the kiss to glance down.

She had been pale, but now was scarlet as she said: "Ah, Blade! You are monstrous big. I begin to feel afraid. I am virgin, Blade. Will it hurt me much?"

He led her toward the bed. "It will hurt, Taleen. But not for long, and in the end you will enjoy the hurting. And I will go as gentle as I can."

But once on the bed she held him off yet awhile. Blade explored and lavished kisses on her breasts, finding them swollen and warm and hard-tipped and fitting perfectly, encupped in his big hands.

He sought to be tender, yet he wanted her terribly by this time and, when still she held him off and cried that she was afraid, he pressed her down and opened her slim legs by main strength and thrust softly into her. Gently at first, then the animal in him took over and he stabbed her to the core and did not hear her moans. Moans that changed gradually to sobs and then to a wild laughter and crying out as she came up to him and entwined about him and bit at him in frenzy. As Blade was himself spending he felt her final convulsive shudder and knew that for the first time in her short life the Princess Taleen had come at a man's urging.

For a long time they lay wrapped in moonlight, gossamer tendrils ensilvering their naked flesh, whilst each made his separate way back from the small death. Taleen, her legs all entwined in his, sighed at last and said most unsteadily: "So *that* is what it is like, Lord Blade! Thank Frigga I know at last—and that it is you who have taught me. What fools young girls are! They jibber and jabber and prate wise of what they know not. But I see the why of it now—making love is not a thing one can guess of. It cannot be known without the doing."

Blade kissed her ear. "You are calling me Lord Blade again. Am I to take it, then, that I am not to be hanged and flayed after all? Not even with a golden rope?"

She thrust her tongue into his mouth for an instant. Then: "I will always call you Lord Blade. You *are* my lord now. For all time. I will never want another."

Blade, with the cynicism of his age, and knowing it did not greatly matter, said nothing to that. Instead: "I am to see your father tonight. What is the clock?"

Taleen stroked his thigh.

"Not this night, my Lord. I have spoken with my father and the audience is put off until tomorrow. He is an old man, and weary from the recent fighting with Fjordar, and it was no great problem."

"I begin to see," Blade chuckled, "who rules in Voth."

"You will rule in Voth," she answered fiercely. "And I at your side. My father will not live long."

Blade, watching her through half closed eyes, wondered at her meaning. She was a marvelous elfin child, barbaric and savage, and blood on her hands was somehow innocent because she knew no difference. Her mind was not as befouled and complex as his had been, and was coming to be again as the computer of Lord Leighton probed again and again for him.

Taleen lay against him and whispered in his ear. "I have talked with Abdias, my father's High Councilor. He operates a net of spies. I have learned much that is of import to us."

Blade, again ready for jousting, would have topped her but she pushed him back. "Nay. Listen to me first. I have heard that the Lady Alwyth is dead and Lycanto taken leave of his wits. I am pleased, and thank Frigga for both, but it is a matter you should know of."

"Why should I care what happens to Lycanto and his lady?" he asked impatiently.

The truth was that his memory of recent events was growing dimmer by the moment. Taleen would never understand that.

She kissed him fiercely. "Be patient and I will tell you why. It is said that Alwyth was taken flagrant in adultery, and plotting against Lycanto, and so stoned to death. Much too easy a death, I think. Lycanto has fallen into drink, will not be parted from his beer horn for a moment, and many say he is lunatic, or stricken by a Dru curse—it really does not matter which—so he no longer rules Alb."

Blade raised on an elbow and feigned interest while kissing one of her firm breasts. "Who does rule in Alb, then?"

"Cunobar the Gray. He has deposed Lycanto—and even now marches north to Voth, with all the Albian army behind him. They will be at our gates in less than a week."

Blade, his lips brushing a rosy nipple, could find no vast excitement in this intelligence. "So what of this? Is not this Cunobar a friend to your father, and you?"

"That is true enough. But there is a difference now, my Lord. And it is all of my doing. Or most of it, for Cunobar the Gray has long wanted me for his wife. He spoke for me when I was still a child, as is the custom. I have liked him, but have not loved him, and I never gave him promise. Until—"

Blade left off kissing her breast. "Until?"

"Until recent days, when I was greatly angered with you. Because you treated me as child and would not see my love. I sent a message to Cunobar the Gray. I—"

It explained so much. Blade held up a hand and said, with a weary laugh, "You asked Cunobar to march up here and win your hand in fair and honorable combat—by killing me!"

She would not meet his eye. "I did. I was regretful in

210

the instant, but the messenger had gone. But it is no matter, Lord."

He followed her glance. She was looking at the great bronze axe, newly burnished by Sylvo, gleaming in the rays of the moon.

"You will slay Cunobar easily enough," said Taleen. "He is not as old as his hair tells of him, and he is a fine warrior, but none can stand up to you. I am not worried."

"Nor am I," answered Blade. "Because I am not going to fight Cunobar, in fair combat or foul. I am weary of blood and sick of killing."

Taleen drew back to stare at him in amazement. "This cannot be Lord Blade that speaks! You *must* fight Cunobar—else he can take me for his own. And name you coward to the world."

A little star of pain exploded in Blade's head. He grimaced and fell into a flurry of temper.

"Let Cunobar take you, then. And the devil too, for that matter!"

The word lingered in the chamber. Devil? The Blade that Taleen knew would have said: Thunor!

Taleen's horror changed to concern. She eyed Blade with a new tenderness. "You are not well? Frigga help me, I know something is wrong. You do not look the same, my Lord Blade, nor do you speak the same. What is it?"

Blade reached for her, not to be denied this time. She resisted, still babbling on, but he bore her down and silenced her with his lunging entry. In a moment she began to move and moan beneath him.

Blade, on the verge of convulsion, felt the pain slamming at his head. Someone screamed and he knew it to be his voice. Then the pain vanished, to be replaced by utter silence and tranquility as he fell into the body of Taleen. She was enormous woman now, world woman, and she opened her chasm to him as he clung like an ant to her smooth female flesh-smelling mountains and shot the scar-

211

let rapids of her veins down into the burning moist heat of her. Falling and falling and sliding—no hand or foothold on these pink slopes and the wet glissade ever increasing and at the end, waiting for him, the edge of eternity drenched in a waterfall of frothing virgin's blood.

For one frantic half breath Blade clung to the precipice of the only reality he knew, fearful of returning to a reality he had lost. In a great brilliant flash of light and knowledge he saw Taleen's face, the room about him, and Aesculp brooding in the corner. This creature threshing about was himself. His hand, flailing, sought beneath a pillow by accident and his fingers closed about a round and smooth object that was of marble size. What?

Words roared at him in tiny balloons, miniscule from an inverted bull horn, and a chorus was crying aloud that it was the black pearl he held. The pearl given him back by Jarl, who had taken it by threat from a reluctant sea robber.

"Such loot is too rich for the likes of them," Jarl explained. "It will only give them ideas—ideas—idea—"

Blade rode the black pearl now, clinging to that smooth convexity, and shot out of a red tunnel into Craghead's mists. Surf cried a dirge for Queen Beata groaning in her cage. Heads were piled high, each picked up and borne away by monster flies, and blood caked on an axe and the mist grew cold—cold—colder.

Aesculp came alive and leaped at Blade from the corner, a terrible creature with a bloodstain for a face. Bronze sparked and the chamber was filled with a dreadful sound of leathern wings.

Blade made a final silent sound in his throat. Not Thunor, not Blade himself, could have explained what it meant.

Chapter Sixteen

"Some of the greatest inventions," said Lord Leighton, "have been discovered quite by accident. I think, J, that this may be one of them."

For a moment J did not answer. He was looking at the big man in the small white bed. Richard Blade slept peacefully, his curling beard and longish hair a dark stain on the pristine pillow. Small electrodes attached here and there led to a large electroencephalograph in one corner of the aseptic room, part of a hospital complex lying far beneath the Tower of London. Here there was silence, broken only by their voices and the occasional hum of a machine, with no encroachment by the insane traffic high over them.

J's benign, aging Establishment face bore traces of harrowing nights and days. As head of Britain's super agency, MI6A, he was accustomed to bearing a heavy load; the past few weeks had been nearly intolerable.

"I thought we had lost him," J said. "I will admit to it now, Lord Leighton. I had given up hope and I was blaming you and your damned blundering. That infernal computer of yours—"

Lord Leighton's yellow eyes were red streaked and his

expensive suit hung on his polio-ruined frame like so many rags. Now and then he twitched and raised an arm, as if trying to ease himself of the hump he must wear forever. He was peering at the encephalograph.

"His brain waves are very nearly back to normal," he told J quietly. "Another few hours and the molecular structure will be restored to what it was. I have sedated him to sleep another twelve hours. When you talk to him again, J, he will be exactly the man you have always known."

J nodded without speaking. He went to the bedside and bent over the sleeping Blade, then lightly touched the bearded face with his fingers. "Wherever he's been, Lord L, he has been in wind and weather. And sun. He is burnt nearly black. That wound in his back—and the healed burns—my God, Lord L! He is going to have a story to tell!"

Lord Leighton paced a few steps—sometimes movement eased the eternal pain in his back—and watched J with a mixture of affection and impatience. J was a spymaster, no scientist, and it was inevitable that he should get the cart before the horse.

"I hope Blade can tell us his story," Lord Leighton began, "but I shouldn't count on it too heavily, J. He simply may not remember very much. I have foreseen that. I am already working on a memory expanding drug which, in conjunction with a sort of booster computer—I call it a chronos computer—should enable Blade to remember *everything* about his next venture. And without any conscious effort on his part."

Lord Leighton beamed at J, remarkably like a crippled old cat that has found a way to attract mice without effort on its own part.

J was not ashamed to let his jaw droop as he stared at the little cripple.

"His next venture? What in hell are you talking about, man?"

Lord Leighton looked long-suffering, patient, and waved a placating hand toward a small table on which lay a thick file bound in green leather.

"It's all in there, J. Everything. Read it in the taxi, on your way to the Prime Minister. It's the highest priority and top top secret, or however you chaps label these things."

J looked from Lord Leighton to the peacefully slumbering Blade and back again at Leighton. "I," he said, "will be eternally damned! I'm going to have something to say about this, Leighton. I'm damned if I stand by and watch you—"

Lord Leighton still wore the expression of an angel whose patience is tried beyond measure. When J's complaints had tailed away into inarticulate mutterings, he said:

"You don't really understand it yet, do you, J? I said a moment ago that many great inventions, or scientific discoveries, are made by accident. This I believe to be one of them. I can't prove it yet, but I think that Blade has been out in another dimension! Not in space, not in time—none of your science-fiction jiggery pokery—but I believe that the computer so disarranged his brain cells that he has been seeing, existing, in a dimension that *we* cannot see or experience, though we may both be living in the very midst of it at this moment. Walking *through* it, as it were, without knowing it is there.

"Put in an absurdly simple way it is nothing more than the dog whistle thing—the dog can hear the whistle, you can't. But the sound *is* there!"

By now J had recovered some of his aplomb. He frowned. "We nearly lost him this time, damn it. Who knows what will happen next time—if there is one."

"There will be one," said Lord Leighton softly. "The Prime Minister will see to it. He is not a fool. This discovery may have unlimited possibilities, J, may open doors that we do not even conceive of now. It could mean the

215

complete renaissance of England as a nation, as a great power. God knows we stand in need of it!"

J was silent. Putting it like that made all the difference. Richard Blade had been risking his life for Britain many years now. He was tops in a most dangerous profession. If this thing were asked of him—Blade would do it without a murmur.

"He is in excellent shape," Leighton said. "We have given him exhaustive tests, as you know, and there will be many more. I find no evidence of any permanent brain damage. Best, and most important, I have finally succeeded in tracing down the computer fault that was responsible. It was not easy, J! It has taken me days of sweat, as you also know. I am, in a way, responsible for that. I built the computer so it would correct its own errors—and this it did. That is why I had to take it completely down, and run so many thousands of tests, before I could duplicate the error, and reverse it, to bring Blade back. But I'll not have to go through that again."

J, still only half convinced, looked again at the sleeping man. Blade was smiling faintly.

Lord Leighton went to the machine and scanned it briefly. "He's dreaming. Distinct REMs now."

J scratched his sharp chin. "I wonder what about? I mean—here or there? This dimension—I'll accept that mumb-jumbo for the moment—or the one he's been to?"

Lord Leighton's smile was crooked as he turned from the machine. "We shall never know—but let me get back, J. The computer made a mistake and then immediately corrected itself, thus making it devilish hard to *find* the mistake. That was the problem all along. If I hadn't thought of that yarn of Stevenson's we might never have gotten Blade back."

"Stevenson? I don't follow."

"The writer, man! The chap that wrote Dr. Jekyll and Mr. Hyde. Don't you recall? Dr. Jekyll could change into Hyde, and back again, because of some impurity—equal to the computer's mistake—in the original batch of salts that Jekyll made into solution and drank. But when *that* batch was gone, so was the obscure impurity, and Jekyll had only *pure* salts. He was stuck in Hyde's body. Surely you see it—I had to find the mistake, which the computer had erased, and then put it back into the programming. Then reverse it to get to Blade. Actually rather simple, once one has the logic of it in mind."

"It still took you long enough," J said tartly. "You must have tried a hundred times."

"Fifty-one," said Leighton. Then, wearily, "Fifty-one times I reached for him, and got him on the fifty-second." He smiled briefly. "I wonder what he was doing when I finally reached him? And if he knew what was happening?"

There was a gentle rap on the door. Lord Leighton opened it and took a small envelope from a uniformed guard. He closed and locked the door and turned to J as he tore open the envelope. A large black pearl rolled into his hand. Lord Leighton tossed the pearl to J, who nearly dropped it.

"Absolute form and purity," read Leighton from the lab report in his hand.

"Lustre unsurpassed, of highest quality, nothing like it known to experts. No record of any such pearl in historic times. No history. Impossible to evaluate in money terms, for it is unique in fullest meaning of the word. And so on and so on—there's a lot of expert's gibberish which I'll not bother reading. But you see the implications now, J? *Blade brought something back!* Call it treasure, if you like, and of no great importance. But on his next trip what might he not bring back? Knowledge, J. Knowledge!"

The big man in the bed moved restlessly and spoke one word.

"Taleen."

Both men caught the word distinctly—in any case the recording tapes were switched on—and they went to the bed and waited.

Nothing more. Richard Blade slumbered on, his lips twitching now and again in what might have been a smile, or the beginnings of a scowl.

J, having taken leave of Lord Leighton, and submitted to the elaborate checking out process that permitted him egress from the tower's underground labyrinth, wandered a bit bemused as he sought for a taxi. It had begun to rain, a slight but annoying drizzle, and taxis were hard to come by.

Spotting an empty at last J waded bravely into the stream of traffic, raised a fawn-gloved hand and shouted: "Taleen—Taleen!"

He caught himself at once and cried "Taxi" and the driver pulled over and stopped. As J piled in he said, "Number Ten Downing, please. And do hurry."

J, clutching the green file to his sparse chest, was slightly distraught. Why had he called out that word—a name?—which he had heard only once in his life. Taleen? Taleen! Taleen. Possibly something Freudian there, and God knows he didn't want to get into *that*. He was a simple civil servant, whose business happened to be managing spies, with a soupcon of counter-espionage, and matters were muddled enough as it was. And yet—Taleen? What could it possibly mean?

The driver of the taxi, a cockney, watched his fare in the mirror. He shook his head slowly. You got all types. The gent was a toff, no doubting that, and must be a nob or he wouldn't be going to Number Ten. *That* was all right—the gent had the Number Ten look. The constables would let him in, right enough.

Looked a little barmy, though. Staring off into nothing, twisting his mouth about and saying something over and over. Must be some sort of facial tick, poor chap.

218

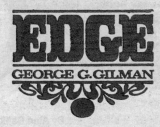